LARGE PRINT

Books should be returned or renewed by the
last date stamped above

GEORGE, Elizabeth

I, Richard

I,
Richard

Elizabeth George

Thorndike Press • **Chivers Press**
Waterville, Maine USA   Bath, England

This Large Print edition is published by Thorndike Press, USA and by Chivers Press, England.

Published in 2003 in the U.S. by arrangement with Bantam Books, an imprint of The Bantam Dell Publishing Group, a division of Random House, Inc.

Published in 2003 in the U.K. by arrangement with Hodder & Stoughton Ltd.

U.S. Hardcover 0-7862-4688-X (Basic Series)
U.K. Hardcover 0-7540-1910-1 (Windsor Large Print)
U.K. Softcover 0-7540-9273-9 (Paragon Large Print)

The text of this Large Print edition is unabridged.
Other aspects of the book may vary from the original edition.

Set in 16 pt. Plantin by Minnie B. Raven.

Printed in the United States on permanent paper.

British Library Cataloguing-in-Publication Data available

Library of Congress Cataloging-in-Publication Data

George, Elizabeth.
    I, Richard / Elizabeth George.
      p. cm.
    ISBN 0-7862-4688-X (lg. print : hc : alk. paper)
    1. Large type books. 2. Detective and mystery stories, American. I. Title.
PS3557.E478 I17 2003
 813'.54—dc21   2002038421

For Rob and Glenda

Contents

Introduction to
Exposure

I first wrote this story for *Sisters in Crime* (Volume II), having been inspired to do so by taking two summer sessions at Cambridge University through a program offered by UCLA. The first session, in 1988, was called "The Country Houses of Great Britain," and from it I took my initial inspiration for a story which I called "The Evidence Exposed." The second session, in 1989, was a course on Shakespeare, and its curious and whimsical look at William Shakespeare as a closet Marxist — no matter the anachronous bent of such a look! — became part of the foundation for a novel I wrote called *For the Sake of Elena*, which was set in Cambridge.

"The Evidence Exposed" was my first attempt at a crime story in abbreviated form. It was also the first short story I'd written in about twenty years. As such, it was a noble effort, but I was never completely happy with it. Indeed, fairly soon after publication, I realized that I'd killed the wrong person, and it became my intention to rewrite the story if I ever had the chance to do so.

A lot of life supervened in the meantime. I always seemed to have other novels under contract, courses to teach, and research to do. Occasionally, even, I was asked to write other short stories and when the request coincided with an idea that I believed could be contained in less than six hundred pages, I'd apply myself once again to the challenging format.

Finally, my Swedish publisher wanted to put out a "slim volume" of my stories — of which, at this point, there were only three. I agreed. My English publisher discovered this book and weighed in with a request to print it in English. My German and French publishers followed suit. And in very short order, my American publisher made the same request. At this point I realized that it was time to rewrite "The Evidence Exposed" as well as to add to the small collection two more stories that I'd been mulling over.

Consequently, I set about revising and rewriting "The Evidence Exposed," and what you have here — for the first time —

is the new version of that older and far clunkier story.

I'm quite pleased with the way it came out. It has a new point of view and a new victim. And Abinger Manor has a new owner. But the rest of the characters remain the same.

Exposure

When members of the history of British architecture class thought about the Abinger Manor Affair later on, each one of them would say that Sam Cleary had been the likeliest candidate for murder. Now, you might ask yourself why anyone would have wanted to kill a harmless American professor of botany who — on the surface at least — had done nothing more than come to Cambridge University with his wife to take part in a summer session at St. Stephen's College. But that's the crux of the matter, you see, the *with his wife* part of it. Old Sam — seventy if he was a day and a spiffy dresser with a bent for bow ties and tweeds even in the middle of the hottest summer England had seen in decades — tended to forget that his wedded Frances had come along for the experience as well. And when Sam forgot that Frances was there, his eyes started wandering in order to take a visual sampling of the other ladies. It appeared to be second nature to the fellow.

This visual sampling might have been something that Frances Cleary could have overlooked. Her husband, after all, couldn't be expected to walk around Cambridge with blinders on, and Cambridge in the summer brought out fine ladies like mayflies looking for barbecues. But when he took to spending long evenings in the college pub, entertaining their classmate Polly Simpson with tales of everything from his childhood spent on a farm in Vermont to his years in 'Nam where, according to Sam, he saved his entire platoon single-handedly . . . well, that was too much for Frances. Not only was Polly young enough to be Sam's granddaughter and then some, she was — if you'll pardon the expression — drop-dead gorgeous and blonde and curvy in a way that poor Frances hadn't been even in her glory years.

So when the night before the Day in Question saw Sam Cleary and Polly Simpson in the college pub laughing, talking, teasing each other as usual, giggling like kids — which at twenty-three Polly still was, as a matter of fact — and acting otherwise like individuals with Something Specific on Their Minds till two in the morning, Frances finally had words with her husband. And her husband wasn't the only one to hear them.

Noreen Tucker was the messenger delivering news of this delicate subject over breakfast the next day, having been awakened by the sound of Frances's accelerating displeasure at two twenty-three in the morning and having been kept awake by the sound of Frances's accelerating displeasure till exactly four thirty-seven. That was when a slamming door punctuated Sam's decision to listen no more to his wife's accusations of heartless insensitivity and insidious infidelity.

Under other circumstances, an unwilling eavesdropper might have kept her own counsel regarding this overheard marital contretemps. But Noreen Tucker was a woman who liked the spotlight. And since she had so far achieved precious little recognition in her thirty years as a romance writer, she took her bows where she could.

That's what she was doing on the morning of the Day in Question, as other members of the History of British Architecture class gathered to break bread together in the cavernous dining hall of St. Stephen's College. Dressed in Laura Ashley and a straw boater in the mistaken belief that projecting youthfulness equated to youthfulness, Noreen imparted the salient details of the Clearys' early-morning argument, and she leaned forward with a glance to the right and the left to underscore both the import and the confidential nature of the information she was sharing.

"I couldn't believe my *ears*," she told her fellow students in breathless summation. "Who looks milder mannered than Frances Cleary, I ask you, who? And to believe she even *knew* such language existed . . . ? Why, I was just *slayed* to hear it, truly. I was completely mortified. I didn't know whether I should knock on the wall to quiet her down or go for help. Although I can't imagine the *porter* would have wanted to get involved, even if I'd gone for him. And anyway, if *I'd* actually gotten involved in some way, there was always the chance that Ralph here might've been pushed into the middle of it, trying to defend me, you know. And I couldn't put *him* at risk, could I? Sam might've asked him to step outside, and Ralph here is in *no* condition to get into a brawl with *anyone*. Are you, sweetheart?"

Ralph here was more a blob in a safari jacket than an actual person, Noreen's shadow and constant companion. No one in the History of British Architecture class had managed to get more than ten words from the man in the eleven days they'd been in Cambridge, and there were those among the larger group of students taking other classes in St. Stephen's College who swore he was altogether mute.

What went for his condition was hypoglycemia, which was the topic Noreen segued into once she was done dissecting the Cleary marriage and Sam's attraction to the ladies in general and Polly Simpson in particular. Ralph here, she informed her listeners, was an absolute martyr to the ailment. Low blood sugar was the curse of Ralph here's family, she explained, and he had the worst case of any of them. He'd even passed out once at the wheel of their car while on the *freeway*, don't you know. It was only through Noreen's quick thinking and even quicker acting that utter disaster was avoided.

"I grabbed the wheel so fast, you'd think I'd been trained as a rescue professional of some sort," Noreen revealed. "It's astonishing the level we can rise to when the worst happens, don't you agree?" As was her bent, she waited for no reply. Instead, she turned to her husband and said, "You've got your nuts and chews to take on the outing today, don't you, sweetie my own? We can't have you passing out cold in the middle of Abinger Manor, now can we?"

"Up 'n the room," Ralph said into his

bowl of corn flakes.

"Just make sure you don't leave them there," his wife replied. "You know how you are."

"How you are is henpecked," was the description offered by Cleve Houghton as he joined their table. "Ralph needs exercise, not that junk you keep feeding him every time he turns around, Noreen."

"Speaking of junk," was Noreen's rejoinder with a meaningful look at the plate he carried, overloaded with eggs, sausage, grilled tomatoes, and mushrooms. "I wouldn't be so quick to cast stones, Cleve dear. Surely that can't be good for your arteries."

"I did eight miles along the backs this morning," he replied. "All the way to Grantchester with no heavy breathing, so my arteries are fine, thank you. The rest of you should try some running. Hell, it's the best exercise known to man." He tossed back his hair — thick and dark, it was, something a man of fifty could be proud of — and caught sight of Polly Simpson just entering the dining room. He amended his comments with, "The second best exercise," and smiled lazily and with hooded eyes in Polly's direction.

Noreen tittered. "Goodness, Cleve. Rein

16

yourself in. I believe she's spoken for already. Or at least she's spoken *about*." Noreen used her own comment as introduction to the topic she'd covered before Cleve's appearance on the scene. But she added a few more thoughts this time round, most of them centering on Polly Simpson as a Natural Born Troublemaker and someone certainly fingered by Noreen on Day One to cause *some* sort of dissension in their midst. After all, when she wasn't sucking up to their instructor — the better to massage her final grade, no doubt — with exclamations over the beauties in *every* slide the tiresome woman foisted daily upon her students, she was cozying up to one man or another in a way that *she* probably thought of as friendly but anyone else with a grain of sense would have called outright provocative. "What's she actually *up* to, I ask you?" Noreen demanded of anyone who was continuing to listen at this point. "There they sit with their heads together night after night, she and Sam Cleary. And doing what? You can't tell *me* they're discussing flowers. They're laying their plans for *afterwards*. Together. You mark my words."

Whether the words were marked was something no one commented upon since

Polly Simpson was fast upon her classmates, carrying a tray on which she'd placed a virtuously weight-conscious single banana and a cup of coffee. She wore her camera slung round her neck as usual, and when she set down her tray, she strode to the end of the table and focused her shutter on the group at their morning meal. On the afternoon of their first session in the History of British Architecture class, Polly had declared to them that she would be the seminar's official historian, and so far she'd been as good as her word. "Believe me, you'll want this as a souvenir," she announced each time she caught someone in her lens. "I promise. People always like my pictures when they see them."

"Jesus, Polly. Not now," Cleve groused as the girl made adjustments to her lens at the far end of the breakfast table, but he sounded good-natured about his complaint and no one missed the fact that he ran one hand back through his hair to give it just the sort of *GQ* tousle that promised to make him look thirty again.

"The whole class isn't present, Polly dear," Noreen said. "And surely you want *everyone* in the picture, don't you?"

Polly looked around, then smiled and

18

said, "Well, here's Em and Howard showing up. We've got most of the crowd."

"But surely not the most *important*
people," Noreen persisted as the other two
students joined them. "Don't you want to
wait for Sam and Frances?"

"Not everyone needs to be in every picture," Polly said, quite as if Noreen's question hadn't been fraught with enough
undercurrents to drown a gorilla.

"All the same . . ." Noreen murmured,
and she asked Emily Guy and Howard
Breen — two San Franciscans who'd
buddy-bonded on the first day of class — if
they'd run into either Sam or Frances on L
staircase where they all had rooms. "They
didn't get much sleep last night," Noreen
said with a meaningful glance in Polly's direction. "I wonder, could they have slept
right through their alarm this morning?"

"Not with Howard singing in the
shower," Emily said. "I heard him from
two floors below."

Howard said, "No day begins right
without a morning tribute to Barbra."

Noreen, not much liking this potential
shift in the topic, put an end to it by
saying, "And here *I* thought Bette Midler
was the rage with all of your sort."

At this, there was an uncomfortable little

silence at the table. Polly's lips parted as she lowered her camera. Emily Guy knotted her eyebrows and did her spinster's-innocence bit of pretending she didn't quite understand what Noreen was implying. Cleve Houghton snorted, always maintaining his manly man pose. And Ralph Tucker kept spooning up corn flakes.

Howard himself was the one to break the silence. He said, "Bette Midler? Nope. I only like Bette if I'm wearing my high heels and fishnets, Noreen. And I can't get into the shower with them on. Water ruins the patent leather."

Polly snickered, Emily smiled, and Cleve stared at Howard a good ten seconds before bellowing an appreciative guffaw. "I'd *like* to see you in heels and fishnets," he said.

"All in good time," Howard replied. "I'll need to eat my breakfast first."

So Noreen Tucker, you see, might also have been a good candidate for murder. She liked stirring the pot to discover what sort of burnt-on goodies were adhering to the bottom, and when she had them good and stirred up, she liked the way they bittered the brew. She didn't realize that she was doing this, however. Her intentions were simple enough, no matter what their outcome actually was. If conversations revolved around topics she had chosen, she could orchestrate the flow of discussion and thereby keep herself at the head of the class. Being at the head of the class meant having all eyes fixed upon her. And having all eyes fixed on her in Cambridge ameliorated the sting of having no eyes fixed upon her anywhere else.

The problem was Victoria Wilder-Scott, their instructor, a dizzy woman who favoured khaki skirts and madras shirts and who habitually and unconsciously sat in class during their discussions in such a way as to show her underpants to the gentleman students. Victoria was there to fill their minds with the minutiae of British architecture. She wasn't the least interested in summer session gossip and she and Noreen had been at polite but deadly loggerheads from the first, a pitched battle to see who was going to control what went for content in the classroom. Noreen always tried to sideline her with probing and generally absurd questions about the personal lives of the architects whose work they were studying: Did Christopher Wren find his name an impediment to acquiring a lasting love in his life? Did Adam's ceilings imply something deeply sensuous and ungovernable within his nature? But Victoria Wilder-Scott merely stared at Noreen like a woman waiting for a translation to be made before she said, "Yes. Well," and brushed Noreen's questions away like the thirsty female mosquitoes they were.

She'd been preparing her History of British Architecture students for the trip to Abinger Manor from the first day of class. Abinger Manor, deep in the Buckinghamshire countryside, reflected every style of architecture known to Great Britain while simultaneously being the repository of everything from priceless rococo silver to paintings by English, Flemish, and Italian masters. Victoria had shown her students endless slides of coved ceilings, broken pediments, gilded capitals on marble pilasters, ornate stone drip spouts, and dogtoothed cornices, and when their brains were saturated with architectural details, she sopped up the overflow with additional slides of porcelain, silver, sculptures, tapestries, and furniture galore. This, she told them, was the crown jewel of English properties. The stately home had only recently been opened to view and the wait to see it among people who were not so fortunate as to be enrolled in the History of British Architecture class at Cambridge University's summer session was a minimum of twelve months. And *that's* only if the eager visitor spent days on end trying to get through by telephone for reservations. "None of this reservations-by-Internet nonsense," Victoria Wilder-Scott told them. "At Abinger Manor, they do things the old-fashioned way." Which was, of course, the proper way to do them.

They would see this monument to days gone by — not to mention to propriety — in a few hours, after a rather long drive across the countryside.

They were to meet that morning after breakfast at the Queen's Gate, which gave way to Garrett Hostel Lane, at the end of which their mini-coach would be waiting for them. It was here, where the assembled students picked up their sack lunches and browsed through them with the usual complaints about institutional food, that they were finally joined by a subdued Sam Cleary and a miserable-looking Frances.

If clothes made a statement about the outcome of their wee-hours discord, Sam had clearly emerged the winner: dapper as always in a trim sports jacket, with his bow tie cleverly complementing the forest green

23

highlights in his tweed trousers. Frances, on the other hand, was dowdiness incarnate in a drab, too-large tunic and a matching too-large pair of trousers. She looked like a refugee from the Cultural Revolution.

Polly seemed eager to mend whatever breach she might have caused between the professor and his wife. After all, she was nearly fifty years Sam's junior and a girl with a boyfriend back home in Chicago to boot. She might have enjoyed the attentions of an older man — a *really* older man, as she would have put it — in the college pub for several nights running, but that was not to say that she would ever have considered fanning the flames of Sam's interest to build to something more. True, he was extremely nice looking with all that gray hair and that blush of good health on his cheeks. But there was no way around the fact that he was also *old,* and he couldn't compare to Polly's own David despite David's so far unshakable and somewhat obsessive interest in developing a career studying howler monkeys.

Polly called out a cheerful good morning to the Clearys and motioned to them with her camera. She'd put on an enormous telephoto lens for their outing, which

24

served her purposes well at the moment. She could take the picture she wanted of Sam and his wife while keeping her distance from them. She said, "Stay right there by the herbaceous border. The colours are sensational with your hair, Frances."

Frances's hair was gray. Not that stunning white that some women are blessed with but battleship gray. She had a lot of it, which was fortunate, but the dullness of its colour made her look dour at even her best moments. And this not being one of her best moments, she looked pretty much the worse for wear.

"Amazing what lack of sleep can do to one, isn't it?" Noreen Tucker murmured with great meaning as the Clearys approached the rest of the students after posing cooperatively — at least on Sam's part — for Polly's picture. "Ralph, you haven't forgotten your nuts and chews, have you, sweetie? We don't want any crises in the hallowed halls of Abinger Manor this morning."

Ralph's answer comprised a downward motion with his thumb in the direction of his waist. This was easily interpretable: The plastic bag in which he kept his trail mix was pluming out of his safari jacket like the tail of an infant marsupial.

"If you feel the shakes coming, you have a handful of that right away," Noreen instructed him. "No waiting around for permission from someone, you hear me, Ralph?"

"Will do, will do." Ralph meandered over to the lunch bags next to the Queen's Gate and huffed his way down to pick two of them out of the wicker basket.

"That guy'll be lucky to make it to sixty," Cleve Houghton said to Howard Breen. "And what're *you* doing to take care of yourself?"

"Showering only with friends," Howard replied.

They were joined then by Victoria Wilder-Scott, who steamed in their direction in her khaki and madras with her glasses perched on the top of her head and a three-ring binder clutched to her bony chest. She squinted at her students as if perplexed by the fact that they were out of focus. A moment later, she realised why.

She said, "Oops, the specs! Right, then," and lowered them to her nose as she continued breezily. "You've all read your brochures, I trust? And the second chapter in *Great Houses of the British Isles*? So we're all perfectly clear on what we're going to see at Abinger Manor? That marvelous collection of Meissen that you saw in your textbook. The finest in England. The paintings by Gainsborough, Le Brun, Turner, Constable, and Reynolds. That lovely piece by Whistler. The Holbein. The rococo silver. Some remarkable furniture. The Italian sculptures. All those wonderful period clothes. The gardens are exquisite, by the way: They rival Sissinghurst. And the park . . . Well, we won't have time to see all of it, but we'll do our best. You have your notebooks? Your cameras?"

"Polly has hers," Noreen pointed out. "I believe that makes any others redundant."

Victoria blinked in the direction of their class historian. From the first, she'd made no secret of the fact that she approved of Polly's zeal, and she only wished more of her students were willing to throw themselves into the Cambridge experience in like manner. To Victoria, that was the trouble with agreeing to teach these summer sessions in the first place: They were generally flooded by well-to-do Americans whose idea of learning stopped at watching television documentaries from the comfort of their living room sofas.

"Yes, well," Victoria said and beamed at

27

Polly. "Have you documented our pending departure?"

"Get over by the gate, you guys," Polly said in answer. "Let's have a group shot before we take off."

"You pose with the others," Victoria said. "I'll take the picture."

"Not with this camera," Polly said. "It's got a light meter fit only for an Einstein. No one can figure it out. It belonged to my grandpa."

"Is your grandfather still alive, then?" Noreen asked archly. "He must be . . . what, Polly? Terribly old. Seventy perhaps?"

"Not a bad guess," Polly said. "He's seventy-two."

"A real antique."

"Yeah. But he's a tough old geezer and completely full of —" Polly stopped herself. Her gaze went to Sam, then to Frances, then to Noreen, who said pleasantly, "Full of what?"

"Full of wit and wisdom, no doubt." Emily Guy put this in. Like Victoria Wilder-Scott, she admired Polly Simpson's energy and enthusiasm and she envied, without being consumed by that emotion, the fact that life was unspooling before her and not closing off as it was for herself.

28

For her own part, Emily Guy had come to Cambridge to forget an unhappy love affair with a married man that had consumed the last seven years of her life, so any indication in another woman of a propensity to involve herself hopelessly in love triangles was something that she reacted to badly. Like Noreen, she'd seen Polly in conversation with Sam Cleary in the evenings. But unlike Noreen, she'd taken it for nothing more than a young girl's kindness towards an older man who was clearly besotted with her. Frances Cleary's jealousy was not Polly Simpson's problem, Emily Guy had decided the first time she saw Frances frown over the tabletop in Polly's direction.

Further to making amends to Frances, though, Polly did her best to stay out of Sam Cleary's sight line for the trip to Abinger Manor. She walked to the minicoach in the company of Cleve Houghton, and she spent the journey to Buckinghamshire riding across the aisle from him and involving him in earnest conversation.

These two activities, of course, were not missed by Noreen Tucker, who as we've seen, liked to start fires wherever she could. "Our Polly definitely wants more than a cracker," she murmured to her silent husband as they rolled along the parched summer countryside. "And you can bet what she's after is made out of gold."

Ralph gave no reply — it was always rather difficult to tell whether he was cognizant or merely somnambulating his way through a day — so Noreen cast around for a more attentive listener, finding it in Howard Breen across the aisle from her. He was leafing through the brochure they'd all been given on the glories of Abinger Manor. She said to him, "Age doesn't matter when money's involved, don't you agree, Howard?"

Howard raised his head, saying, "Money? For what?"

"Money for baubles. Money for travel. Money for living a fancier life. He's a doctor. Divorced. Got piles of cash. And she's been drooling over those slides of Victoria's since the first day of class, if you haven't noticed. So wouldn't she just love a nice antique or two to take home to Chicago as a souvenir? And isn't Cleve Houghton just the man to buy her one now Sam Cleary's been brought into line by Frances?"

Howard lowered his brochure and looked to his companion on the journey —

Emily Guy — for an interpretation of Noreen's remarks. "She's talking about Polly and Cleve Houghton," Emily said and added in a low voice, "having moved on from Polly and Sam."

"It's all *about* money with a girl like that," Noreen said. "Believe me, if you had a bucket or two, she'd be after you as well, Howard, no matter your . . . well, your sexual preferences if I may call them that. Consider yourself lucky to be escaping."

Howard cast a glance in the direction of Polly, who was in the process of illustrating some point she was making by gesturing with her hands. He said, "Damn. Escaping? I don't want that. I can always go either AC *or* DC. If the moon's full and the wind's blowing from the east, I'm ripe for the plucking. Matter of fact, Noreen, *you've* started to look pretty damn good to me in the past few days."

Noreen looked flustered. "Why I hardly think —"

"I noticed," Howard grinned.

Noreen wasn't someone to take a put-down lightly, nor was she a woman who chose to respond with a frontal attack. She merely smiled and said, "Well, if you're bent that way today, Howard, I'm afraid I can't help you as I'm spoken for. But I'm sure our Emily will be happy to oblige. In fact, I'll bet that's just what she's been hoping for. A man's interest can make a woman feel . . . well, like *anything's* possible, can't it? Even that an AC might become a DC on a permanent basis. I expect you'd like that, Emily. Every woman needs a man, after all."

Emily grew hot despite the fact that there was no way on earth that Noreen Tucker could have known anything about her recent past: the hopes she'd invested in a love affair that had seemed like a case of star-crossed lovers meeting at last and had turned out to be nothing more than a squalid little attempt to make something special from what was actually a series of hurried couplings in hotels that had left her feeling lonelier than before.

So she wasn't the first person that day to think that Noreen Tucker might serve a greater purpose for mankind by being rubbed off the planet.

At the front of the coach, Victoria Wilder-Scott had spent most of the trip across the countryside expatiating by microphone on the beauties of Abinger Manor. She appeared to be making the peroration of her remarks as the tour coach turned down a leafy lane. "Thus, the family remained staunchly Royalist to the end. In the north tower, you'll see a priest's hole where King Charles was hidden prior to his escape to the Continent. And in the long gallery, you'll be challenged to find a Gibb door that's completely concealed. It was through this door that the king began his escape on that fateful night. And it was because of the family's continued loyalty to him that the owner was later elevated to the rank of earl. That title has passed down through the family, of course, and while the present earl comes only at the weekends to the estate, his mother — who herself, by the way, is the daughter of the sixth earl of Asherton — lives on the grounds, and I wouldn't be surprised if we ran into her. She's known for mixing in with the guests. A bit of an eccentric . . . as these types frequently are."

When the tour coach made its final turn and the History of British Architecture class got their first glimpse of Abinger Manor, an appreciative murmur went up among them despite whatever else was on their minds. Victoria Wilder-Scott turned in her seat, delighted to hear their reaction to the place. She said, "I promised you, didn't I? It does not disappoint."

Across a moat that was studded with lily pads, two crenellated towers stood at the sides of the building's front entry. They rose five stories, and on either side of them, crowstepped gables were surmounted by impossibly tall, impossibly decorated chimneys. Bay windows, a later addition to the house, extended over the moat and gave inhabitants a view of the extensive garden. This was edged on one side by a tall yew hedge and on the other by a brick wall against which grew an herbaceous border of lavender, aster, and dianthus. The History of British Architecture class wandered towards this with a quarter hour to explore it prior to their scheduled tour.

They were not the only visitors to the manor that morning. A large tour coach pulled into the environs of the manor directly behind them, and from it debouched a crowd of German tourists who immediately joined Polly Simpson in taking photographs of the front of the manor house. Two family groups arrived simultaneously in Range Rovers and immediately struck out for the maze, in which they quickly became lost and began shouting at each other to help them find their way. And a silver Bentley joined the other vehicles moments later, gliding to a stop in near perfect silence.

From this final vehicle, a handsome couple stepped: the man tall and blond and dressed with the sort of casual flair that suggests money; the woman dark and lithe and yawning, as if she'd slept for most of the journey.

Unbeknownst to the rest of the visitors to Abinger Manor on this Day in Question, these last two arrivals were Thomas Lynley and his intended bride Lady Helen Clyde. And they had a vested interest in being there since the primary inhabitant of Abinger Manor was Lynley's own fearsome aunt Augusta, the aforementioned dowager countess, who wished her nephew to see for himself that one could open one's property to view without disaster dancing attendance. She wanted him to do the same with his own extensive property in Cornwall, but so far she'd not made much progress persuading him of the idea's efficacy.

"We're not all the Duchess of Devonshire," Lynley would tell her gently.

"If a next-to-nothing *Mitford* can do it and bring it off, then so bloody well can I," was her reply.

But they didn't go in search of Aunt

Augusta, as well they might have done, considering the relationship. Instead, Thomas Lynley and Helen Clyde joined the others in the garden and admired what his aunt had done to keep it blooming despite the drought.

Of course, the others had no way of knowing that this Thomas Lynley who quietly walked round the garden with his arm lightly dropped round his future wife's shoulders was actually a member of the family who now lived in a single wing of the stately building. But more importantly — especially considering the events that were to occur within that building — the others had no way of knowing that his means of employment was as a detective with New Scotland Yard. Instead what they saw was what people generally saw when they looked upon Thomas Lynley and Helen Clyde: the careful expenditure of money on an unostentatious quality of appearance and of dress; the polite and deferential silence of years of good breeding; and a bond of love that looked like friendship because it was from friendship that that love had blossomed.

In other words, they were grossly out of place among the visitors to Abinger Manor that day.

When the bell rang for the tour to begin, the group assembled at the front door. They were greeted by a determined-looking girl in her mid-twenties with spots on her chin and too much eye makeup. She ushered them inside, locked the door behind them in case anyone had any ideas of absconding with a precious — not to mention portable — knickknack — and she began speaking in the sort of English that suggested she'd been well prepared for foreigners. Simple words, simply spoken, with plenty of pauses.

They were, she told them, in the original screens passage of the manor house. The wall to their left was the original screen. They would be able to admire its carving when they got to the other side of it. If they would please stay together and not stray behind the corded-off areas . . . Photographs were permitted only without a flash.

Things went well at first. The group maintained a respectful silence, and pictures were taken dutifully without flash. The only questions asked were asked by Victoria Wilder-Scott and if the guide offered apocryphal answers, no one was the wiser.

It was in this manner that they came to

the Great Hall, a magnificent room that was everything Victoria Wilder-Scott had promised her students it would be. While the guide catalogued its features for them, the group dutifully took note of the towering coved ceiling, of the minstrel gallery and its intricate fretwork, of the tapestries, the portraits, the fireplaces, and the carpets. Cameras focused and clicked. Appreciative murmurs rose. Somewhere in the room, a clock delicately chimed half past ten.

As if in accompaniment to this, a ferocious growl interrupted the guide's programmed speech. Someone giggled and a few people turned to see Polly Simpson clutching her stomach. "Sorry," she said. "Only a banana for breakfast."

This remark lit something of a fire beneath the normally taciturn Ralph Tucker. While the tour group attended back to their guide, he sidled over to Polly and gallantly offered her the front of his safari jacket.

"Energy boost," he said. "Good for the blood."

She smiled her thanks at him and dipped her hand inside to scoop out some trail mix. He did the same. Of course, they had to eat surreptitiously and they did it like two naughty school kids, with attendant snickers of mischief. It was easy enough to carry off since their guide was leading them out of the Great Hall, where they went up a flight of stairs and into a narrow, corridor-like room.

"This long gallery," the guide informed them as they assembled behind a velvet cord that ran the length of the room, "is one of the most famous in England. It contains not only the finest collection of rococo silver in the country, part of which you can see arranged to the left of the fireplace on that demi-lune table — that's a Sheraton piece, by the way — but also a Le Brun, two Gainsboroughs, a Reynolds, a Holbein, a charming Whistler, two Turners, three Van Dycks, and a number of lesser known artists. In the case at the end of the room, you'll find a hat, gloves, and stockings that belonged to Elizabeth the First. And here's one of the most remarkable features in the entire house." She walked to the left of the Sheraton table and pushed lightly on a section of the paneling. A door swung open, previously hidden by the structure of the wall.

Several of the German tourists clapped appreciatively. The guide said, "It's a Gibb door. Clever, isn't it? Servants could come and go through it and never be seen in the public rooms of the house."

Cameras clicked in the guide's direction. Necks craned. Voices murmured.

And that's when it happened.

The guide was saying, "I'd like you to especially take note of —" when events conspired to interrupt her.

Someone gasped, "Hon! Nor! Hon!" and someone else cried, "Oh my God!" A third voice called out, "Watch out! Ralph's going down!"

And in short order, that's exactly what happened. Ralph Tucker gave an inarticulate cry and crashed down onto one of Abinger Manor's valuable satinwood tables. He upset an enormous flower arrangement, smashed a porcelain bowl of potpourri which sent its contents flying across the Persian carpet, and toppled the table onto its side. This, in effect, ripped the velvet cord from its brass posts down the entire length of the room as Ralph landed in an unmoving heap on the floor.

Noreen Tucker shrieked, "Ralph! Sweetie pie!" and plunged through the crowd to get to her spouse. She pulled on his shoulder as chaos broke out around her. People pressed forward, others backed away. Someone began praying, someone else cursing. Three

German women fell onto sofas that were available now that the line of demarcation was gone. A man shouted for water while another called for air.

There were thirty-two people in the room with absolutely no one in charge since the guide — whose training had been limited to memorizing salient details about the furnishings of Abinger Manor and not first aid — stood rooted to the floor as if she herself had had some part in whatever had just happened to Ralph Tucker.

Voices came from every direction.

"Is he . . . ?"

"Jesus. He *can't* be . . ."

"Ralph! Ralphie!"

"Sie ist gerade ohnmächtig geworden, nicht wahr . . ."

"Someone call an ambulance, for God's sake." This last was said by Cleve Houghton, who'd managed to fight his way through the crowd and who had dropped to his knees, had taken one look at Ralph Tucker's face, and had begun administering CPR. "Now!" he shouted at the guide who finally roused herself, flew through the Gibb door, and pounded up the stairs.

"Ralphie! Ralphie!" Noreen Tucker wailed as Cleve paused, took Ralph's pulse, and went back to CPR.

"Kann er nicht etwas unternehmen?" one of the Germans cried as another said, *"Schauen Sie sich die Gesichtsfarbe an."*

It was then that Thomas Lynley joined Cleve, removing his jacket and handing it over to Helen Clyde. He eased through the crowd, straddled the elephantine figure of Ralph Tucker, and took over the heart massage as Cleve Houghton moved to Ralph's mouth and continued blowing into the man's lungs.

"Save him, *save* him!" Noreen cried. "Help him. Please!"

Victoria Wilder-Scott reached her side. She said, "They're helping him, dear. If you'll come this way . . ."

"I won't leave my Ralph! He just needed to *eat*."

"Is he choking?" someone asked.

"Have you tried the Heimlich?"

And the tour guide crashed back into the room. She called out, "I've just phoned . . ." But her words faltered, then stopped. She could see as well as everyone else that the two men working on the body on the floor were attempting to revive what was already a corpse.

Thomas Lynley took charge at this point. He brought forth his warrant card and showed it to the guide, saying quietly, "Thomas Lynley. New Scotland Yard. Have someone tell my aunt — Lady Fabringham — there's been a mishap in the gallery, but for God's sake keep her out of here, all right?" He knew Augusta's propensity for involving herself in matters not her concern, and the last thing they needed was to have her tramping round giving orders which would only complicate matters. An ambulance was on its way, after all, and there was nothing more to be done other than to get this unfortunate individual to hospital where he'd be pronounced dead by an official employed for just that purpose. Lynley suggested that the others continue on their tour if for no other reason than to clear the room for the arrival of the rescue crew.

No one much felt like going forward to see the further glories of Abinger Manor at this juncture, but leaving the weeping Noreen Tucker behind, the rest of the company filed obediently out of the room. This was not before Lynley bent to the body on the floor, however, and opened the fist that was clenched in death.

Cleve Houghton said to him, "Heart failure. I've seen them go like this before," but while Lynley nodded, he made no reply. Instead he examined the remains of the trail mix that dribbled from Ralph's fingers onto the floor. When he looked up, it was not at Cleve but rather at the departing group. And he looked at them with serious speculation because it was more than clear to the country-born Thomas Lynley if to no one else at the moment that Ralph Tucker had been murdered.

While Noreen Tucker sank weeping into a priceless Chippendale chair and Helen Clyde went to her and put a comforting hand upon her shoulder, the door closed behind the tour group and within moments they were being asked to admire the drawing room, especially the pendant plasterwork of its remarkable ceiling. It was called the King Edward Drawing Room, their much-subdued guide told them, its name taken from the statue of Edward IV that stood over the mantelpiece. It was a three-quarter-size statue, she explained, not life-size, for unlike most men of his time, Edward IV was well over six feet tall. In fact, when he rode into London on the twenty-sixth of February in 1460 . . .

Frankly, no one could believe that the young woman was going on. There was

44

something indecent about being asked to admire chandeliers, flocked wallpaper, eighteenth-century furniture, Chinese vases, and a French chimneypiece in the face of Ralph Tucker's death. No matter that the man was essentially no one to any of them. He was still dead and out of respect for his passing, they might have abandoned the rest of the tour.

So everyone was restless and uneasy. The air was close. Composure seemed brittle. When Cleve Houghton finally rejoined them in the winter dining room with the news that Ralph Tucker's body had been taken away, he passed along the information that Thomas Lynley had also put out a call for the local police.

"Police?" Emily Guy whispered, horrified by the implication.

The word quickly swept through the rest of the company. The students of the History of British Architecture class began eyeing each other with grave suspicion.

Everyone knew it had to be the trail mix. The difficulty was the same for all of them, however: No one could root out the answer to the pressing question of why anyone on earth or anywhere else would want to murder Ralph Tucker. Noreen Tucker, yes. She'd stuck her nose into everyone else's business from day one, and she was certainly the least likely among them to win the Congeniality Award. Or perhaps Sam Cleary, done in by his wife for stepping outside the vows of marriage one time too many for her liking. Or even Frances herself, eliminated by Sam to give him a clear shot at Something More with Polly Simpson. But Ralph? No. It didn't make sense.

Everyone's thoughts thus went in the same general direction. It was when they ended up with Polly Simpson that several individuals remembered a terrible but significant detail: Polly too had eaten from Ralph Tucker's trail mix and not for the first time, as a matter of fact. For hadn't she also dipped into it on their very first outing when Ralph, in a moment of bonhomie that was not repeated, generously offered the mix round the tour coach in place of afternoon tea on their way back to Cambridge after a long day looking at properties in Norfolk? Yes, she had. She alone certainly had. So it was possible that *she* had been fingered for murder, with Ralph Tucker merely an unfortunate casualty who'd had to be done away with as well.

This made more than one person watch Polly with some concern, waiting for the least sign that she too was about to collapse from whatever it was that had taken Ralph from them. Someone even quietly suggested that she might want to retire to a lavatory and do what she could to upchuck just in case. But Polly, who didn't seem to understand the implication being made, merely grimaced at the suggestion and went on taking her pictures, albeit noticeably subdued from her usual ebullience.

Death by trail mix naturally brought up the question of poison in people's minds. And that made people ask themselves how someone was supposed to get a poison in Cambridge. You couldn't just walk into the local pharmacy and ask for something fast-acting, untraceable, and non-messy. So it stood to reason that the poison in question had been brought from home. And *that* led people into thinking more seriously about Noreen Tucker and whether her devotion to dear Ralph was all that it seemed.

The group was in the library when Thomas Lynley and his lady rejoined them, with Lynley running his speculative gaze over everyone in the room. His companion did much the same, having been brought into the picture while poor Ralph was being loaded into the ambulance. They separated and took up positions in different parts of the crowd. Neither of them paid the slightest attention to what the guide was saying. Instead they gave their full attention to the visitors to Abinger Manor.

From the library they went into the chapel, accompanied by the sounds of their own footsteps, the echoing voice of the guide, the occasional snapping of cameras. Lynley moved through the group, saying nothing to anyone save his companion, with whom he spoke a few words at the door. Again they separated.

From the chapel they went to the armory. From there into the billiard room. From there into the music room. From there, they traipsed down two flights of stairs and went into the kitchen. The buttery beyond it had been turned into a gift shop, and the Germans made for this as the Americans did likewise. It was at this moment that Lynley spoke.

"If I might see everyone together," he said as they began to scatter. "If you'll just stay here in the kitchen for a moment."

Mild protests rose from the German group. The Americans said nothing.

"We've a problem to consider, I'm afraid," Lynley said, "with regard to Mr. Tucker's death."

"Problem?" Sam Cleary asked the question as others chimed in with "What's going on?" and "What do you want with us?"

"It was heart failure," Cleve Houghton asserted. "I've seen enough of that to tell you —"

"As have I," a heavily accented voice put in. The remark came from a member of the German party, and he looked none too pleased that their tour was once again being disrupted. "I am a doctor. I, too, have seen heart failure. I know what I see."

This begged the question, naturally, of why the man hadn't done something to help out during the crisis, but no one mentioned that fact. Instead, Thomas Lynley extended his hand. In his palm lay half a dozen seeds. "It looks like heart failure," he explained. "That's what an alkaloid does. It paralyzes the heart in a matter of minutes. These are yew, by the way."

"Yew?" someone asked. "What was yew —"

"Those would be from the potpourri," Victoria Wilder-Scott pointed out. "It spilled all over the carpet when Mr. Tucker fell."

Lynley shook his head. "They were mixed in with the nuts in his hand," he said. "And the bag he was carrying in his jacket was peppered with them. He was murdered, I'm afraid."

So everyone's secret fears had been harped aright. And while some of them dwelled once more on the question of why Ralph Tucker had been murdered, the rest of them looked to the only person in the kitchen who would know beyond a doubt the potential harm contained in a bit of yew.

The Germans, in the meantime, were protesting heartily. The doctor led them. "You have no business with us," he said. "That man was a stranger. I insist that we be allowed to leave."

"Of course," Thomas Lynley said. "I agree. And leave you shall, just as soon as we solve the problem of the silver."

"What are you talking about?"

"It appears that one of you took the opportunity of the chaos in the gallery to remove two pieces of rococo silver from the table by the fireplace. They're milk jugs. Rather small, extremely ornate, and definitely missing. This isn't my jurisdiction, of course, but until the local police arrive to start their inquiries into Mr. Tucker's death, I'd like to take care of this small detail of the silver myself." He could, of course, only too easily imagine what his aunt Augusta would have to say about the matter if he *didn't* take care of it.

"What are you going to do?" Frances Cleary asked fearfully.

"Do you plan to keep us here until one of us admits to something?" the German doctor scoffed. "You cannot search us without some authority."

"That's correct, of course," Thomas Lynley said. "Unless you agree to be searched."

Silence ensued. Into it, feet shuffled. A throat cleared. Urgent conversation was conducted in German. Someone rustled papers in a notebook.

Cleve Houghton was the first to speak. He looked over the group. "Hell, I have no objection."

"But the women . . ." Victoria Wilder-Scott pointed out with some delicacy.

Lynley nodded to his companion, who was standing by a display of copper kettles at the edge of the group. "This is Lady Helen Clyde," he told them. "She'll search the women."

And so they searched: the men in the scullery and the women in the warming room across the corridor.

Both Thomas Lynley and Helen Clyde

made a thorough job of it. Lynley was all business. Helen employed a more gentle touch. Each of them had the individuals in their keeping undress and redress. Each of them emptied pockets, bags, rucksacks, and canvas totes. Lynley did all of this in a grim silence designed to intimidate. Helen chatted with the women in a manner designed to put them at ease.

In neither case did they find anything, however. Even Victoria Wilder-Scott and the tour guide had been searched.

Lynley told them to wait in the tearoom. He turned back to the stairway at the far end of the kitchen.

"Where's he going now?" Polly Simpson asked, hands clutching her camera to her chest.

"He'll have to look for the silver in the rest of the house," Emily Guy pointed out.

"But that could take *forever,*" Frances Cleary whispered.

"It doesn't matter, does it? We're going to have to wait for the local police anyway."

"Hell no, this was heart failure," Cleve Houghton said. "There's no silver missing. It's probably being cleaned somewhere."

But this, alas, was not the case, as Lynley discovered when he made the report he did not wish to make to his paternal aunt.

Augusta was all suitable horror and compassion when told that a visitor to her home had died on the premises. But she was vengeance incarnate when she learned that a "sneaky little criminal" had had the sheer *audacity* to take possession of one of her priceless treasures. She expounded for a good five minutes on what she intended to do to the perpetrator of this crime, and it was only by assuring his aunt that the Law — in the person of himself — would work tirelessly on her behalf that Lynley was able to prevent the woman from accosting the visitors herself. He left Augusta to the ministrations of her three corgis, and retraced his steps to find the tour group.

They had left the buttery and were being held in the courtyard, and Lynley could see them from the windows in the private wing where his aunt now lived. He studied them, taking note of the fact that even in crisis people tended to adhere to cultural stereotypes. The Germans stood grimly in tiny clusters of people with whom they were already intimate. Husbands with their wives. Wives and husbands with their children. In-laws with their offspring and grandchildren. Students with their compatriots. They did not venture beyond the boundaries of these already established groups and for the most part they stood in stiff silence. The Americans, on the other hand, mingled not only with each other but also with the English family groups who'd been on the tour with them. They spoke to each other, some somberly and some with a fair degree of animation. And one among them even took a few pictures.

Lynley had noted Polly Simpson earlier, as a reflex reaction that grew from the fact that he'd once been in love with a young photographer. He wasn't so many years away from that affair that he hadn't noticed — as he would have done during the time of that involvement — the equipment which Polly was using. It was odd, he thought as he watched her, how our attachment to a person allows us to learn things that we never expect to learn. Not only about ourselves, not only about them, but about aspects of life that we might otherwise remain in ignorance of. Watching Polly below him in the courtyard, Lynley was able to imagine his former lover in the same circumstance, with the same enthusiasm for light and texture and composition, able to concentrate on the work she was doing by dismissing what had just preceded it.

This was part of the resilience of youth, he decided (somewhat pompously since he himself was not yet forty), and having spent fifteen years in pursuit of the criminal element, he allowed himself a moment wistfully watching Polly Simpson at work with her camera before retracing his steps to the group. He was crossing through the kitchen on his way to the buttery when the significance of what he'd just seen in the courtyard finally struck him. And even then it only struck him because he'd recalled more than once playing the pack mule for his former lover's photographic equipment, hearing her say more to herself than to him, "I'll need the twenty-eight millimeter to get this shot," and then standing patiently by while she made the switch in her lenses.

More than that, he realised that all throughout the tour and before it — as he and Helen had made a circuit of the grounds among the other visitors to Abinger Manor — he'd seen a truth without actually registering *what* he was seeing. Which was so easy to do, he thought, when you don't consider the logic behind what's in front of your eyes.

He strode through the buttery. From there, he went out into the courtyard. So sure he was of what he was about to do that he dismissed the Germans and the two English families and waited in grim silence while they left the courtyard. When they had done so, he sought out Polly Simpson and without ceremony, he took the camera from her shoulder.

She protested with, "Hey! That's mine. What're you —"

He silenced her by opening the first of the film containers that were affixed to the strap of the camera. It was empty. As were the others. He said, "I've been noticing you taking pictures since we arrived. How many would you say you've exposed?"

She said, "I don't know. I don't keep count. I just keep taking them till I run out."

"But you've brought no extra film, have you?"

"I didn't think I'd need it."

"No? Curious. You began taking pictures the moment you stepped into the garden. You haven't stopped, except during the crisis in the gallery, I expect. Or did you photograph that as well?"

Emily Guy gasped. Sam Cleary said, "See here . . ." and would have gone further had his wife not clutched at his arm.

"What's this all about?" Victoria Wilder-

Scott said. "Everyone knows Polly always takes pictures."

"Indeed? With this lens?" Lynley asked.

"It's a macro zoom," Polly said, and as Lynley grasped the lens forcefully, she cried, "Hey! Don't! That thing cost a mint."

"Did it," Lynley said. He twisted it off. He upended it smartly against the palm of his hand. Two pieces of silver tumbled out.

Several people gasped.

"A dummy," Cleve Houghton said soberly.

And every eye in the courtyard went to Polly Simpson.

It was a sombre History of British Architecture class that returned to Cambridge late that evening. They were, of course, minus three of their members. What remained of Ralph Tucker was undergoing the postmortem knife while his widow made the most of her circumstances by accepting the hospitality of a solicitous Augusta, dowager countess of Fabringham, who was well aware of Americans' bent towards litigation at the drop of the hat and was eager to avoid a close encounter with any form of American jurisprudence. And Polly Simpson was in the custody of the local police, charged with the primary crime of murder and the secondary thwarted crime of burglary.

Polly Simpson was heavily on the minds of her fellow students, needless to say. And needless to say, they all felt rather differently about her.

Sam Cleary, for one, felt a perfect fool for having failed to recognize that Polly's fascination with him had in reality extended only as far as his knowledge of botany. She'd hung on his every word and story, it was true, but hadn't she guided him most towards his work, till she had what she needed from him: a poison she could put her hands on simply by taking a walk along the college backs in Cambridge.

Frances Cleary, for another, felt reassured. True, Ralph Tucker was dead so the cost was high, but she'd learned that her husband wasn't the object of young girls' fatal attraction that she'd thought he was, so she rested far more secure in her marriage. Secure enough, indeed, to allow Sam to ride home in the mini-coach right next to Emily Guy.

Emily Guy and Victoria Wilder-Scott felt disappointed and depressed by the day's events, but for different reasons. Vic-

toria Wilder-Scott had just lost the first en-
thusiastic student she'd had in a summer
session from America in years while Emily
Guy had discovered that a pretty young
girl, so much admired because she had no
weakness for men, had a weakness for
something else instead.

And the men themselves — Howard
Breen and Cleve Houghton? They thought
of Polly's arrest as a loss. For his part,
Cleve mourned the fact that her arrest
would put an end to his hopes of getting
her to bed despite the twenty-seven years
between their respective ages. And for *his*
part, Howard Breen was happy to see the
last of her . . . since her departure left
Cleve Houghton available to him. After all,
one could always hope, at the end of the
day.

And that's what the Americans actually
ended up learning in the History of British
Architecture class that summer in Cambridge: Hope hadn't worked for Polly
Simpson. But that's not to say it wouldn't
work for the rest of them.

Introduction to
The Surprise of His Life

The inspiration for this story came from a double homicide that caught my attention in the early 1990s. It received a great deal of publicity at the time and although the defendant was found not guilty of the charges, I spent a lot of time considering his potential for guilt and how, if indeed he committed the crime, the killing might have come about. Here's what I concluded:

Although there were two victims of that crime — a young man and a slightly older woman — it seemed to me that the wife was the target.

The husband was an obsessive man estranged from his wife. His life was dominated by thoughts of her, specifically with thoughts of how she had left him and, in leaving him, how she had humiliated him. He was a minor celebrity. In his mind, she was nothing. Yet *she* walked out on *him* and, to make matters worse, she no longer gave any indication that things might work out eventually between them. She'd initially said she wanted a cooling-off period because their relationship was so volatile. He'd agreed to that. But now she was talking about divorce and the d-word made him feel like a fool. Not only would he probably lose his kids — they had two of them, a boy and a girl — but a divorce was going to cost him a bucket and she didn't deserve a dime of what he had.

Thoughts like these began swarming in his mind until every hour of every day was torture for the husband. Only when he slept was he free from the wife and from her plans to take his kids, take his money, and no doubt hook up with some young stud . . . all at *his* expense. But even then, at night, the husband dreamed about her. And the thoughts during the day and the dreams at night were driving him so crazy, he thought he'd die if he couldn't do something about them.

It seemed to him that the only way to wipe her out of his mind was to kill her. She deserved it anyway. He'd always watched how she came on to men. She'd probably been unfaithful to him a dozen times already. She was a lousy wife and a lousy mother and he'd be doing his kids a favor at the same time as he'd be wiping her out of his mind if he just got rid of her.

So he laid his plans.

He and the wife lived no great distance apart. If he got his timing down to the second, he could zip over to her house, kill her, and be back at his own place . . . all within about fifteen minutes. Maybe less. But he knew that the cops would want him to account for every second on the night his wife was murdered, so he decided to set things up for a night when he had a flight to catch to another part of the country. To make things look even tighter, he'd phone a limousine to take him to the airport. Who the heck, he thought, would *ever* figure that a killer would off his wife barely a half hour before a limo was picking him up?

The question of the weapon was a tricky one. He couldn't use a gun for obvious reasons: It was a crowded neighborhood and one gunshot would have everyone out in the street wondering what was going on. He couldn't shoot her inside her house, either, because their children would be upstairs in bed and the last thing he wanted was to have them wake up and come running down to find their dad standing over their mother's body with a smoking gun.

There was always a garrote, but that allowed her to be able to fight him off. So, no. He needed something quick like a gun but silent like a garrote, and a knife seemed like the only answer.

So on the night in question, he dressed in black. So as not to leave any forensic evidence behind, he wore gloves on his hands and a knitted cap on his head. He was a big man — tall, hefty, muscular, and strong — and she was small. If everything went according to plan, he'd have her out of the way in less than a minute and *then* he'd be free of her at last.

He went to her house, a townhouse which was set back from the street behind a wall. He knocked on the door. She had a dog, but the dog knew him and shouldn't be a problem.

Oddly enough, she opened the door to his knock instead of asking who it was the way she normally did. But that also was of no account. He asked her if she'd just step outside so they could talk for a minute without waking up the kids.

I'm heading out in an hour, he told her. I wanted to talk to you about . . .

What? His decision to go ahead and not contest the divorce? The settlement she wanted? One or both of their children?

It doesn't matter because whatever he asked to talk to her about was what got her to step outside the house. And when she did that, he was upon her so quickly that she never knew what hit her. He spun her around, plunged the knife into her neck, and he slashed it across her throat with a power that came from the fury he felt toward her: because she wouldn't get out of his mind, because she was going to take his children, because she was going to rob him blind, just *because*.

It was over in an instant. He lowered her dead and bloody body to the ground and turned to leave . . . just as the gate opened and a young man entered.

He was on a friendly errand: simply returning a pair of sunglasses to their owner. He was on his way home from work and the last thing he expected to see was the husband with a knife in his hand and his wife's mutilated body on the ground before him.

The young man's first reaction was to draw a breath in shock. He said, What the — but he had time for no more. The husband leapt upon him with the knife in his hand, slashing and stabbing.

There was no noise. This was not a Hollywood movie where men fight for their lives to the accompaniment of sound effects and music. This was real. And in a real fight, there is only silence broken by grunts or groans, neither of which are audible behind a wall.

During the fight, the husband lost the knitted hat he had on. He lost one of the gloves. He was covered with blood and his own knife had cut him on the hand. But he prevailed. The young man died, his only crime being helpful.

The husband now had a problem on his hands, though. Valuable time had been lost in the second killing. He couldn't stop to find the hat and the glove. He also had to get home, throw his clothes into the washer, get into the shower, and get out to that limousine.

This was what he did, losing the second glove in his haste.

As for the knife, that was not a problem. He put it in his golf bag which he was taking with him on his trip. The golf bag might have been X-rayed at the airport with the baggage set to go into the hold of the jet. But among the golf clubs, it would hardly be noticed and even if it was, it didn't constitute an explosive so it would hardly be remarked upon.

When he arrived at his destination, his

plan was simple to execute. He dressed in sweats and went out for an early-morning run. He took the knife with him and disposed of it somewhere along the route.

Within a scant few hours, he would be notified of his wife's murder. But he had his alibi and even if that didn't hold up, he had plenty of money to hire lawyers to get him out of whatever mess that kid with the sunglasses caused him.

When I considered that crime and the husband's potential for guilt, it triggered within me the idea for the short story that follows. In it, a husband begins obsessing about his young wife's faithlessness . . . with unexpected results.

The Surprise of His Life

When Douglas Armstrong had his first consultation with Thistle McCloud, he had no intention of murdering his wife. His mind, in fact, didn't turn to murder until two weeks after consultation number four.

At that time, Douglas watched closely as Thistle prepared herself for a revelation from another dimension. She held his wedding band in the palm of her left hand. She closed her fingers around it. She hovered her right hand over the fist that she'd made, and she hummed five notes that sounded suspiciously like the beginning of "I Love You Truly." Gradually, her eyes rolled back, up, and out of view beneath her yellow-shaded lids, leaving him with the disconcerting sight of a thirty-something female in a straw boater, striped vest, white shirt, and polka-dotted tie, looking as if she were one quarter of a barbershop quartet in desperate hope of finding her partners.

When he'd first seen Thistle, Douglas had appraised her attire — which in subsequent visits had not altered in any appreciable fashion — as the insidious getup of a charlatan who wished to focus her clients' attention on her personal appearance rather than on whatever machinations she would be going through to delve into their pasts, their presents, their futures, and — most importantly — their wallets. But he'd come to realize that Thistle's odd getup had nothing to do with distracting anyone. The first time she held his old Rolex watch and began speaking in a low, intense voice about the prodigal son, about his endless departures and equally endless returns, about his aging parents who welcomed him always with open arms and open hearts, about his brother who watched all this with a false fixed smile and a silent shout of *What about me? Do I mean nothing?*, he had a feeling that Thistle was exactly what she purported to be: a psychic.

He'd first come to her storefront operation because he'd had forty minutes to kill prior to his yearly prostate exam. He dreaded the exam and the teeth-grating embarrassment of having to answer his doctor's jovial, rib-poking "Everything up and about as it should be?" with the truth, which was that Newton's law of gravity had begun asserting itself lately to his dearest appendage. And since he was six weeks short of his fifty-fifth birthday, and since every disaster in his life had occurred in a year that was a multiple of five, if there was a chance of knowing what the gods had in store for him and his prostate, he wanted to be able to do something to head off the chaos.

These things had all been on his mind as he spun along Pacific Coast Highway in the dim gold light of a late December afternoon. On a drearily commercialized section of the road — given largely to pizza parlors and boogie board shops — he had seen the small blue building that he'd passed a thousand times before and read PSYCHIC CONSULTATIONS on its hand-painted sign. He'd glanced at his gas gauge for an excuse to stop and while he pumped super unleaded into the tank of his Mercedes across the street from that small blue building, he made his decision. What the hell, he'd thought. There were worse ways to kill forty minutes.

So he'd had his first session with Thistle McCloud, who was anything but what he'd expected of a psychic since she used no crystal ball, no tarot cards, nothing at all but a piece of his jewelry. In his first three visits, it had always been the Rolex watch from which she'd received her psychic emanations. But today she'd placed the watch to one side, declared it diluted of power, and set her fog-colored eyes on his wedding ring. She'd touched her finger to it, and said, "I'll use that, I think. If you want something further from your history and closer to your heart."

He'd given her the ring precisely because of those last two phrases: *further from your history and closer to your heart.* They told him how very well she knew that the prodigal son business rose from his past while his deepest concerns were attached to his future.

Now, with the ring in her closed fist and with her eyes rolled upward, Thistle stopped the five-note humming, breathed deeply six times, and opened her eyes. She observed him with a melancholia that made his stomach feel hollow.

"What?" Douglas asked.

"You need to prepare for a shock," she said. "It's something unexpected. It comes from nowhere and because of it, the essence of your life will be changed forever. And soon. I feel it coming very soon."

Jesus, he thought. It was just what he needed to hear three weeks after having an indifferent index finger shoved up his ass to see what was the cause of his limp-dick syndrome. The doctor had said it wasn't cancer, but he hadn't ruled out half a dozen other possibilities. Douglas wondered which one of them Thistle had just tuned her psychic antennae onto.

Thistle opened her hand and they both looked at his wedding ring where it lay on her palm, faintly sheened by her sweat. "It's an external shock," she clarified. "The source of upheaval in your life isn't from within. The shock comes from outside and rattles you to your core."

"Are you sure about that?" Douglas asked her.

"As sure as I can be, considering the armor you wear." Thistle returned the ring to him, her cool fingers grazing his wrist. She said, "Your name isn't David, is it? It never was David. It never will be David. But the *D* I feel is correct. Am I right?"

He reached into his back pocket and brought out his wallet. Careful to shield his driver's license from her, he clipped a fifty-dollar bill between his thumb and index finger. He folded it and handed it over.

"Donald," she said. "No. That isn't it, either. Darrell, perhaps. Dennis. I sense two syllables."

"Names aren't important in your line of work, are they?" Douglas said.

"No. But the truth is always important. Someday, Not-David, you're going to have to learn to trust people with the truth. Trust is the key. Trust is essential."

"Trust," he told her, "is what gets people screwed."

Outside, he walked across the highway to the cramped side street that paralleled the ocean. Here he always parked his car when he visited Thistle. With its vanity license plate DRIL4IT virtually announcing who owned the Mercedes, Douglas had decided early on that it wouldn't encourage new investors if someone put the word out that the president of South Coast Oil had begun seeing a psychic regularly. Risky investments were one thing. Placing money with a man who could be accused of using parapsychology rather than geology to find oil deposits was another. He wasn't doing that, of course. Business never came up in his sessions with Thistle. But try telling that to the board of directors. Try telling that to anyone.

He unarmed the car and slid inside. He headed south, in the direction of his office. As far as anyone at South Coast Oil knew, he'd spent his lunch hour with his wife, having a romantic winter's picnic on the bluffs in Corona del Mar. The cellular phone will be turned off for an hour, he'd informed his secretary. Don't try to phone and don't bother us, please. This is time for Donna and me.

Any mention of Donna always did the trick when it came to keeping South Coast Oil off his back for a few hours. She was warmly liked by everyone in the company. She was warmly liked by everyone period. Sometimes, he reflected suddenly, she was too warmly liked. Especially by men.

You need to prepare for a shock.

Did he? Douglas considered the question in relation to his wife.

When he pointed out men's affinity for her, Donna always acted surprised. She told him that men merely recognized in her a woman who'd grown up in a household of brothers. But what he saw in men's eyes when they looked at his wife had nothing to do with fraternal affection. It had to do with getting her naked, getting down and dirty, and getting laid.

It's an external shock.

Was it? What sort? Douglas thought of the worst.

Getting laid was behind every man-woman interaction on earth. He knew this well. So while his recent failures to get it up and get it on with Donna frustrated him, he had to admit that he was feeling concerned that her patience with him was trickling away. Once it was gone, she'd start looking around. That was only natural. And once she started looking, she was going to find or be found.

The shock comes from outside and rattles you to your core.

Shit, Douglas thought. If chaos was about to steamroller into his life as he approached his fifty-fifth birthday — that rotten bad luck integer — Douglas knew that Donna would probably be at the wheel. She was twenty-nine, four years in place as wife number three, and while she acted content, he'd been around women long enough to know that still waters did more than simply run deep. They hid rocks that could sink a boat in seconds if a sailor didn't keep his wits about him. And love made people lose their wits. Love made people go a little bit nuts.

Of course, *he* wasn't nuts. He had his wits about him. But being in love with a woman nearly thirty years his junior, a woman whose scent caught the nose of every male within sixty yards of her, a woman whose physical appetites he himself was failing to satisfy on a nightly basis . . . and had been failing to satisfy for weeks

. . . a woman like that . . .

"Get a grip," Douglas told himself brusquely. "This psychic stuff is baloney, right? Right." But still he thought of the coming shock, the upset to his life, and its source: external. Not his prostate, not his dick, not an organ in his body. But another human being. "Shit," he said.

He guided the car up the incline that led to Jamboree Road, six lanes of concrete that rolled between stunted liquidambar trees through some of the most expensive real estate in Orange County. It took him to the bronzed glass tower that housed his pride: South Coast Oil.

Once inside the building, he navigated his way through an unexpected encounter with two of SCO's engineers, through a brief conversation with a geologist who simultaneously waved an ordnance survey map and a report from the EPA, and through a hallway conference with the head of the accounting department. His secretary handed him a fistful of messages when he finally managed to reach his office. She said, "Nice picnic? The weather's unbelievable, isn't it?" followed by "Everything all right, Mr. Armstrong?" when he didn't reply.

He said, "Yes. What? Fine," and looked

through the messages. He found that the names meant nothing to him.

He walked to the window behind his desk and looked at the view through its enormous pane of tinted glass. Below him, Orange County's airport sent jet after jet hurtling into the sky at an angle so acute that it defied both reason and aerodynamics, although it did protect the delicate auditory sensibilities of the millionaires who lived in the flight path below. Douglas watched these planes without really seeing them. He knew he had to answer his telephone messages, but all he could think about was Thistle's words: *an external shock.*

What could be more external than Donna?

She wore Obsession. She put it behind her ears and beneath her breasts. Whenever she passed through a room, she left the scent of herself behind.

Her dark hair gleamed when the sunlight hit it. She wore it short and simply cut, parted on the left and smoothly falling just to her ears.

Her legs were long. When she walked, her stride was full and sure. And when she walked with him — at his side, with her hand through his arm and her head held back — he knew that she caught the attention of everyone. He knew that together they were the envy of all their friends and of strangers as well.

He could see this reflected in the faces of people they passed when he and Donna were together. At the ballet, at the theater, at concerts, in restaurants, glances gravitated to Douglas Armstrong and his wife. In women's expressions he could read the wish to be young like Donna, to be smooth-skinned again, to be vibrant once more, to be fecund and ready. In men's expressions he could read desire.

It had always been a pleasure to see how others reacted to the sight of his wife. But now he saw how dangerous her allure really was and how it threatened to destroy his peace.

A shock, Thistle had said to him. *Prepare for a shock. Prepare for a shock that will change your world.*

That evening, Douglas heard the water running as soon as he entered the house: fifty-two-hundred square feet of limestone floors, vaulted ceilings, and picture windows on a hillside that offered an ocean view to the west and the lights of Orange County to the east. The house had cost him a fortune, but that had been all right

79

with him. Money meant nothing. He'd bought the place for Donna. But if he'd had doubts about his wife before — born of his own performance anxiety, growing to adulthood through his consultation with Thistle — when Douglas heard the water running, he began to see the truth. Because Donna was in the shower.

He watched her silhouette behind the blocks of translucent glass that defined the shower's wall. She was washing her hair. She hadn't noticed him yet, and he watched her for a moment, his gaze traveling over her uplifted breasts, her hips, her long legs. She usually bathed — languorous bubble baths in the raised oval tub that looked out on the lights of the city of Irvine. Taking a shower suggested a more earnest and energetic effort to cleanse herself. And washing her hair suggested . . . Well, it was perfectly clear what that suggested. Scents got caught up in the hair: cigarette smoke, sautéing garlic, fish from a fishing boat, or semen and sex. Those last two were the betraying scents. Obviously, she would have to wash her hair.

Her discarded clothes lay on the floor. With a hasty glance at the shower, Douglas fingered through them and found her lacy underwear. He knew women. He knew his wife. If she'd actually been with a man that afternoon, her body's leaking juices would have made the panties' crotch stiff when they dried, and he would be able to smell the afterscent of intercourse on them. They would give him proof. He lifted them to his face.

"Doug! What on earth are you doing?"

Douglas dropped the panties, cheeks hot and neck sweating. Donna was peering at him from the shower's opening, her hair lathered with soap that streaked down her left cheek. She brushed it away.

"What are *you* doing?" he asked her. Three marriages and two divorces had taught him that a fast offensive maneuver threw the opponent off balance. It worked.

She popped back into the water — clever of her, so he couldn't see her face — and said, "It's pretty obvious. I'm taking a shower. God, what a day."

He moved to watch her through the shower's opening. There was no door, just a partition in the glass-block wall. He could study her body and look for the telltale signs of the kind of rough lovemaking he knew that she liked. And she wouldn't know he was even looking, since her head was beneath the shower as she rinsed off her hair.

81

"Steve phoned in sick today," she said, "so I had to do everything at the kennels myself."

She raised chocolate Labradors. He had met her that way, seeking a dog for his youngest son. Through a reference from a veterinarian, he had discovered her kennels in Midway City — less than one square mile of feedstores, other kennels, and dilapidated postwar stucco and shake roofs posing as suburban housing. It was an odd place for a girl from the pricey side of Corona del Mar to end up professionally, but that was what he liked about Donna. She wasn't true to type, she wasn't a beach bunny, she wasn't a typical Southern California girl. Or at least that's what he had thought.

"The worst was cleaning the dog runs," she said. "I didn't mind the grooming — I never mind that — but I hate doing the runs. I completely reeked of dog poop when I got home." She shut off the shower and reached for her towels, wrapping her head in one and her body in the other. She stepped out of the stall with a smile and said, "Isn't it weird how some smells cling to your body and your hair while others don't?"

She kissed him hello and scooped up her

clothes. She tossed them down the laundry chute. No doubt she was thinking, Out of sight, out of mind. She was clever that way.

"That's the third time Steve's phoned in sick in two weeks." She headed for the bedroom, drying off as she went. She dropped the towel with her usual absence of self-consciousness and began dressing, pulling on wispy underwear, black leggings, a silver tunic. "If he keeps this up, I'm going to let him go. I need someone consistent, someone reliable. If he's not going to be able to hold up his end . . ." She frowned at Douglas, her face perplexed. "What's wrong, Doug? You're looking at me so funny. Is something wrong?"

"Wrong? No." But he thought, That looks like a love bite on her neck. And he crossed to her for a better look. He cupped her face for a kiss and tilted her head. The shadow of the towel that was wrapped around her hair dissipated, leaving her skin unmarred. Well, what of it? he thought. She wouldn't be so stupid as to let some heavy breather suck bruises into her flesh, no matter how turned on he had her. She wasn't that dumb. Not his Donna.

But she also wasn't as smart as her husband.

★ ★ ★

At five forty-five the next day, he went to the personnel department. It was a better choice than the Yellow Pages because at least he knew that whoever had been doing the background checks on incoming employees at South Coast Oil was simultaneously competent and discreet. No one had ever complained about some two-bit gumshoe nosing into his background.

The department was deserted, as Douglas had hoped. The computer screens at every desk were set to the shifting images that preserved them: a field of swimming fish, bouncing balls, and popping bubbles. The director's office at the far side of the department was unlit and locked, but a master key in the hand of the company president solved that problem. Douglas went inside and flipped on the lights.

He found the name he was looking for among the dog-eared cards of the director's Rolodex, a curious anachronism in an otherwise computer-age office. *Cowley and Son, Inquiries,* he read in faded typescript. This was accompanied by a telephone number and by an address on Balboa Peninsula.

Douglas studied both for the space of

two minutes. Was it better to know or to live in ignorant bliss? he wondered at this eleventh hour. But he wasn't living in bliss, was he? And he hadn't been living in bliss from the moment he'd failed to perform as a man was meant to. So it was better to know. He had to know. Knowledge was power. Power was control. He needed both.

He picked up the phone.

Douglas always went out for lunch — unless a conference was scheduled with his geologists or the engineers — so no one raised a hair of an eyebrow when he left South Coast Oil before noon the following day. He used Jamboree once again to get to the Coast Highway, but this time instead of heading north toward Newport where Thistle made her prognostications, he drove directly across the highway and down the incline where a modestly arched bridge spanned an oily section of Newport Harbor that divided the mainland from an amoeba-shaped portion of land that was Balboa Island.

In summer the island was infested with tourists. They bottled up the streets with their cars and rode bicycles in races on the sidewalk around the island's perimeter. No local in his right mind ventured onto Balboa Island during the summer without good reason or unless he lived there. But in winter, the place was virtually deserted. It took less than five minutes to snake through the narrow streets to the island's north end where the ferry waited to take cars and pedestrians on the eye-blink voyage across to the peninsula.

There a stripe-topped carousel and a Ferris wheel spun like two opposing gears of an enormous clock, defining an area called the Fun Zone, which had long been the summertime bane of the local police. Today, however, no bands of juveniles roved with cans of spray paint at the ready. The only inhabitants of the Fun Zone were a paraplegic in a wheelchair and his bike-riding companion.

Douglas passed them as he drove off the ferry. They were intent upon their conversation. The Ferris wheel and carousel did not exist for them. Nor did Douglas and his blue Mercedes, which was just as well. He didn't particularly want to be seen.

He parked just off the beach, in a lot where fifteen minutes cost a quarter. He pumped in four. He armed the car and headed west toward Main Street, a tree-shaded lane some sixty yards long that began at a faux New England restaurant overlooking Newport Harbor and ended at Balboa Pier, which stretched out into the Pacific Ocean, gray-green today and unsettled by roiling waves from a winter Alaskan storm.

Number 107-B Main was what he was looking for, and he found it easily. Just east of an alley, 107 was a two-story structure whose bottom floor was taken up by a time-warped hair salon called JJ's — heavily devoted to macramé, potted plants, and posters of Janis Joplin — and whose upper floor was divided into offices that were reached by means of a structurally questionable stairway at the north end of the building. Number 107-B was the first door upstairs — JJ's Natural Haircutting appeared to be 107-A — but when Douglas turned the discolored brass knob below the equally discolored brass nameplate announcing the business as COWLEY AND SON, INQUIRIES, he found the door locked.

He frowned and looked at his Rolex. His appointment was for twelve-fifteen. It was currently twelve-ten. So where was Cowley? Where was his son?

He returned to the stairway, ready to head to his car and his cellular phone, ready to track down Cowley and give him hell for setting up an appointment and failing to be there to keep it. But he was three steps down when he saw a khaki-clad man coming his way, sucking up an Orange Julius with the enthusiasm of a twelve-year-old. His thinning gray hair and sun-lined face marked him at least five decades older than twelve, however. And his limping gait — in combination with his clothes — suggested old war wounds.

"You Cowley?" Douglas called from the stairs.

The man waved his Orange Julius in reply. "You Armstrong?" he asked.

"Right," Douglas said. "Listen, I don't have a lot of time."

"None of us do, son," Cowley said, and he hoisted himself up the stairway. He nodded in a friendly fashion, pulled hard on the Orange Julius straw, and passed Douglas in a gust of aftershave he hadn't smelled for a good twenty years. Canoe. Jesus. Did they still sell that?

Cowley swung the door open and cocked his head to indicate that Douglas was to enter. The office comprised two rooms: One was a sparsely furnished waiting area through which they passed; the other was obviously Cowley's demesne. Its centerpiece was an olive-green steel desk. Filing cabinets and bookshelves of the same issue matched it.

The investigator went to an old oaken office chair behind the desk, but he didn't sit. Instead, he opened one of the side drawers, and just when Douglas was expecting him to pull out a fifth of bourbon, he dug out a bottle of yellow capsules instead. He shook two of them into his palm and knocked them back with a long swig of Orange Julius. He sank into his chair and gripped the arms.

"Arthritis," he said. "I'm killing the bastard with evening primrose oil. Give me a minute, okay? You want a couple?"

"No." Douglas glanced at his watch to make certain Cowley knew that his time was precious. Then he strolled to the steel bookshelves.

He was expecting to see munitions manuals, penal codes, and surveillance texts, something to assure the prospective clients that they'd come to the right place with their troubles. But what he found was poetry, volume after volume neatly arranged in alphabetical order by author, from Matthew Arnold to William Butler Yeats. He wasn't sure what to think.

The occasional space left at the end of a

bookshelf was taken up by photographs. They were clumsily framed, snapshots mostly. They depicted grinning small children, a gray-haired grandma type, several young adults. Among them, encased in Plexiglas, was a military Purple Heart. Douglas picked this up. He'd never seen one, but he was pleased to know that his guess about the source of Cowley's limp had been correct.

"You saw action," he said.

"My butt saw action," Cowley replied. Douglas looked his way, so the PI continued. "I took it in the butt. Shit happens, right?" He moved his hands from their grip on the arms of his chair. He folded them over his stomach. Like Douglas's own, it could have been flatter. Indeed, the two men shared a similar build: stocky, quickly given to weight if they didn't exercise, too tall to be called short and too short to be called tall. "What can I do for you, Mr. Armstrong?"

"My wife," Douglas said.

"Your wife?"

"She may be . . ." Now that it was time to articulate the problem and what it arose from, Douglas wasn't sure that he could. So he said, "Who's the son?"

Cowley reached for his Orange Julius

and took a pull on its straw. "He died," he said. "Drunk driver got him on the Ortega Highway."

"Sorry."

"Like I said. Shit happens. What shit's happened to you?"

Douglas returned the Purple Heart to its place. He caught sight of the graying grandma in one of the pictures and said, "This your wife?"

"Forty years my wife. Name's Maureen."

"I'm on my third. How'd you manage forty years with one woman?"

"She has a sense of humor." Cowley slid open the middle drawer of his desk and took out a legal pad and the stub of a pencil. He wrote ARMSTRONG at the top in block letters and underlined it. He said, "About your wife . . ."

"I think she's having an affair. I want to know if I'm right. I want to know who it is."

Cowley carefully set his pencil down. He observed Douglas for a moment. Outside, a gull gave a raucous cry from one of the rooftops. "What makes you think she's seeing someone?"

"Am I supposed to give you proof before you'll take the case? I thought that's why I was hiring you. To give *me* proof."

"You wouldn't be here if you didn't have suspicions. What are they?"

Douglas raked through his memory. He wasn't about to tell Cowley about trying to smell up Donna's underwear, so he took a moment to examine her behavior over the last few weeks. And when he did so, the additional evidence was there. How the *hell* had he missed it? She'd changed her hair; she'd bought new underwear — the black lacy Victoria's Secret stuff; she'd been on the phone twice when he'd come home and as soon as he walked into the room, she'd hung up hastily; there were at least two long absences with insufficient excuse for them; there were six or seven engagements that she said were with friends.

Cowley nodded thoughtfully when Douglas listed his suspicions. Then he said, "Have you given her a reason to cheat on you?"

"A reason? What is this? I'm the guilty party?"

"Women don't usually stray without there being a man behind them, giving them a reason." Cowley examined him from beneath unclipped eyebrows. One of his eyes, Douglas saw, was beginning to form a cataract. Jeez, the guy was ancient, a real antique.

"No reason," Douglas said. "I don't cheat on her. I don't even want to."

"She's young, though. And a man your age . . ." Cowley shrugged. "Shit happens to us old guys. Young things don't always have the patience to understand."

Douglas wanted to point out that Cowley was at least ten years his senior, if not more. He also wanted to exclude himself from membership in the club of *us old guys*. But the PI was watching him compassionately, so instead of arguing, Douglas told the truth.

Cowley reached for his Orange Julius and drained the cup. He tossed it into the trash. "Women have needs," he said, and he moved his hand from his crotch to his chest, adding, "A wise man doesn't confuse what goes on here" — the crotch — "with what goes on here" — the chest.

"So maybe I'm not wise. Are you going to help me out or not?"

"You sure you want help?"

"I want to know the truth. I can live with that. What I can't live with is not knowing. I just need to know what I'm dealing with here."

Cowley looked as if he were taking a reading of Douglas's level of veracity. He finally appeared to make a decision, but one he didn't like because he shook his head, picked up his pencil, and said, "Give me some background, then. If she's got someone on the side, who are our possibilities?"

Douglas had thought about this. There was Mike, the poolman who visited once a week. There was Steve, who worked with Donna at her kennels in Midway City. There was Jeff, her personal trainer. There were also the postman, the FedEx man, the UPS driver, and Donna's youthful gynecologist.

"I take it you're accepting the case?" Douglas said to Cowley. He pulled out his wallet from which he extracted a wad of bills. "You'll want a retainer."

"I don't need cash, Mr. Armstrong."

"All the same . . ." All the same, Douglas had no intention of leaving a paper trail via a check. "How much time do you need?" he asked.

"Give it a few days. If she's seeing someone, he'll surface eventually. They always do." Cowley sounded despondent.

"Your wife cheat on you?" Douglas asked shrewdly.

"If she did, I probably deserved it."

That was Cowley's attitude, but it was one that Douglas didn't share. He didn't deserve to be cheated on. Nobody did. And when he found out who was doing the job on his wife . . . Well, they would see a kind of justice that even Attila the Hun was incapable of extracting.

His resolve was strengthened in the bedroom that evening when his hello kiss to his wife was interrupted by the telephone. Donna pulled away from him quickly and went to answer it. She gave Douglas a smile — as if recognizing what her haste revealed to him — and shook back her hair as sexily as possible, running slim fingers through it as she picked up the receiver.

Douglas listened to her side of the conversation while he changed his clothes. He heard her voice brighten as she said, "Yes, yes. Hello . . . No . . . Doug just got home and we were talking about the day . . ."

So now her caller knew he was in the room. Douglas could imagine what the bastard was saying, whoever he was: *"So can you talk?"*

To which Donna, on cue, answered, "Nope. Not at all."

"Shall I call you later?"

"Gosh, that would be great."

"Today was what was great. I love to fuck you."

95

"Really? Outrageous. I'll have to check it out."

"I want to check you out, baby. Are you wet for me?"

"I sure am. Listen, we'll connect later on, okay? I need to get dinner started."

"Just so long as you remember today. It was the best. You're the best."

"Right. Bye." She hung up and came to him. She put her arms round his waist. She said, "Got rid of her. Nancy Talbert. God. Nothing's more important in her life than a shoe sale at Neiman Marcus. Spare me. Please." She snuggled up to him. He couldn't see her face, just the back of her head where it was reflected in the mirror.

"Nancy Talbert," he said. "I don't think I know her."

"Sure you do, honey." She pressed her hips against him. He felt the hopeful but useless heat in his groin. "She's in Soroptimists with me. You met her last month after the ballet. Hmm. You feel nice. Gosh, I like it when you hold me. Should I start dinner or d'you want to mess around?"

Another clever move on her part: He wouldn't think she was cheating if she still wanted it from him. No matter that he couldn't give it to her. She was hanging in there with him and this moment proved it. Or so she thought.

"Love to," he said and smacked her on the butt. "But let's eat first. And after, right there on the dining room table . . ." He managed what he hoped was a lewd enough wink. "Just you wait, kiddo."

She laughed and released him and went off to the kitchen. He walked to the bed where he sat, disconsolately. The charade was torture. He had to know the truth.

He didn't hear from Cowley and Son, Inquiries, for two agonizing weeks during which he suffered through three more coy telephone conversations between Donna and her lover, four more phony excuses to cover unscheduled absences from home, and two more midday showers sloughed off to Steve's absence from the kennels again. By the time he finally made contact with Cowley, Douglas's nerves were shot.

Cowley had news to report. He said he'd hand it over as soon as they could meet. "How's lunch?" Cowley asked. "We could do Tail of the Whale over here."

No lunch, Douglas told him. He wouldn't be able to eat anyway. He would meet Cowley at his office at twelve forty-five.

"Make it the pier, then," Cowley said.

"I'll catch a burger at Ruby's and we can talk after. You know Ruby's at the end of the pier?"

He knew Ruby's. A fifties coffee shop, it sat at the end of Balboa Pier, and he found Cowley there as promised at twelve forty-five, polishing off a cheeseburger and fries with a manila envelope sitting next to his strawberry milkshake.

Cowley wore the same khakis he'd had on the day they'd met. He'd added a panama hat to his ensemble. He touched his index finger to the hat's brim as Douglas approached him. His cheeks were bulging with the burger and fries.

Douglas slid into the booth opposite Cowley and reached for the envelope. Cowley's hand slapped down onto it. "Not yet," he said.

"I've got to know."

Cowley slid the envelope off the table onto the vinyl seat next to himself. He twirled the straw in his milkshake and observed Douglas through opaque eyes that seemed to reflect the sunlight outside. "Pictures," he said. "That's all I've got for you. Pictures aren't the truth. You got that?"

"Okay. Pictures."

"I don't know what I'm shooting. I just

98

tail the woman and I shoot what I see. What I see may not mean shit. You understand?"

"Look. Just show me the pictures."

"Outside."

Cowley tossed a five and three ones onto the table, called, "Catch you later, Susie," to the waitress and led the way. He walked to the railing where he looked out over the water. A whale-watching boat was bobbing about a quarter mile offshore. It was too early in the year to catch sight of a pod migrating to Alaska, but the tourists on board probably wouldn't know that. Their binoculars winked in the light.

Douglas joined the PI. Cowley said, "You got to know that she doesn't act like a woman guilty of anything. She just seems to be doing her thing. She met a few men — I won't mislead you — but I couldn't catch her doing anything cheesy."

"Give me the pictures."

Cowley gave him a sharp look instead. Douglas knew his voice was betraying him. "I say we tail her for another two weeks," Cowley said. "What I've got here isn't much to go on." He opened the envelope. He stood so that Douglas only saw the back of the pictures. He chose to hand them over in sets.

The first set was taken in Midway City not far from the kennels, at the feed and grain store where Donna bought food for the dogs. In these, she was loading fifty-pound sacks into the back of her Toyota pickup. She was being assisted by a Calvin Klein type in tight jeans and a T-shirt. They were laughing together, and in one of the pictures Donna had perched her sunglasses on the top of her head to look directly at her companion.

She appeared to be flirting, but she was a young, pretty woman and flirting was normal. This set seemed okay. She could have looked less happy to be chatting with the stud, but she was a businesswoman and she was conducting business. Douglas could deal with that.

The second set was of Donna in the Newport gym where she worked with a personal trainer twice a week. Her trainer was one of those sculpted bodies with a head of hair on which every strand looked as if it had been seen to professionally on a daily basis. In the pictures, Donna was dressed to work out — nothing Douglas had not seen before — but for the first time he noted how carefully she assembled her workout clothes. From the leggings to the leotard to the headband she wore, everything enhanced her. The trainer appeared to recognize this because he squatted before her as she did her vertical butterflies. Her legs were spread and there was no doubt what he was concentrating on. This looked more serious.

He was about to ask Cowley to start tailing the trainer when the PI said, "No body contact between them other than what you'd expect," and handed him the third set of pictures, saying, "These are the only ones that look a little shaky to me, but they may mean nothing. You know this guy?"

Douglas stared with *know this guy, know this guy* ringing in his skull. Unlike the other pictures in which Donna and her companion-of-the-moment were in one location, these showed Donna at a view table in an oceanfront restaurant, Donna on the Balboa ferry, Donna walking along a dock in Newport. In each of these pictures she was with a man, the same man. In each of the pictures there was body contact. It was nothing extreme because they were out in public. But it was the kind of body contact that betrayed: an arm around her shoulders, a kiss on her cheek, a full body hug that said, Feel me up, baby, 'cause I ain't limp like him.

Douglas felt that his world was spinning, but he managed a wry grin. He said, "Oh hell. Now I feel like a class-A jerk. This guy?" Douglas indicated the athletic-looking man in the picture with Donna. "This is her brother."

"You're kidding."

"Nope. He's a walk-on coach at Newport Harbor High. His name is Michael. He's a free-spirit type." Douglas gripped the railing with one hand and shook his head with what he hoped looked like chagrin. "Is this all you've got?"

"That's it. I can tail her for a while longer and see —"

"Nah. Forget it. Jesus, I sure feel dumb." Douglas ripped the photographs into confetti. He tossed them into the water where they formed a mantle that was quickly shredded by the waves that arced against the pier's pilings. "What do I owe you, Mr. Cowley?" he asked. "What's this dumb ass got to pay for not trusting the finest woman on earth?"

He took Cowley to Dillman's on the corner of Main and Balboa Boulevard, and they sat at the snakelike bar with the locals, where they knocked back a couple of brews apiece. Douglas worked on his affability act, playing the abashed husband who suddenly realizes what a dickhead he's been. He took all Donna's actions over the past weeks and reinterpreted them for Cowley. The unexplained absences became the foundation of a treat she was planning for him: the purchase of a new car, perhaps; a trip to Europe; the refurbishing of his boat. The secretive telephone calls became messages from his children who were in the know. The new underwear metamorphosed into a display of her wish to make herself desirable for him, to work him out of his temporary impotence by giving him a renewed interest in her body. He felt like a total idiot, he told Cowley. Could they burn the damn negatives together?

They made a ceremony of it, torching the negatives of the pictures in the alley behind JJ's Natural Haircutting. Afterward, Douglas drove in a haze to Newport Harbor High School. He sat numbly across the street from it. He waited two hours. Finally, he saw his youngest brother arrive for the afternoon's coaching session, a basketball tucked under his arm and an athletic bag in his hand.

Michael, he thought. Returned from Greece this time, but always the prodigal son. Before Greece, it was a year with Greenpeace on the *Rainbow Warrior*. Before that, it was an expedition up the Amazon. And before that, it was marching against apartheid in South Africa. He had a resumé that would be the envy of any prepubescent kid out for a good time. He was Mr. Adventure, Mr. Irresponsibility, and Mr. Charm. He was Mr. Good Intentions without any follow-through. When a promise was due to be kept, he was out of sight, out of mind, and out of the country. But everyone loved the son of a bitch. He was forty years old; the baby of the Armstrong brothers, and he always got precisely what he wanted.

He wanted Donna now, the miserable bastard. No matter that she was his brother's wife. That made having her just so much more fun.

Douglas felt ill. His guts rolled around like marbles in a bucket. Sweat broke out in patches on his body. He couldn't go back to work like this. He reached for the phone and called his office.

He was sick, he told his secretary. Must have been something he ate for lunch. He was heading home. She could catch him there if anything came up.

In the house, he wandered from room to

room. Donna wasn't at home — wouldn't be home for hours — so he had plenty of time to consider what to do. His mind reproduced for him the pictures that Cowley had taken of Michael and Donna. His intellect deduced where they had been and what they'd been doing prior to those pictures being taken.

He went to his study. There in a glass curio cabinet, his collection of ivory erotica mocked him. Miniature Asians posed in a variety of sexual postures, having themselves a roaring good time. He could see Michael and Donna's features superimposed on the creamy faces of the figurines. They took their pleasure at his expense. They justified their pleasure by using his failure. No limp dick here, Michael's voice taunted. What's the matter, big brother? Can't hold on to your wife?

Douglas felt shattered. He told himself that he could have handled her doing anything else, he could have handled her seeing someone else. But not Michael, who had trailed him through life, making his mark in every area where Douglas had previously failed. In high school it had been in athletics and student government. In college it had been in the world of fraternities. As an adult it had been in embracing adventure rather than in tackling the grind of business. And now, it was in proving to Donna what real manhood was all about.

Douglas could see them together as easily as he could see his pieces of erotica intertwined. Their bodies joined, their heads thrown back, their hands clasped, their hips grinding against each other. God, he thought. The pictures in his mind would drive him mad. He felt like killing.

The telephone company gave him the proof he required. He asked for a printout of the calls that had been made from his home. And when he received it, there was Michael's number. Not once or twice, but repeatedly. All of the calls had been made when he — Douglas — wasn't home.

It was clever of Donna to use the nights when she knew Douglas would be doing his volunteer stint at the Newport suicide hotline. She knew he never missed his Wednesday evening shift, so important was it to him to have the hotline among his community commitments. She knew he was building a political profile to get himself elected to the city council, and the hotline was part of the picture of himself he wished to portray: Douglas Armstrong, husband, father, oilman, and compassionate listener to the emotionally distressed. He needed something to put into the balance against his environmental lapses. The hotline allowed him to say that while he may have spilled oil on a few lousy pelicans — not to mention some miserable otters — he would never let a human life hang there in jeopardy.

Donna had known he'd never skip even part of his evening shift, so she'd waited till then to make her calls to Michael. There they were on the printout, every one of them made between six and nine on a Wednesday night.

Okay, she liked Wednesday night so well. Wednesday night would be the night that he killed her.

He could hardly bear to be around her once he had the proof of her betrayal. She knew something was wrong between them because he didn't want to touch her any longer. Their thrice-weekly attempted couplings — as disastrous as they'd been — fast became a thing of the past. Still, she carried on as if nothing and no one had come between them, sashaying through the bedroom in her Victoria's Secret selection-of-the-night, trying to entice him into making a fool of himself so she could share the laughter with his brother Michael.

No way, baby, Douglas thought. You'll be sorry you made a fool out of me.

When she finally cuddled next to him and murmured, "Doug, is something wrong? You want to talk? You okay?" it was all he could do not to shove her from him. He wasn't okay. He would never be okay again. But at least he'd be able to salvage a measure of his self-respect by giving the little bitch her due.

It was easy enough to plan once he decided on the very next Wednesday.

A trip to Radio Shack was all that was necessary. He chose the busiest one he could find, deep in the barrio in Santa Ana, and he deliberately took his time browsing until the youngest clerk with the most acne and the least amount of brainpower was available to wait on him. Then he made his purchase with cash: a call diverter, just the thing for those on-the-go SoCal folks who didn't want to miss an incoming phone call. Once Douglas programmed the diverter with the number he wanted incoming calls diverted to, he would have an alibi for the night of his wife's murder. It was all so easy.

Donna had been a real numbskull to try to cheat on him. She had been a bigger numbskull to do her cheating on Wednesday nights because the fact of her doing it on Wednesday nights was what gave him the idea of how to snuff her. The volunteers on the hotline worked it in shifts. Generally there were two people present, each manning one of the telephone lines. But Newport Beach types actually didn't feel suicidal very frequently, and if they did, they were more likely to go to Neiman Marcus and buy their way out of their depression. Mid-week especially was a slow time for the pill poppers and wrist slashers, so the hotline was manned on Wednesdays by only one person per shift.

Douglas used the days prior to Wednesday to get his timing down to a military precision. He chose eight-thirty as Donna's death hour, which would give him time to sneak out of the hotline office, drive home, put out her lights, and get back to the hotline before the next shift arrived at nine. He was carving it out fairly thin and allowing only a five-minute margin of error, but he needed to do that in order to have a believable alibi once her body was found.

There could be neither noise nor blood, obviously. Noise would arouse the neighbors. Blood would damn him if he got so much as a drop on his clothes, DNA typing being what it was these days. So he chose his weapon carefully, aware of the irony of his choice. He would use the satin belt of one of her Victoria's Secret slay-him-where-he-stands dressing gowns. She had half a dozen, so he would remove one of them in advance of the murder, separate it from its belt, dispose of it in a Dumpster behind the nearest Vons in advance of the killing — he liked that touch, getting rid of the evidence *before* the crime, what killer ever thought of that? — and then use the belt to strangle his cheating wife on Wednesday night.

The call diverter would establish his alibi. He would take it to the suicide hotline, plug the phone into it, program the diverter with his cellular phone number, and thus appear to be in one location while his wife was being murdered in another. He made sure Donna was going to be at home by doing what he always did on Wednesdays: by phoning her from work before he left for the hotline.

"I feel like dogshit," he told her at five-forty.

"Oh Doug, no!" she replied. "Are you ill or just feeling depressed about —"

"I'm feeling punk," he interrupted her. The last thing he wanted was to listen to

110

her phony sympathy. "It may have been lunch."

"What did you have?"

Nothing. He hadn't eaten in two days. But he told her shrimp because he'd gotten food poisoning from shrimp a few years back and he thought she might remember that, if she remembered anything at all about him at this point. He went on, "I'm going to try to get home early from the hotline. I may not be able to if I can't pull in a substitute to take my shift. I'm heading over there now. If I can get a sub, I'll be home pretty early."

He could hear her attempt to hide dismay when she replied. "But Doug . . . I mean, what time do you think you'll make it?"

"I don't know. By eight at the latest, I hope. What difference does it make?"

"Oh. None at all, really. But I thought you might like dinner . . ."

What she really thought was that she was going to have to cancel her hot romp with his baby brother. Douglas smiled at the realization on how nicely he'd just unhooked her little caboose.

"Hell, I'm not hungry, Donna. I just want to go to bed if I can. You be there to rub my back? You going anywhere?"

"Of course not. Where would I be going? Doug, you sound strange. Is something wrong?"

Nothing was wrong, he told her. What he didn't tell her was how right everything was, felt, and was going to be. He had her where he wanted her now: She'd be home, and she'd be alone. She might phone Michael and tell him that his brother was coming home early so their tryst was off, but even if she did that, Michael's statement after her death would conflict with Douglas's uninterrupted presence at the suicide hotline that night.

Douglas just had to make sure that he was back at the hotline with time to disassemble the call diverter. He'd get rid of it on the way home — nothing could be easier than flipping it into the trash behind the huge movie theater complex that was on his route from the hotline to the neighborhood where he lived — and then he'd arrive at his usual time of nine-twenty to "discover" the murder of his beloved.

It was all so easy. And so much cleaner than divorcing the little whore.

He felt remarkably at peace, considering everything. He'd seen Thistle again and she'd held his Rolex, his wedding band,

and his cuff links to take her reading. She'd greeted him by telling him that his aura was strong and that she could feel the power pulsing from him. And when she closed her eyes over his possessions, she'd said, "I feel a major change coming into your life, not-David. A change of location, perhaps, a change of climate. Are you taking a trip?"

He might be, he told her. He hadn't had one in months. Did she have any suggested destinations?

"I see lights," she responded, going her own way. "I see cameras. I see many faces. You're surrounded by those you love."

They'd be at Donna's funeral, of course. And the press would cover it. He was somebody after all. They wouldn't ignore the murder of Douglas Armstrong's wife. As for Thistle, she'd find out who he really was if she read the paper or watched the local news. But that made no difference since he'd never mentioned Donna and since he'd have an alibi for the time of her death.

He arrived at the suicide hotline at five fifty-six. He was relieving a UCI psych student named Debbie who was eager enough to be gone. She said, "Only two calls, Mr. Armstrong. If your shift is like mine, I

113

hope you brought something to read."

He waved his copy of Money magazine and took her place at the desk. He waited ten minutes after she'd left before he went back out to his car to get the call diverter.

The hotline was located in the dock area of Newport, a maze of narrow one-way streets that traversed the top of Balboa Peninsula. By day, the streets' antique stores, marine chandleries, and second-hand clothing boutiques attracted both locals and tourists. By night, the place was a ghost town, uninhabited except for the new-wave beatniks who visited a coffee dive three streets away, where anorexic girls dressed in black read poetry and strummed guitars. So no one was on the street to see Douglas fetch the call diverter from his Mercedes. And no one was on the street to see him leave the suicide hotline's small cubbyhole behind the real estate office at eight-fifteen. And should any desperate individual call the hotline during his drive home, that call would be diverted onto his cellular phone and he could deal with it. God, the plan was perfect.

As he drove up the curving road that led to his house, Douglas thanked his stars that he'd chosen to live in an environment in which privacy was everything to the homeowners. Every estate sat, like Douglas's, behind walls and gates, shielded by trees. On one day in ten, he might actually see another resident. Most of the time — like tonight — there was no one around.

Even if someone had seen his Mercedes sliding up the hill, however, it was January dark and his was just another luxury car in a community of Rolls-Royces, Bentleys, BMWs, Lexuses, Range Rovers, and other Mercedes. Besides, he'd already decided that if he saw someone or something suspicious, he would just turn around, go back to the hotline, and wait for another Wednesday.

But he didn't see anything out of the ordinary. He didn't see anyone. Perhaps a few more cars were parked on the street, but even these were empty. He had the night to himself.

At the top of his drive, he shut off the engine and coasted to the house. It was dark inside, which told him that Donna was in the back, in their bedroom.

He needed her outside. The house was equipped with a security system that would do a bank vault proud, so he needed the killing to take place outside where a peeping Tom gone bazooka or a burglar or a serial killer might have lured her. He thought of Ted Bundy and how he'd snagged his victims by appealing to their maternal need to come to his aid. He'd go the Bundy route, he decided. Donna was nothing if not eager to help.

He got out of the car silently and paced over to the door. He rang the bell with the back of his hand, the better to leave no trace on the button. In less than ten seconds, Donna's voice came over the intercom. "Yes?"

"Hi, babe," he said. "My hands are full. Can you let me in?"

"Be a sec," she told him.

He took the satin belt from his pocket as he waited. He pictured her route from the back of the house. He twisted the satin around his hands and snapped it tight. Once she opened the door, he'd have to move like lightning. He'd have only one chance to fling the cord around her neck. The advantage he already possessed was surprise.

He heard her footsteps on the limestone. He gripped the satin and prepared. He thought of Michael. He thought of her together with Michael. He thought of his Asian erotica. He thought of betrayal, failure, and trust. She deserved this. They both deserved it. He was only sorry he couldn't kill Michael right now, too.

When the door swung open, he heard her say, "Doug! I thought you said your hands —"

And then he was on her. He leapt. He yanked the belt around her neck. He dragged her swiftly out of the house. He tightened it and tightened it and tightened it and tightened it. She was too startled even to fight back. In the three seconds it took her to get her hands to the belt in a reflex attempt to pull it away from her throat, he had it digging into her skin so deeply that her scrabbling fingers could find no slip of material to grab on to.

He felt her go limp. He said, "Jesus. Yes. *Yes.*"

And then it happened.

The lights went on in the house. A mariachi band started playing. People started shouting, "Surprise! Surprise! Sur—"

Douglas looked up, panting, from the body of his wife, into popping flashes and a video camcorder. The joyous shouting from within his house was cut off by a female shriek. He dropped Donna to the ground and stared without comprehension into the entry and beyond that the living

117

room. There, at least two dozen people were gathered beneath a banner that said SURPRISE, DOUGIE! HAPPY FIFTY-FIVE!

He saw the horrified faces of his brothers and their wives and children, of his own children, of his parents. Of one of his former wives. Among them, his colleagues and his secretary. The chief of police. The mayor.

He thought, What is this, Donna? Some kind of a joke?

And then he saw Michael coming from the direction of the kitchen, Michael with a birthday cake in his hands, Michael saying, "Did we surprise him, Donna? Poor Doug. I hope his heart —" And then saying nothing at all when he saw his brother and his brother's wife.

Shit, Douglas thought. What have I done?

That, indeed, was the question he'd be asking — and answering — for the rest of his life.

Introduction to
Good Fences Aren't Always Enough

So often I'm asked where my ideas for stories come from. I always answer in the same way: Story ideas come from everywhere and anywhere. I might see a wire service article in the LA *Times* and realize that it contains the kernel for a novel, as I did when I wrote *Well-Schooled in Murder*. I might see an exposé in a British newspaper and decide that it can serve as the foundation for a novel, as I did when I wrote *Missing Joseph*. I might want to use a specific location in one of my books, so I'll design a story that fits into that location, as I did when I wrote *For the Sake of Elena*. I might see someone on the street or in the underground, overhear a conversation between two individuals, listen to someone's experience, study a photograph, or determine that a particular type of character would be interesting to write about. Or sometimes what stimulates the story idea is a combination of any of these things.

Often, when I've completed a project, I can't remember what got me started on it in the first place. But that's not the case with the following short story.

In October of 2000, I went on a walking and hiking tour of Vermont after I'd completed the second draft of my novel *A Traitor to Memory*. I'd long wanted to see the New England fall colors, and this trip was to be my reward for a long and enervating time spent at the computer over the fifteen months of writing two drafts of a complicated book. My intention was to see and to photograph the landscape.

As I was traveling on my own, I decided to sign up for a tour of other like-minded individuals interested in the exercise and the atmosphere. We stayed in country inns at night, and during the day we hiked through some of the most spectacular foliage I've ever seen. We had two guides, Brett and Nona. What one of them didn't know about the flora, the fauna, the topography, and the geography of the region, the other one did.

It was while we were on one of these hikes that Nona told me the story of an eccentric woman who once lived near her own home. As soon as I heard the tale, I knew I was listening to the kernel of a short story that I would write.

And when I got home from hiking in Vermont, that's what I did. It seemed fitting to use a variation of a line from Robert Frost — that famous literary New Englander — as the title for my piece.

Good Fences Aren't Always Enough

Twice each year a neighborhood in the attractive old town of East Wingate managed to achieve perfection. Whenever this happened — or perhaps as an indication *that* it had happened — the *Wingate Courier* celebrated the fact with a significant spread of appropriately laudatory column inches dead in the center of its small-town pages, photos included. Citizens of East Wingate who wanted to better their social standing, their quality of life, or their circle of friends then tended to flock to that neighborhood eagerly, with the hope of picking up a piece of real estate there.

Napier Lane was just the sort of place that could at any moment and in the right circumstances be named A Perfect Place to Live. It was very high on potential if not quite there in every respect. It had atmosphere provided by enormous lots, houses over a century old, oaks, maples and sycamores even older, sidewalks cracked with time and character, picket fences, and brick paths that wound through front yards lapping against the sort of friendly porches where neighbors gather on summer nights. If every house had not yet been restored by some young couple with a lot of energy and inclined to nostalgia, there was in Napier Lane's curves and dips an open promise that renovation would come to them all, given enough time.

On the rare occasion that a house on Napier Lane came up for sale, the entire neighborhood held its breath to see who the buyer would be. If it was someone with money, the purchased house might join the ranks of those painted, glistening sisters who were raising the standard of living one domicile at a time. And if it was someone with easy access to that money and a profligate nature to boot, chances were that the renovation of the property in question might even occur quickly. For it had been the case that a family now and then had bought a house on Napier Lane with restoration and renovation in mind, only to discover upon embarking on the job how tedious and costly it actually was. So more than once, someone began the Augean project that's known as Restoring a Historic Property, but within six months admitted defeat and raised the for sale sign of surrender without getting even within shouting distance of completion.

Such was the situation at 1420. Its prior inhabitants had managed to get its exterior painted and its front and back yards cleared of the weeds and debris that tend to collect upon a property when its owners aren't hypervigilant, but that was the extent of it. The old house sat like Miss Havisham fifty years after the wedding that didn't happen: dressed to the nines externally but a ruin inside and languishing in a barren landscape of disappointed dreams. Literally everyone within sight of 1420 was anxious to have someone take on the house and set it to rights.

Except Willow McKenna, that is. Willow, who lived next door, just wanted good neighbors. At thirty-four and trying to get pregnant with her third of what would ultimately be — some years hence — seven children, Willow hoped merely for a family who shared her values. These were simple enough: a man and a woman committed to their marriage who were loving parents to an assortment of moderately well behaved children. Race, color, creed, national origin, political affiliation, automotive inclination, taste in interior decoration . . . none of that mattered. She was just hopeful that whoever bought 1420 would be a positive addition to what was, in her case, a blessed life. A solid family represented that, one in which the dad went out to a white collar if not distinguished job, the mom remained at home and saw to the needs of her children, and the children themselves were imaginative but obedient, with evident respect for their elders, happy, and carrying no infectious diseases. The number of children didn't matter. The more the better, as far as Willow was concerned.

Having grown up with no relations of her own but always clinging to the futile hope that one set of foster parents or another would actually want to adopt her, Willow had long made family her priority. When she'd married Scott McKenna, whom she'd known since her sophomore year in high school, Willow had set about making for herself what fate and a mother who'd abandoned her in a grocery store had long denied her. Jasmine came first. Max followed two years later. If all went according to plan, Cooper or Blythe would arrive next. And her own life, which had lately felt dark, cold, and cavernous with Max's entry into kindergarten, would once more stretch and fill and bustle, relieving the nagging press of anxiety that she'd been experiencing for the last three months.

"You could go to work, Will," her husband Scott had counseled. "Part-time, I mean. If you'd like, that is. No need financially and you'd want to be here when the kids get home from school anyway."

But a job wasn't what Willow wanted. She wanted the void filled in a way only another baby could fill it.

That was where her inclinations lay: toward family and babies and not toward neighborhoods that might or might not be designated Perfect Places to Live. So when the sold sign appeared over the realtor's name on 1420, what she wondered was not when the new neighbors might logically be expected to make the necessary improvements to their environment — a front yard edged by a new picket fence would be a good place to start, thought the Gilberts who lived on the *other* side of 1420 — but rather how big the family was and would the mom want to exchange any recipes.

Everyone, it turned out, was disappointed. For not only did no instant transformation take place in 1420 Napier Lane, but no family moved a plethora of belongings into the old Victorian house at all. Make no mistake: A plethora of items *were* delivered. But as for the mom, the dad, the teeming happy shouting children that were meant to accompany those items . . . They did not materialize. In their place came one lone woman, one lone and — it must be said — rather odd woman.

She was called Anfisa Telyegin, and she was the sort of woman about whom rumors spring up instantly.

First, there was her general appearance, which can largely be described by the single word *gray*. Gray as to hair, gray as to complexion, gray as to teeth and eyes and lips, gray as to personality as well. She was much like chimney smoke in the dark — definitely present but indecipherable as to its source. *Creepy*, the youngsters on Napier Lane called her. And it wasn't a leap of too much imagination to expand from that to the less pleasant *witch*.

Her behavior didn't help matters. She returned neighborly hellos with the barest courtesy. She never answered her doorbell to children selling Girl Scout cookies, candy, magazines, or wrapping paper. She wasn't interested in joining the Thursday morning mothers' coffee that rotated among the houses of the stay-at-home moms. And — this was perhaps her biggest sin — she showed no inclination to join in a single one of the activities that Napier Lane was certain would help it top the short list of spots designated in East Wingate as models of perfection. So invitations to progressive dinners were ignored. The Fourth of July barbecue might not have occurred at all. Christmas caroling did not see her participate. And as for using part of her yard for the Easter egg hunt . . . The idea was unthinkable.

Indeed, six months into her acquisition of 1420 Napier Lane, all anyone knew of Anfisa Telyegin was what they heard and what they saw. What they heard was that she taught Russian language and Russian literature at night at the local community college. What they saw was a woman with arthritic hands, a serious and regrettable case of dowager's hump, no interest in fashion, a tendency to talk to herself, and a great passion for her yard.

At least, that was how it seemed at first because no sooner had Anfisa Telyegin removed the for sale sign from the dusty plot that was her front yard but she was out there murmuring to herself as she planted English ivy which she proceeded to fertilize, water, and baby into a growth spurt unparalleled in the history of the lane.

It seemed to people that Anfisa Telyegin's English ivy grew overnight, crawling along the packed earth and sending out tendrils in every direction. Within a month, the shiny leaves were flourishing like mongrel dogs saved from the pound. In five months more, the entire front yard was a veritable lake of greenery.

People thought at this point that she would tackle the picket fence, which sagged like knee-highs on an eighty-year-old. Or perhaps the chimneys, of which there were six and all of them guano streaked and infested with birds. Or even the windows, where the same drunken venetian blinds had covered the glass — without being dusted or changed — for the last fifty years. But instead, she repaired to the backyard, where she planted more ivy, put in a hedge between her property and her neighbors' yards, and built a very large chicken coop into which and out of which she disappeared and emerged at precise intervals morning and night with a basket on her arm. It was filled with corn on the access route. It was empty — or so it seemed to anyone who caught a glimpse of the woman — on the egress.

"What's the old bag doing with all the eggs?" asked Billy Hart who lived across the street and drank far too much beer.

"I haven't seen any eggs," Leslie Gilbert replied, but she wouldn't have, naturally, because she rarely moved from her sofa to the window during the daytime when the television talk shows were claiming her attention. And she couldn't be expected to see Anfisa Telyegin at night. Not in the dark and between the trees that the woman had planted along the property line just beyond the hedge, trees that like the ivy seemed to grow with preternatural speed.

Soon, the children of Napier Lane were reacting to the solitary woman's strange habits the way children will. The younger ones crossed over to the other side of the street whenever passing 1420. The older ones dared each other to enter the yard and slap hands against the warped screen door that had lost its screen the previous Hallowe'en.

Things might have gotten out of hand at this point had not Anfisa Telyegin herself taken the bull by the horns: She went to the Napier Lane Veterans' Day Chili Cook-off. While it's true that she didn't take any chili with her, it's also true that she did not show up empty-handed. And no matter that Jasmine McKenna found a long gray hair embedded in the lime Jell-O salad with bananas that was Anfisa's contribution to the event. It was the thought that counted — at least to her mother if not to the rest of the neighbors — and that proffered Jell-O encouraged Willow to look with a compassionate eye upon the strange elderly woman from that moment forward.

"I'm going to take her a batch of my drop-dead brownies," Willow told her husband Scott one morning not long after the Veterans' Day Chili Cook-off (won by Ava Downey, by the way, for the third consecutive and maddening year). "I think she just doesn't know what to make of us all. She's a foreigner, after all," which is what the neighbors had learned from the woman herself at the cook-off: born in Russia when it was still part of the USSR, a childhood in Moscow, an adulthood far in the north somewhere till the Soviet Union fell apart and she herself made her way to America.

Scott McKenna said, "Hmm," without really registering what his wife was telling him. He'd just returned from the graveyard shift at TriOptics Incorporated where, as a support technician for TriOptics' complicated software package, he was forced to spend hours on the phone with Europeans, Asians, Australians, and New Zealanders who phoned the help line nightly — or for them, daily — wanting an immediate solution for whatever mindless havoc they'd just wreaked upon their operating system.

"Scott, are you listening to me?" Willow asked, feeling the way she always felt when his response lacked the appropriate degree of commitment to their conversation: cut off and floating in outer space. "You know I hate it when you don't listen to me." Her voice was sharper than she intended and her daughter Jasmine — at the present moment stirring her Cheerios to reduce them to the level of sogginess that she preferred — said, "Ouch, Mom. Chill."

"Where'd she get that?" Scott McKenna looked up from his study of the financial pages of the daily newspaper while five-year-old Max — always his sister's echo if not her shadow — said, "Yeah, Mom. Chill," and stuck his fingers into the yolk of his fried egg.

"From Sierra Gilbert, probably," Willow said.

"Hmph," Jasmine countered with a toss of her head. "Sierra Gilbert got it from *me*."

"Whoever got it from who," Scott said, snapping his paper meaningfully, "I don't want to hear it said to your mother again, okay?"

"It only means —"

"Jasmine."

"Poop." She stuck out her tongue. She'd cut her bangs again, Willow saw, and she sighed. She felt defeated by her strong-willed daughter on the fast path to adolescence, and she hoped that little Blythe or Cooper — with whom she was finally and blessedly pregnant — might be more the sort of child she'd had in mind to bring into the world.

It was clear to Willow that she wasn't going to receive Scott's acknowledgment of — much less his benediction on — her plan for the drop-dead brownies unless and until she made it clear why she thought a neighborly gesture was called for at this point. She waited to do so until the kids were off to school, safely escorted to the bus stop at the end of the street and attended there — despite Jasmine's protests — until the yellow doors closed upon them. Then she returned to the house and found her husband preparing for the daily five hours of sleep he allotted himself prior to sitting down to work on the six consulting accounts that so far described what went for McKenna Computing Designs. Nine more accounts and he would be able to leave TriOptics and maybe then their lives would be a little more normal. No more regimented sex in the hours between the kids' going to bed and Scott's leaving for work. No more long nights alone listening to the creaking floorboards and trying to convince herself it was only the house settling.

Scott was in the bedroom, casting his clothes off. He left everything where it fell and fell himself onto the mattress, where he turned on his side and pulled the blankets over his shoulder. He was twenty-seven seconds away from snoring, when Willow spoke.

"I've been thinking, hon."

No response.

"Scott?"

"Hmmm?"

"I've been thinking about Miss Telyegin." Or Mrs. Telyegin, Willow supposed. She'd not yet learned if the woman next door was married, single, divorced, or widowed. Single seemed most likely to Willow for some reason that she couldn't quite explain. Maybe it had to do with the woman's habits, which were becoming more apparent — and patently stranger — as the days and weeks passed. Most notable were the hours she kept, which were almost entirely nocturnal. But beyond that, there was the oddity of things like the venetian blinds on 1420 being always closed against the light; of Miss Telyegin wearing rubber boots rain or shine whenever she did emerge from her house; of the fact that she not only never entertained visitors, but she never went anywhere besides to work and home again precisely at the same time each day.

"When does she buy her groceries?" Ava Downey asked.

"She has them delivered," Willow replied.

"I've seen the truck," Leslie Gilbert confirmed.

"So she never goes out in the daytime at all?"

"Never before dusk," Willow said.

Thus was *vampire* added to *witch,* but only the children took that sobriquet seriously. Nonetheless, the other neighbors began to shy away from Anfisa Telyegin, which prompted Willow's additional sympathy and made Anfisa Telyegin's effort at the Veterans' Day Chili Cook-off even more worthy of admiration and reciprocation.

"Scott," she said to her drowsy husband, "are you listening to me?"

"Can we talk later, Will?"

"This'll only take a minute. I've been thinking about Anfisa."

He sighed and flipped onto his back,

putting his arms behind his head and exposing what Willow least liked to see when she looked upon her spouse: armpits as hairy as Abraham's beard. "Okay," he said without a display of anything resembling marital patience. "What *about* Anfisa?"

Willow sat on the edge of the bed. She placed her hand on Scott's chest to feel his heart. Despite his present impatience, he had one. A very big one. She'd seen it first at the high school sock hop where he'd claimed her for a partner, rescuing her from life among the wallflowers, and she depended now upon its ability to open wide and embrace her idea.

"It's been tough with your parents so far away," Willow said. "Don't you agree?"

Scott's eyes narrowed with the suspicion of a man who'd suffered comparisons to his older brother from childhood and who'd only too happily moved his family to a different state to put an end to them. "What d'you mean, tough?"

"Five hundred miles," Willow said. "That's a long way."

Not long enough, Scott thought, to still the echoes of "Your brother the cardiologist" which followed him everywhere.

"I know you want the distance," Willow continued, "but the children could benefit from their grandparents, Scott."

"Not from these grandparents," Scott informed her.

Which was what she expected her husband to say. So it was no difficult feat to segue from there into her idea. It seemed to her, she told Scott, that Anfisa Telyegin had extended a hand of friendship to the neighborhood at the Chili Cook-off and she wanted to reciprocate. Indeed, wouldn't it be lovely to get to know the woman on the chance that she might become a foster grandparent to their children? She — Willow — had no parents whose wisdom and life experience she could offer to Jasmine, Max, and little Blythe-or-Cooper. And with Scott's family so far away . . .

"Family doesn't have to be defined as blood relations," Willow pointed out. "Leslie's like an aunt to the children. Anfisa could be like a grandmother. And anyway, I hate to see her alone the way she is. With the holidays coming . . . I don't know. It seems so sad."

Scott's expression changed to show the relief he felt at not having Willow suggest they move back to be near his loathsome parents. She sympathized with — if she didn't understand — his unwillingness to expose himself to any more comparisons to his vastly more successful sibling. And that empathy of hers, which he'd always seen as her finest quality, was something he accepted as not being limited to an application only to himself. She *cared* about people, his wife Willow. It was one of the reasons he loved her. He said, "I don't think she wants to mix in with us, Will."

"She came to the cook-off. I think she wants to try."

Scott smiled, reached up and caressed his wife's cheek. "Always rescuing strays."

"Only with your blessing."

He yawned. "Okay. But don't expect much. She's a dark horse, I think."

"She just needs some friendship extended to her."

And Willow set about doing exactly that the very same day. She made a double batch of drop-dead brownies and arranged a dozen artfully on a green plate of Depression glass. She covered them carefully in Saran Wrap and fixed this in place with a jaunty plaid ribbon. As carefully as if she were bearing myrrh, she carried her offering next door to 1420.

It was a cold day. It didn't snow in this part of the country and while autumns were generally long and colorful, they could also be icy and gray. That was the case when Willow left the house. Frost still lay on her neat front lawn, on the pristine fence, on the crimson leaves of the liquid-ambar at the edge of the sidewalk, and a bank of fog was rolling determinedly down the street like a fat man looking for a meal.

Willow stepped watchfully along the brick path that led from her front door to the gate, and she held the drop-dead brownies against her chest as if exposure to the air might somehow harm them. She shivered and wondered what winter would be like if this was what a day in autumn could do.

She had to set her plate of brownies on the sidewalk for a moment when she reached the front of Anfisa's house. The old picket gate was off one hinge and instead of pushing it open, one needed to lift it, swing it, and set it down again. And even then, it wasn't an easy maneuver with the ivy now thickly overgrowing the front yard path.

Indeed, as Willow approached the house, she noticed what she hadn't before. The ivy that flourished under Anfisa's care had begun to twine itself up the front steps and was crawling along the wide front porch and twisting up the rails. If Anfisa didn't

140

trim it soon, the house would disappear beneath it.

On the porch, where Willow hadn't stood since the last inhabitants of 1420 had given up the effort at DIY and moved to a brand-new — and flavorless — development just outside of town, Willow saw that Anfisa had made another alteration to the home in addition to what she'd done with the yard. Sitting next to the front door was a large metal chest with *grocery delivery* stenciled in neat white letters across its lid.

Odd, Willow thought. It was one thing to have your groceries delivered . . . Wouldn't *she* like to have that service if she could ever bear the thought of someone other than herself selecting her family's food. But it was quite another thing to leave it outside where it could spoil if you weren't careful.

Nonetheless, Anfisa Telyegin had lived to the ripe old age of . . . whatever it was. She must, Willow decided, know what she was doing.

She rang the front bell. She had no doubt that Anfisa was at home and would be home for many hours still. It was daylight, after all.

But no one answered. Yet Willow had

141

the distinct impression that there *was* someone quite nearby, listening just behind the door. So she called out, "Miss Telyegin? It's Willow McKenna. It was such a nice thing to see you at the Chili Cook-off the other night. I've brought you some brownies. They're my specialty. Miss Telyegin? It's Willow McKenna. From next door? 1418 Napier Lane? To your left?"

Again, nothing. Willow looked to the windows but saw that they were, as always, covered by their venetian blinds. She decided that the front bell had not worked, and she knocked instead on the green front door. She called out, "Miss Telyegin?" once more before she began to feel silly. She realized that she was making something of a fool of herself in front of the whole neighborhood.

"There was our Willow bangin' away on that woman's front door like an orphan of the storm," Ava Downey would say over her gin and tonic that afternoon. And her husband Beau, who was always at home from the real estate office in time to mix the Beefeaters and vermouth for his wife just the way she liked it, would pass along that information to his pals at the weekly poker game, from which those men would carry it home to their wives till everyone knew without a doubt how needy Willow McKenna was to forge connections in her little world.

She felt embarrassment creep up on her like the secret police. She decided to leave her offering and phone Anfisa Telyegin about it. So she lifted the lid of the grocery box and set the drop-dead brownies inside.

She was lowering the heavy lid when she heard a rustling in the ivy behind her. She didn't think much about it till a skittering sounded against the worn wood of the old front porch. She turned then, and gave out a shriek that she smothered with her hand. A large rat with glittering eyes and scaly tail was observing her. The rodent was not three feet away, at the edge of the porch and about to dive into the protection of the ivy.

"Oh my God!" Willow leapt onto the metal food box without a thought of Ava Downey, Beau, the poker game, or the neighborhood seeing her. Rats were terrifying — she couldn't have said why — and she looked around for something to drive the creature off.

But he took himself into the ivy without her encouragement. And as the last of his gray bulk disappeared, Willow McKenna didn't hesitate to do so herself. She leapt from the food box and ran all the way home.

"It *was* a rat," Willow insisted.

Leslie Gilbert took her gaze away from the television. She'd muted the sound upon Willow's arrival but hadn't completely torn herself away from the confrontation going on there. *My Father Had Sex With My Boyfriend* was printed on the bottom of the screen, announcing the day's topic among the combatants.

"I know a rat when I see one," Willow said.

Leslie reached for a Dorito and munched thoughtfully. "Did you let her know?"

"I phoned her right away. But she didn't answer and she doesn't have a machine."

"You could leave her a note."

Willow shivered. "I don't even want to go into the yard again."

"It's all that ivy," Leslie pointed out. "Bad thing to have ivy like that."

"Maybe she doesn't know they like ivy. I mean, in Russia, it'd be too cold for rats, wouldn't it?"

Leslie took another Dorito. "Rats're like cockroaches, Will," she said. "It's never too anything for them." She fastened her eyes

144

to the television screen. "Least we know why she has that box for her groceries. Rats bite through anything. But they don't bite through steel."

There seemed nothing for it but to write a note to Anfisa Telyegin. Willow did this promptly but felt that she couldn't deliver such news to the reclusive woman without also proffering a solution to the problem. So she added the words, "I'm doing something to help out," and she bought a trap, baited it with peanut butter, and bore it with her to 1420.

The next morning at breakfast, she told her husband what she had done, and he nodded thoughtfully over his newspaper. She said, "I put our phone number in the note, and I thought she'd call, but she hasn't. I hope she doesn't think I think it's a reflection on her that there's a rat on her property. Obviously, I didn't mean to insult her."

"Hmm," Scott said and rattled his paper.

Jasmine said, "Rats? *Rats?* Yucky yuck, Mom."

And Max said, "Yucky yucky yuck."

Having started something with the deposit of the trap on Anfisa Telyegin's front porch, Willow felt duty bound to finish it. So she returned to 1420 when Scott was asleep and the children had gone off to school.

She walked up the path with far more trepidation than she'd felt on her first visit. Every rustle in the ivy was the movement of the rat, and surely the *scritching* sound she could hear was the rodent creeping up behind her, ready to pounce on her ankles.

Her fears came to nothing, though. When she mounted the porch, she saw that her effort at trapping the critter had been successful. The trap held the rat's broken body. Willow shuddered when she saw it, and hardly registered the fact that the rodent looked somewhat surprised to find his neck broken right when he was helping himself to breakfast.

She wanted Scott there to help her, then. But realizing that he needed his sleep, she'd come prepared. She'd carried with her a shovel and a garbage bag in the hope that her first venture in vermin extermination would have been successful.

She knocked on the door to let Anfisa Telyegin know what she was doing, but as before there was no answer. As she turned to face her task with the rat, though, she saw the venetian blinds move a fraction. She called out, "Miss Telyegin? I've put a trap down for the rat. I've got him. You don't need to worry about it," and she felt a bit put out that her neighbor didn't open

146

the front door and thank her.

She steeled herself to the job before her — she'd never liked coming across dead animals, and this occasion was no different from finding roadkill adhering to the treads of her tires — and she scooped the rat up with the shovel. She was just about to deposit the stiffened body into the garbage sack, when a susurration of the ivy leaves distracted her, followed by a skittering that she recognized at once.

She whirled. Two rats were on the edge of the porch, eyes glittering, tails swishing against the wood.

Willow McKenna dropped the shovel with a clatter. She made a wild dash for the street.

"Two more?" Ava Downey sounded doubtful. She rattled the ice in her glass and her husband Beau took it for the signal it was and went to refresh her gin and tonic. "Darlin', you sure you're not sufferin' from somethin'?"

"I know what I saw," Willow told her neighbor. "I let Leslie know and now I'm telling you. I killed one, but I saw two more. And I swear to God, they *knew* what I was doing."

"Intelligent rats, then?" Ava Downey

asked. "My Lord, what a perplexin' situation." She pronounced it *per*plexing in her southern drawl, Miss North Carolina come to live among the mortals.

"It's a neighborhood problem," Willow said. "Rats carry disease. They breed like . . . well, they breed . . ."

"Like rats," Beau Downey said. He gave his wife her drink and joined the ladies in Ava Downey's well-appointed living room. Ava was an interior decorator by avocation if not by career, and everything she touched was instantly transformed into a suitable vignette for *Architectural Digest*.

"Very amusin', darlin'," Ava said to her husband, without smiling. "My oh my. Married all these years and I had no idea you have such a quick wit."

Willow said, "They're going to infest the neighborhood. I've tried to talk to Anfisa about it, but she's not answering the phone. Or she's not at home. Except there're lights on, so I think she's home and . . . Look. We need to do something. There're children to consider."

Willow hadn't thought of the children till earlier that afternoon, after Scott had risen from his daily five hours. She'd been in the backyard in her vegetable garden, picking the last of the autumn squash.

She'd reached for one and in doing so had dug her fingers into a pile of animal droppings. She'd recoiled from the sensation and pulled the squash out hastily from the tangle of its vine. The vegetable, she saw, had been scarred with tooth marks.

The droppings and tooth marks had told the tale. There weren't just rats in the yard next door. There were rats on the move. Every yard was vulnerable.

Children played in those yards. Families held their summer barbecues there. Teenagers sunned themselves there in the summer and men smoked cigars on warm spring nights. These yards weren't meant to be shared with rodents. Rodents were dangerous to everyone's health.

"The problem's not rats," Beau Downey said. "The problem's the woman, Willow. She probably thinks having rats is normal. Hell, she's from Russia. What d'you want?"

What Willow wanted was peace of mind. She wanted to know that her children were safe, that she could let Blythe-or-Cooper crawl on the lawn without having to worry that a rat — or rats' droppings — would be out there.

"Call an exterminator," Scott told her.

"Burn a cross on her lawn," Beau Downey advised.

She phoned Home Safety Exterminators, and in short order a professional came to call. He verified the evidence in Willow's vegetable plot, and for good measure, he paid a call on the Gilberts on the other side of 1420 and did much the same there. This, at least, got Leslie off the sofa. She dragged a set of kitchen steps to the fence and peered over at 1420's backyard.

Aside from a path to the chicken coop, ivy grew everywhere, even up the trunks of the fast-growing trees.

"This," Home Safety Exterminator pronounced, "is a real problem, lady. The ivy's got to go. But the rats have to go first."

"Let's do it," Willow said.

But there was a problem as things turned out. Home Safety Exterminators could trap rats on the McKennas' property. They could trap rats in the Gilberts' yard. They could walk down the street and see to the Downeys' and even cross over and deal with the Harts'. But they couldn't enter a yard without permission, without contracts being signed and agreements reached. And that couldn't happen unless and until someone made contact with Anfisa Telyegin.

The only way to manage this was to waylay the woman when she left one night to teach one of her classes at the local college. Willow appointed herself neighborhood liaison, and she took up watch at her kitchen window, feeding her family takeout Chinese and pizzas for several days so as not to miss the moment when the Russian woman set off for the bus stop at the end of Napier Lane. When that finally happened, Willow grabbed her parka and dashed out after her.

She caught up to her in front of the Downeys' house which, as always, was already ablaze with Christmas lights despite the fact that Thanksgiving had not yet arrived. In the glow from the Santa and reindeer on the roof, Willow explained the situation.

Anfisa's back was to the light, so Willow couldn't see her reaction. Indeed, she couldn't see the Russian woman's face at all, so shrouded was she in a head scarf and a wide-brimmed hat. It seemed reasonable enough to Willow to assume that a passing along of information would be all that the unpleasant situation required. But she was surprised.

"There are no rats in the yard," Anfisa Telyegin said with considerable dignity, all things considered. "I fear you are mistaken, Mrs. McKenna."

"Oh no," Willow contradicted her. "I'm not, Miss Telyegin. Truly, I'm not. Not only did I see one when I brought you those brownies . . . Did you get them, by the way? They're my specialty . . . But when I set a trap, I actually caught it. And then I saw two more. And then when I found the droppings in my yard and called the exterminator and *he* looked around . . ."

"Well, there you have it," Anfisa said. "The problem is with your yard, not mine."

"But —"

"I must be on my way."

And so she walked off, with nothing settled between them.

When Willow shared this information with Scott, he decided a neighborhood war council was called for, which was another term for a poker night at which poker wasn't played and to which wives were invited. Willow found herself overwrought at the idea of what might happen once the neighborhood became involved in the problem. She didn't like trouble. But by the same token, she wanted her children to be safe from vermin. She spent most of the meeting anxiously chewing on her nails.

Every position taken on the situation

was a turn of the prism that is human nature. Scott wanted to go the legal route in keeping with his by-the-book personality. Start with the health department, bring in the police if that didn't work, turn to lawyers subsequently. But Owen Gilbert didn't like this idea at all. He didn't like Anfisa Telyegin for reasons having more to do with her refusal to let him do her income taxes than with the rodents that were invading his property, and he wanted to call the F.B.I. and the I.R.S. and have them deal with her. Surely she was involved in something. Everything from tax dodging to espionage was possible. Mention of the I.R.S. brought the I.N.S. into Beau Downey's mind, which was more than enough to enflame *him*. He was of the persuasion that immigrants are the ruination of America and since the legal system and the government clearly weren't about to do a damn thing to keep the borders closed to the invading hordes, Beau said *they* should at least do something to close their neighborhood to them.

"Let's let this gal know she ain't welcome here," he said, to which suggestion his wife Ava rolled her eyes. She never made a secret of the fact that she considered Beau good for mixing her drinks, servicing her sexual needs, and not much more.

"How d'you suggest we do that, darlin'?" Ava asked. "Paint a swastika on her front door?"

"Hell, we need a family in there anyway," Billy Hart said, chugging his beer. It was his seventh and his wife had been counting them, as had Willow, who wondered why Rose didn't stop him from making a fool of himself every time he went out in public instead of just sitting there with an agonized expression on her face. "We need a couple our own age, people with kids, maybe even a teenage daughter . . . one with decent tits." He grinned and gave Willow a look she didn't like. Her own breasts — normally the size of teacups — were swelling with her pregnancy and he fixed his eyes to them and winked at her.

With so many opinions being expressed, is there any doubt that nothing was settled? The only thing that occurred was passions being enflamed. And Willow felt responsible for having enflamed them.

Perhaps, she thought, there was another way to deal with the situation. But wrack her brains though she did for the next several days, she could come up with no approach to the problem.

It was when a letter went misdelivered to her house that Willow came up with what seemed a likely plan of action. For stuck within a collection of catalogues and bills was a manila envelope forwarded to Anfisa Telyegin from an address in Port Terryton, a small village on the Weldy River some ninety-five miles north of Napier Lane. Perhaps, Willow thought, someone in Anfisa's former neighborhood could help her present neighbors learn how best to approach her.

So on a crisp morning when the children were in school and Scott was tucked away for his well-earned five hours, Willow got out her state atlas and plotted a route that would take her to Port Terryton before noon. Leslie Gilbert went, too, despite having to miss her daily intake of dysfunction on the television set.

Both of the ladies had heard of Port Terryton. It was a picturesque village some three hundred years old, set amidst an old-growth deciduous forest that flourished right to the banks of the Weldy River. Money lived in Port Terryton. Old money, new money, stock market money, dot com money, inherited money. Mansions built in the eighteenth and nineteenth centuries served as display pieces for inordinate wealth.

There were inferior areas in the village as well, streets of visually pleasing cottages where the day help and the lesser souls lived. Leslie and Willow found Anfisa's former residence in one of these areas: a charming and well-painted gray and white saltbox structure shaded by a copper-leafed maple with a clipped front lawn and flowerbeds planted with a riot of pansies.

"So what're we trying to find out, exactly?" Leslie asked as Willow pulled to a stop by the curb. Leslie had brought along a box of glazed donuts, and she'd spent most of the drive gorging herself upon them. She licked her fingers as she asked the question, bending down to squint through the window at Anfisa's former house.

"I don't know," Willow said. "Something that could help."

"Owen's idea was the best," Leslie said loyally. "Call in the Feds and hand her over."

"There's got to be something less . . . well, less brutal than that. We don't want to destroy her life."

"We're talking about a yard full of rats," Leslie reminded her. "A yard of

156

rats that she denies exists."

"I know, but maybe there's a *reason* why she doesn't know they're there. Or why she can't face admitting they're there. We need to be able to help her confront this."

Leslie blew out a breath and said, "Whatever, sweetie."

They'd come to Port Terryton without much of a plan of what they'd do once they got there. But as they looked fairly harmless — one of them just beginning to show a pregnancy and the other placid enough to inspire trust — they decided to knock on a few doors. The third house they tried was the one that provided them with the insight they'd been looking for. It was, however, not an insight that Willow would have liked to unearth.

From Barbie Townsend across the street from Anfisa Telyegin's home, they received cups of tea with lemon, chocolate chip cookies, and a wealth of information. Barbie had even kept a scrapbook of the Rat Lady Affair, as the Port Terryton newspaper had come to call it.

Leslie and Willow hardly spoke on the drive home. They'd planned to have lunch in Port Terryton, but neither of them had an appetite once they were finished talking to Barbie Townsend. They were both intent upon getting back to Napier Lane and informing their husbands of what they'd learned. Husbands, after all, were intended to deal with this sort of situation. What else were they for? They were supposed to be the protectors. Wives were the nurturers. That's the way it was.

"They were everywhere," Willow told her husband, interrupting him in the midst of a phone call to a prospective client. "Scott, the newspaper even had *pictures* of them."

"Rats," Leslie informed her Owen. She went directly to his office and barged right in, trailing her paisley shawl behind her like a security blanket. "The yard was infested. She'd planted ivy. Just like here. The health department and the police and the courts all got involved . . . The neighbors sued, Owen."

"It took five years," Willow told Scott. "My God, five years. Jasmine will be *twelve* in five years. Max will be ten. And we'll have Blythe-or-Cooper as well. And probably two more. Maybe three. And if we haven't solved this problem by then . . ." She began to cry, so afraid for her children was she becoming.

"It cost them a fortune in lawyers' fees,"

Leslie Gilbert told Owen. "Because every time the court ordered her to do something, she countered with a lawsuit herself. Or she appealed. We don't have the kind of money they have in Port Terryton. What're we going to do?"

"She's sick in some way," Willow said to Scott. "I know that, and I don't want to hurt her. But still, she's got to be made to *see* . . . Only how can we make her see if she denies there's a problem in the first place? *How?*"

Willow wanted to go the mental health route. While the Napier Lane menfolk gathered nightly to come up with a plan of action that would take care of the problem posthaste, Willow did some research on the Internet. What she learned opened her heart to the Russian woman who, she realized, clearly wasn't responsible in full for the infestation of her property.

"Read this," Willow said to her husband. "It's a sickness, Scott. It's a mental disorder. It's like . . . You know when people have too many cats? Women, usually? Older women? You can take all their cats away but if you don't deal with the mental problem, they just go out and get more cats."

"You're saying she collects *rats?*" Scott

asked her. "I don't think so, Willow. If you want to take the psychological viewpoint, then let's call this what it is: denial. She can't admit that she's got rats because of what rats imply."

The men agreed with Scott, especially Beau Downey who pointed out that, as a foreigner — or furinner, as he pronounced it — Anfisa Telyegin probably didn't know a damn thing about hygiene, personal or otherwise. God only knew what the *inside* of her house was like. Had any of them seen it? No? Well, then, he rested his case. They ought to just set up a little accident over at 1420. A fire, say, started by bad wiring or maybe by gas leaking at the side of the house.

Scott wouldn't hear of that and Owen Gilbert began making noises to distance himself from the whole situation. Rose Hart — who lived across the street and didn't have as much invested in the situation — pointed out that they didn't really know how many rats there were, so perhaps they were getting too excited about what was really a simple situation. "Willow only saw three: the one she trapped and two others. It could be we're getting too riled up. It could be this is a simpler problem than we think."

"But in Port Terryton, it was an *infestation*," Willow cried, wringing her hands. "And even if there're only two more, if we don't get rid of them, there'll soon be twenty. We *can't* ignore this. Scott? Tell them . . ."

Several women exchanged knowing glances. Willow McKenna had never been able to stand on her own two feet, even now.

It was Ava Downey — who would have believed it? — who offered a potential solution. "If she's in denial as you suggest, Scott darlin'," Ava said, "why don't we simply do somethin' to make her fantasy world real?"

"What would that be?" Leslie Gilbert asked. She didn't like Ava, whom she saw as being after every woman's husband, and she generally avoided speaking to her. But the circumstances were dire enough that she was willing to put her aversion aside and listen to anything that promised to solve the problem quickly. She had, after all, just that morning tried to start her car only to find that wires in the engine had been chewed up by vermin.

"Let's get rid of the creatures for her," Ava said. "Two or three or twenty. Let's just get rid of them."

Billy Hart gulped down what was the last of his ninth beer of the evening and pointed out that no exterminator would take on the job, even if the neighbors paid to have it done, not without Anfisa Telyegin's cooperation. Owen concurred as did Scott and Beau. Didn't Ava remember what the agent from Home Safety Exterminators had told Leslie and Willow?

" 'Course I remember," Ava said. "But what I'm suggestin' is that we take on the work ourselves."

"It's her property," Scott said.

"She might call in the cops and have us arrested if we go settin' traps all around her yard, honey," Beau Downey added.

"Then we'll have to do it when she's not home."

"But she'll see the traps," Willow said. "She'll see the dead rats in them. She'll know —"

"You're misunderstandin' me, darlin'," Ava purred. "I'm not suggestin' we use traps at all."

Everyone living near 1420 knew everyone else's habits: what time Billy Hart staggered out for the morning paper, for example, or how long Beau Downey revved up the motor of his SUV before he finally

162

blasted off for work each day. This was part of being on friendly terms with one another. So no one felt compelled to remark upon the fact that Willow McKenna could say to the minute exactly when Anfisa Telyegin went to work at the community college each evening and when she returned home.

The plan was simple: After Owen Gilbert obtained the appropriate footwear for them all — no man wanted to traipse through what might be rat-infested ivy in his loafers — they would make their move. Eight Routers — as they called themselves — would form a shoulder-to-shoulder line and move slowly through the ivy-covered front yard in heavy rubber boots. This line would drive the rats toward the house where the Terminators would be waiting for them as they emerged from the ivy on the run from the rubber boots. And the Terminators would be armed with bats, with shovels, and with anything else that would eliminate the nasty creatures. "It seems to me it's the only way," Ava Downey pointed out. Because while no one truly wanted Anfisa Telyegin to have to find her property littered with rats killed by traps, so also did no one want to find rats in their own yard where the creatures might manage to stagger before succumbing to a crawl-off-and-die-somewhere-else poison, if that's the route the neighbors chose.

So hand-to-rodent combat appeared to be the only answer. And as Ava Downey put it in her inimitable fashion: "I don't expect you fine big strong men mind gettin' a little blood on your hands . . . not in a cause good as this."

What were they to say to such a challenge to their masculinity? A few feet shuffled and someone murmured, "I don't know about this," but Ava countered with, "I just don't see any other way to do it. Course I'm willin' to listen to any other suggestions."

There were no others. So a date was chosen. And everyone set about preparing himself.

Three nights later, all the children gathered at the Harts' house to keep them out of the way and out of sight of what was going to happen at 1420. No one wanted their offspring to hear or see the destruction that was planned. Children are sensitive to this sort of thing, the wives informed their husbands after a morning-coffee agreement to stand as one. The less they knew about what their daddies were up to, the better for them all, the women said. No bad memories and no bad dreams.

The men among them who didn't like blood, violence, or death bolstered themselves with two thoughts. First, they considered their children's health and safety. Second, they dwelt upon the Higher Good. One or two of them reminded himself that a yard of rats wouldn't go over well with the *Wingate Courier*, nor would it get Napier Lane very far toward achieving Perfect Place to Live status. Others just kept telling themselves that it was only two rats they were talking about. Two rats and nearly ten times that in men . . . ? Well, those were odds that anyone could live with.

Thirty minutes after Anfisa Telyegin left 1420 and headed for the bus stop and the ride to the community college and her Russian literature class, the men made their move in the darkness. And much was the relief of the faint-at-heart when the Routers managed to drive only four rats into the waiting line of Terminators. Beau Downey was among this latter group and he was happy to dispatch all four rats himself, yelling, "Gimme some light over here!

Scare the hell out of 'em!" as he chased down one rodent after another. Indeed, later it would be said that he took a little *too* much pleasure in the process. He wore his blood-spattered jumpsuit with the distinction of a man who's never fought in a real battle. He talked about "nailin' the little bastards" and gave a war whoop as his bat made contact with rat number four.

Because of this, he was the one who pointed out that the backyard had to be dealt with, too. So the same process was gone through there, with the net result being five more furry corpses, five more bodies in the garbage bag.

"Nine rats, not so bad after all," Owen Gilbert said with the relief of someone who'd made sure up front he was among the Routers and consequently forever free of the blood of the innocent.

"That don't seem right to me," Billy Hart pointed out. "Not with the droppings all over the McKennas' yard and not with Leslie's engine wires getting chomped. I don't think we got them all. Who's for crawling under the house? I got a smoke bomb or three we could use to scare 'em out."

So a smoke bomb was set off and three more rats met the fate of their fellows. But

166

a fourth got away from the best of Beau's efforts and made a dash for Anfisa's chicken coop.

Someone shouted, "Get him!" but no one was fast enough. He slithered beneath the shelter and disappeared from view.

What was odd was that the chickens didn't notice a rat in their midst. From inside the coop came not a single rustling wing or protesting squawk. It was as if the chickens had been drugged or, more ominously . . . eaten by rats.

Clearly, someone was going to have to see if the latter was the case. But no one leapt to the opportunity. The men advanced on the chicken coop, leery, and those with flashlights found that they could barely hold them steady upon the little structure.

"Grab that door and swing it open, Owen," one of the men said. "Let's get that last mother and get out of here."

Owen hesitated, unanxious to be confronted by several dozen mutilated chicken corpses. And chicken corpses certainly seemed very likely, since even with the approach of the men, no sound came from within the coop.

Beau Downey said, "Hell," in disgust when Owen didn't move. He lurched past him and yanked open the door himself and threw a smoke bomb inside.

And that's when it happened.

Rats poured through the opening. Rats by the dozen. Rats by the hundred. Small rats. Large rats. Obviously well-fed rats. They flooded from the chicken coop like boiling oil from a battlement and began to shoot off in every direction.

The men flailed clubs and bats and shovels at them, every which way. Bones crunched. Rats squealed and screamed. Blood spurted in the air. Flashlights captured the carnage in pools of bright illumination. The men didn't speak. They merely grunted as one after another the rats were chased down. It was like a primitive battle for territory, engaged in by two primordial species only one of which was going to survive.

By the end, Anfisa Telyegin's yard was littered with the blood, bones, and bodies of the enemy. Any rats that escaped had done so to either the McKennas' or the Gilberts' yard, and they would be dealt with there by professionals. As to the land that those few remaining rats had left behind in their flight . . . It was like the scene of any other disaster: not a place that can be cleaned up quickly and certainly not a place that would soon be forgotten.

But the men had promised their wives that the job would be done without signs left behind, so they did their best to scrape up broken furry bodies and wash the ivy and the outside of the chicken coop free of blood. They discovered in doing this that there had never been chickens in the coop in the first place and what this implied about Anfisa Telyegin's daily delivery of corn to the coop . . . Indeed what this implied about Anfisa Telyegin herself. . . .

It was Billy Hart who said, "She's nuts," and Beau Downey who suggested, "We gotta get her out of the goddamn neighborhood." But before either of these comments could be mooted in any way, the decrepit front gate of 1420 opened and Anfisa herself stepped into the yard.

The plan hadn't been thought out enough to allow for midterm exams that ended class earlier than usual that night. It also hadn't been thought out enough to consider what a line of eight men tramping through ivy was likely to do to that greenery. So Anfisa Telyegin took one look at the mess in her yard — sufficiently lit by the streetlight in front of her house — and she gave a horrified cry that could be heard all the way to the bus stop.

She cried out not so much because she loved her ivy and mourned the exfoliation brought about by eight pairs of boot-shod feet. Rather she cried out because she knew intuitively what that trodden-down ivy meant.

"My God!" she keened. "No! My God!"

There was no way out of her yard save through the front, so the men emerged one by one. They found Anfisa kneeling in the midst of the trampled ivy, her arms clutched across her body, swaying side to side.

"No, no!" she cried, and she began to weep. "You do not understand what you have done!"

The men were not equipped to handle this. Clubbing rats, yes. That was right up their alley. But offering comfort to a stranger whose suffering made no sense to them . . . ? That was quite another matter. Good God, they'd done the mad woman a favor, hadn't they? Jesus. So they'd mutilated a little bit of ivy in the process. Ivy grew like weeds, especially in this yard. It would all be back to normal in a month.

"Get Willow," Scott McKenna said as "I'll get Leslie," Owen Gilbert muttered. And the rest of them dispersed as quickly as they could, with the furtive air of little boys who've had perhaps too much fun doing something for which they will soon be punished.

Willow and Leslie came on the run from Rose Hart's house. They found Anfisa weeping and swaying, beating her fists against her breasts.

"Can you get her inside?" Scott McKenna asked his wife.

Owen Gilbert said to Leslie, "Jeez, make her see it's just ivy, Les. It'll grow back. And it had to be done."

Willow, for whom empathy was actually something of a curse, was herself fighting back an onslaught of emotion in the presence of the Russian woman's anguish. She hadn't expected to feel *anything* other than relief upon the disposal of the rats, so the guilt and the sorrow she was experiencing confused her mightily. She cleared her throat and said to Leslie, "Will you . . . ?" and bent to take Anfisa's arm. "Miss Telyegin," she said, "it's all right. Really. It'll be all right. Will you come inside please? May we make you some tea?"

With Leslie helping, she got the sobbing woman to her feet and as the rest of the neighborhood wives began to gather on Rose Hart's front lawn, Willow and Leslie mounted the front steps of 1420 and helped Anfisa open the door.

Scott followed. After what he'd seen in the chicken coop, he wasn't about to let his wife walk into that house without him. God only knew what they would find inside. But his imagination had fed him inaccurate images. For inside Anfisa Telyegin's house, there was not a sign of anything as much as a hair being out of place. He saw this, felt ashamed of what he'd been anticipating, and excused himself, leaving Leslie and Willow to comfort Anfisa where and how they could.

Leslie put water on to boil. Willow looked for cups and tea. And Anfisa sat at the kitchen table, shoulders shaking as she sobbed, "Forgive. Please forgive."

"Oh, Miss Telyegin," Willow murmured. "These things happen sometimes. There's nothing to forgive."

"You trusted me," Anfisa wept. "I am so sorry for what I have done. I shall sell. I shall move. I shall find —"

"There's no *need* for that," Willow said. "We don't want you to move. We just want you to be safe on your property. We all want to be safe."

"What I've done to you," Anfisa cried.

"Not once, but twice. You cannot forgive."

It was the *but twice* that caused Leslie Gilbert to realize uneasily that, hard as it was to accept, the Russian woman and Willow McKenna were actually talking at cross-purposes. She said, "Hey, Will . . ." in a monitory tone just as Anfisa said, "My dearest little friends. All of you gone."

Which was when Willow, feeling a chill run over her, finally climbed aboard the locomotive of comprehension.

She looked at Leslie. "Does she mean . . . ?"

"Yeah, Will. I think she does."

It was only when Anfisa Telyegin posted a for sale sign in front of her house on Napier Lane two weeks later that Willow McKenna managed to get the complete story from the immigrant woman. She'd gone to 1420 bearing a plate of Christmas cookies as a peace offering and unlike the previous occasion of the drop-dead brownies, this time Anfisa opened the door. She beckoned Willow inside with a nod of her head. She took her into the kitchen and made her tea. It seemed that the passage of two weeks had been sufficient to allow the older woman not only time to grieve but also time to decide to bring Willow a partial step into her world.

"Twenty years," she said as they sat at the table. "I would not become who they wanted me to be, and I would not be silent. So they sent me away. Lubyanka first, do you know what that is? Run by KGB? Yes? A dreadful place. And from there, Siberia."

Willow said, "Prison?" in a whisper. "You've been in prison?"

"Prison would be nice. Concentration camp, this was. Oh, I've heard your people laugh about this place Siberia. To them it is a joke: the salt mines in Siberia. I have heard this. But to be there. With no one. Year after year. To be forgotten because one's lover was the important voice, the voice that counted, while until he died one was merely a helpmate, never taken seriously by anyone till the authorities took one seriously. It was a terrible time."

"You were . . . ?" What did they call it? Willow tried to remember. "A dissident?"

"A voice they didn't like. Who would not be still. Who taught and wrote until they came to fetch her. And then it was Lubyanka. And then it was Siberia. And there in that cell, the little ones came. I was afraid at first. The filth. The disease. I drove them off. But still they came. They came and they watched me. And then I saw. They wanted very little and they were afraid too. So I offered them bits. Some bread. A sliver of meat when I had it. And so they stayed and I wasn't alone."

"The rats . . ." Willow tried to keep the aversion from her voice. "They were your friends."

"To this day," she replied.

"But, Miss Telyegin," Willow said, "you're an educated woman. You've read. You've studied. You must know rats carry diseases."

"They were good to me."

"Yes. I see you believe that. But that was then, when you were in prison and desperate. You don't need rats now. Let people take their place."

Anfisa Telyegin lowered her head. "Invasion and killing," she said. "Some things cannot be forgotten."

"But they can be forgiven. And no one wants you to leave. We know . . . I know you had to leave your home once before. In Port Terryton. I know about what happened there. The police, the lawsuits, the courts . . . Miss Telyegin, you've got to see that if you move away and start over again and if you encourage rats to live on your property again . . . Don't you see that you'll just be back where you started? No one's going to let you choose rats over people."

"I will not do that again," Anfisa said. "But I cannot stay here. Not after what has happened."

"Just as well, darlin'," Ava Downey said over her gin and tonic. Eight months had passed since the Night of the Rats, and Anfisa Telyegin was gone from their midst. The neighborhood had returned to normal and the new occupants of 1420 — a family called Houston with an attorney husband, a pediatrician wife, a Danish au pair, and two well-scrubbed children of eight and ten who wore uniforms to their private school and carried their books to and from the car in neat satchels — were finally doing what the local inhabitants had long desired. For weeks on end, painters wielded their brushes, wallpapers carried rolls into the house, wood finishers sanded and stained, drapers created masterworks for the windows . . . The chicken coop was carted off and burnt, the ivy was removed, the picket fence was replaced, and a lawn and flowerbeds were planted in front of the house while an English garden was designed for the back. And six months after that, Napier Lane was finally designated A Perfect Place to Live by the *Wingate Courier*, with 1420 the house that was chosen to symbolize the beauties of the neighborhood.

And there was no jealousy over that fact, although the Downeys were rather cool when the rest of the neighbors offered the Houstons their congratulations on having 1420 selected by the newspaper as the model of domiciliary perfection. After all, the Downeys had restored their own house first and Ava had from the beginning been so kind as to offer her expertise in interior design to Madeline Houston. . . . No matter that Madeline had chosen to ignore virtually all of those suggestions, common courtesy demanded that the Houstons decline the pictorial honor presented to them, passing it along to the Downeys who were — if nothing else — mentors to everyone when it came to restoration and interior decoration. But the Houstons apparently didn't see it that way, so they posed happily at the gate of 1420 when the newspaper photographers came to call and they framed the subsequent front page of the *Wingate Courier* and placed it in their front hallway so everyone — including the green-eyed Downeys — could see it when they came to call.

So "Just as well, darlin'," was said with some mixed feelings by Ava Downey when Willow McKenna stopped to chat in the midst of a walk with little Cooper snoozing in his stroller. Ava was sitting in her faux wicker rocking chair on the front porch, celebrating a warm spring day with her first outdoor gin and tonic of the season. She was referring to the departure of Anfisa Telyegin from their midst, something that Willow herself hadn't quite come to terms with, despite the advent of the Houstons who — with their children, their au pair, and their commitment to home improvement — were so much more suited to Napier Lane. "C'n you imagine what we'd be goin' through right now if we *hadn't* taken steps to deal with the problem?" Ava asked.

"But if you'd seen her that night . . ." Willow couldn't remove from her mind the image of the Russian woman as she'd been on her knees, weeping in the ivy. "And then to learn about what the rats meant to her . . . I just feel so —"

"Extended postpartum," Ava said. "That's what this is. What you need is a drink. Beau! Beau, honey, you in there,

178

darlin'? Fix Willow here —"

"Oh no. I've got to get dinner. And the kids're alone. And . . . It's just I can't stop feeling sad about it all. It's like we drove her off, and I never thought I'd do something like that, Ava."

Ava shrugged and rattled her ice cubes. "All for the best," she noted.

What Leslie Gilbert said darkly was, "Sure Ava would feel that way. Southerners are used to driving people off their property. It's one of their sports." But she said this mostly because she'd watched Ava zero in on Owen at the New Year's Eve party. She hadn't yet forgotten that they'd used their tongues when they'd kissed, although Owen was still denying that fact.

Willow said, "But she didn't need to leave. I'd forgiven her. Hadn't you?"

"Sure. But when someone's ashamed . . . What're they supposed to do?"

Ashamed was how Willow herself felt. Ashamed that she'd panicked, ashamed that she'd tracked down Anfisa's previous residence, and ashamed most of all that, having tracked down the truth in Port Terryton, she hadn't given the Russian woman the chance to rectify matters before the men acted. Had she done that, had she told Anfisa what she'd unearthed about her, surely Anfisa would have taken steps to make sure that what had happened in Port Terryton didn't happen in East Wingate.

"I didn't really give her a chance," she told Scott. "I should have told her what we intended to do if she wouldn't bring in the exterminators. I think I should tell her that now: that what we did was right but *how* we did it was wrong. I think I'll feel better if I do that, Scott."

Scott McKenna thought no explanations to Anfisa Telyegin were necessary. But he knew Willow. She wouldn't rest until she'd made whatever peace she felt she needed to make with their erstwhile neighbor. He personally considered it a waste of her time, but the truth was that he was so caught up in meeting the needs of — praise God — the *twelve* clients he had now at McKenna Computing Designs that he really didn't do more than murmur, "Whatever you think's right, Will," when his wife at last mentioned going to see Anfisa.

"She was in *prison*," Willow reminded him. "In a concentration camp. If we'd known that at the time, I'm sure we would have done things differently. Wouldn't we?"

Scott was only half listening, so he said, "Yeah. I guess."

Which Willow took for agreement.

It wasn't difficult to trace Anfisa. Willow did it through the community college, where a sympathetic secretary in Human Resources met her for coffee and slipped across the table to her an address in Lower Waterford, one hundred and fifteen miles away.

Willow didn't take Leslie Gilbert this time. Instead she asked if she would baby-sit Cooper for a day. Since Cooper was at the stage where he slept, ate, eliminated, and spent the rest of the time cooing at the mobiles above his crib, Leslie knew that she'd not be distracted from her daily intake of talk shows, so she agreed. And since she'd been looking forward to the topic of the day on her favorite show — *I Had Group Sex With My Son's Friends* — she didn't ask Willow where she was going, why she was going there, or if she wanted company.

This was just as well. Willow wanted to talk to Anfisa Telyegin alone.

She found Anfisa's new house on Rosebloom Court in Lower Waterford, and when she saw it, she felt a new onslaught of guilt, comparing it to her previous homes both in Port Terryton and on

Napier Lane. Those houses were both historical properties. This was not. They had been reflective of the time period during which they'd been built. This was reflective of nothing more than a tract-home designer's desire to make as much money as he could from as little creative effort as possible. It was the sort of place families had moved into in droves after World War II: with stucco walls, a concrete driveway with a crack down the middle from which weeds grew, and a tarpaper roof. Willow's spirits sank when she saw it.

She sat in her car and regretted everything, but most of all she regretted her propensity to panic. If she hadn't panicked when she saw the first rat, if she hadn't panicked when she found the droppings in her vegetable garden, if she hadn't panicked when she learned about Anfisa's trouble in Port Terryton, perhaps she wouldn't have condemned the poor woman to life in this dismal cul-de-sac with its barren one-tree lawns, its warped garage doors that dominated the house fronts, and its patchy, uneven sidewalks.

"It was her choice, darlin'," Ava Downey would have said. "And let's not forget the chicken coop, Willow. She didn't have to encourage rats to take up residence in her yard, now, did she?"

This last question resonated in Willow's mind as she sat in front of Anfisa's house. It prompted her to recognize that there was more of a difference between this house and the last house than was described by the structure itself. For unlike the house on Napier Lane, this yard had no ivy anywhere. Indeed, it had nothing in which a rat could live. All it comprised were flowerbeds neatly planted with neatly trimmed shrubs and a front lawn clipped as smooth as an ice rink.

Perhaps, Willow thought, it had taken two houses and two neighborhoods in an uproar for Anfisa Telyegin to learn that she couldn't share her property with rats and hope to go unnoticed.

Willow had to make sure that some good had come of what had happened in her neighborhood, so she got out of her car and crept quietly up to the backyard fence to have a look. A chicken coop, doghouse, or toolshed would be a very bad sign. But a glance over the fence to the patio, the lawn, and the rosebushes proved that no habitat for rodents had been provided this time around by the Russian woman.

"Sometimes people've got to learn their lessons the hard way, Willow," Ava

Downey would have said.

And it certainly looked as if Anfisa Telyegin had learned, hard way or not.

Willow felt somewhat redeemed by what she saw, but she knew that full absolution wouldn't come until she assured herself that Anfisa was doing well in her new environment. Indeed, she hoped that a conversation with her former neighbor would evolve into an expression of gratitude from Anfisa to the Napier Lane residents who'd managed — however dramatically — to bring her to her senses. That would be something that Willow could carry home to her husband and her friends and thus redeem herself in their eyes as well, for she, after all, had instigated everything.

Willow knocked at the door, which was sunk into a small, square entry defined by a single concrete step. She felt a twinge of concern when a window curtain on the entry flicked, and she called out, "Miss Telyegin, are you home? It's Willow McKenna," with the hope of reassuring the woman.

Her greeting seemed to do the trick. The door cracked open three inches, revealing a shaft of Anfisa Telyegin from head to toe.

Willow smiled. "Hel*lo*. I hope you don't mind my dropping by. I was in the area and I wanted to see . . ." Her voice drifted off. Anfisa was looking at her with no comprehension at all. Willow said, "Willow McKenna? Your next-door neighbor on Napier Lane? D'you remember me? How *are* you, Miss Telyegin?"

Anfisa's lips curved suddenly at this, and she stepped away from the door, roused by the mention of Napier Lane. Willow took this movement for permission to enter, so she gave a little push to the door and went inside.

Everything seemed fine. The house was as neat as a surgeon's brain: swept, dusted, and polished. True, there was a slightly peculiar odor in the air, but Willow put that down to the fact that none of the windows were open despite the fine spring day. The place had probably been closed up all winter with the heater sealing in everything from cooking odors to cleaning scents.

"How *are* you?" Willow said to the older woman. "I've been thinking about you for quite a long time. Are you working in a college in this area now? You're not commuting down to East Wingate, are you?"

Anfisa smiled beatifically. "I am well," she said. "I am so well. Will you have tea?"

The relief Willow felt at being greeted so warmly was like a down comforter on an icy night. She said, "Have you forgiven me, Anfisa? Have you been able to *truly* forgive me?"

What Anfisa said in reply couldn't have been more of a comfort had Willow written the words herself. "I learned much on Napier Lane," she murmured. "I do not live as I lived then."

"Oh my gosh," said Willow, "I am *so* glad."

"Sit, sit," Anfisa said. "In here. Please. Let me make tea."

Willow was only too happy to draw a chair from the table and watch as Anfisa bustled contentedly around the kitchen. She chatted as she filled a kettle and pulled teacups and saucers out of a cupboard.

This was a good place for her to settle, Anfisa told Willow. It was a simpler neighborhood, she said, more suited to someone like herself with simpler needs and simpler tastes. The houses and yards were plain, like her, and people kept mostly to themselves.

"This is better for me," Anfisa said. "It is more what I am accustomed to."

"I'd hate to think you consider Napier Lane a mistake, though," Willow said.

"I learned much about life in Napier Lane," Anfisa told her, "much more than I have learned anywhere else. For that, I am grateful. To you. To everyone. I would not be as I am this moment if it were not for Napier Lane."

And how she was at this moment was at peace, she said. Not in so many words but in her actions, in the expressions of pleasure, delight, and satisfaction that flickered across her face as she talked. She wanted to know about Willow's family: How was her husband? Her little girl and boy? And there was another small one, wasn't there? And would there be more? Surely, yes, there would be more, wouldn't there?

Willow blushed at this last question and what it implied about Anfisa's intuition. Yes, she admitted to the Russian, there would be more. In fact, she hadn't told her husband yet, but she was fairly certain that she was already pregnant with the fourth McKenna.

"I hadn't intended it to be so soon after Cooper," Willow confessed. "But now that it's happened, I've got to say I'm thrilled. I love big families. It's what I always wanted."

"Yes," Anfisa smiled. "Little ones. How they make life good."

Willow returned the smile and felt so gratified by the reception that Anfisa was giving her, by Anfisa's every exclamation of pleasure over each piece of news Willow imparted, that she leaned forward and squeezed the Russian woman's hand. She said, "I am *so* glad I came to see you. You seem like a different person here."

"I am a different person," Anfisa said. "I do not do what I did before."

"You *learned*," Willow said. "That's what life is about."

"Life is good," Anfisa agreed. "Life is very full."

"Nothing could be better to hear. This is like music to my ears, Anfisa. May I call you that? May I call you Anfisa? Is that all right? I'd like to be friends."

Anfisa clasped Willow's hand much as Willow had just clasped hers. "Friends," she said, "yes. That would be good, Willow."

"Perhaps you can come to East Wingate to visit us," Willow said. "And we can come here to visit you. We have no family within five hundred miles, and we'd be thrilled to have you be . . . well, like a grandmother to my children, if you'd be willing. In fact, that's what I was hoping for when you first moved to Napier Lane."

Anfisa brightened, put a hand on her chest. "Me? You thought of me as a grandmother to your little ones." She laughed, clearly delighted at the prospect. "I will love to be that. I will love it through and through. And you —" She grasped Willow's hand once more — "you are too young to be a grandmother. So you must be the aunt."

Willow said, "The aunt?" and she smiled, although mystified.

"Yes, yes," Anfisa said. "The aunt to my little ones as I will be the grandmother to yours."

"To your . . ." Willow swallowed. She couldn't stop herself from looking around. She forced a smile and went on, saying, "You have little ones yourself? I didn't know that, Anfisa."

"Come." Anfisa rose and put her hand on Willow's shoulder. "You must meet them."

Without wanting her feet to do what they were doing, Willow followed Anfisa from the kitchen to the living room and from the living room down a narrow hall. The odor she'd first smelled when she'd entered the house was stronger here and stronger still when Anfisa opened one of the bedroom doors.

"I keep them in here," Anfisa said to Willow over her shoulder. "The neighbors don't know and you mustn't tell. I learned so very very much from living as I did on Napier Lane."

Introduction to
Remember, I'll Always Love You

This story was one I thought about for a long time. A number of years ago, a friend of mine related to me a situation in which a man had made a "deathbed" declaration of love to his wife that, in context, seemed like nothing that had any resemblance to love at all. My initial reaction to the brief tale was outrage. My secondary reaction was anger. My third reaction was something typical to anyone who is born to write: I thought about what a good story it would make.

The tough part was trying to decide what circumstances in the life of the man and wife in this story would culminate in his final declaration of love for her, not to mention the situation in which he made that declaration. I considered just about everything. I went on a hike in Italy's Cinque Terre and thought about placing the story there. I did the same in the Italian lakes and seriously considered Isola di Pescatori as a perfect spot to place my tale. The only problem was that *nothing* aside from potential settings was actually coming to me. And you can't exactly write a short story if there is nothing but location to drive it.

Finally, in a conversation with my fiancé, I arrived at the kernel for this story, which was the *reason* that the husband dies. Once I had that, I was on my way. I sent my assistant to the library and the Internet to gather some information for me and while she did that, I began creating the characters who would people the world of Eric and Charlotte Lawton. I soon saw that I didn't need an exotic location for this story at all. Indeed, I saw that the story would sit well right here in Southern California, in my own backyard.

When I completed my eleventh novel, I finally had the time to write this story. So here it is, my answer to why that unknown man in a tale told me by one of my girlfriends said, "Remember, I'll always love you" to his wife just before he died.

Remember, I'll Always Love You

Charlie Lawton didn't cry at her husband's burial. She'd done her crying already, when it first happened and then at the funeral. In the aftermath of his horrible death, she'd wept buckets and she was all cried out. So she just watched the proceedings numbly.

They'd earlier given her all the graveside options. She could have the minister say another prayer — this one brief — and then she could depart immediately for a somber reception at which the mourners would be given food and drink and a final chance to murmur inadequate words of comfort to Eric Lawton's widow. Or she could remain and watch as the hastily chosen coffin was lowered into the ground. She could then pick a flower from the funeral wreath that she herself had purchased only two days earlier from within a fog and through anguish-smeared vision. She could toss this flower into the grave, which would encourage the other mourners to do likewise, and then she could walk off to the waiting limousine. Or she could remain for every second of the burial, right down to the moment when the backhoe — parked at a discreet distance — rumbled across the lawn to the grave. She could stay until the vault was sealed and the soil was packed and the squares of lawn replaced. She could even watch them affix the plastic tag to a pole that would mark the site until the gravestone arrived. She could read his name *Eric Lawton* as if that might help her absorb the fact that he was gone, and she could fill in the rest herself: Eric Lawton, beloved husband of Charlotte. Eric Lawton, dead at forty-two.

She chose the first option. It was easier to turn away than to watch the coffin disappear into forever. As for giving the other mourners an opportunity to show a sign of their affection for Eric by dropping flowers into his grave . . . She didn't want to do anything that might remind her how few mourners there actually were.

At the house later, grief struck her like a virus. She stood at the window, her throat tight and hot, and she felt as if a fever were coming upon her. She looked out at the backyard into whose landscaping she and her husband had put such thought and had maintained with such loving care while behind her, the voices were hushed in keeping with both the dolor and the delicacy of the situation.

Tragedy. She overheard the whisper.

Fine man was murmured several times.

Fine man in every way was spoken once.

In every way but one, Charlie thought.

She felt an arm slip round her and she leaned into the longtime friendship of Bethany Franklin, who'd driven out from Hollywood to this soulless suburb of soulless Los Angeles the very night Charlie had phoned her with the news. She'd shrieked, "Eric! Bethie! Oh my God!" and Bethany had come on the run. She'd said, "That God damn *motorcycle,*" in a voice that told Charlie her teeth were clenched round the final word and then, "I'm on my way. D'you hear me, Charlie? I'm on my way."

Now she said quietly, "How you holding up, chickadee? You want I should show these folks the front door?"

With an effort, Charlie put her own hand on Bethany's where it rested on her shoulder. She said, "Everything started when I let him buy the Harley, Beth."

"You didn't *let* him do anything, Charles. It doesn't work that way."

"He'd got a tattoo as well. Did I tell you that? First the tattoo. It was only on his arm and I thought, 'Well, why not. It's a guy thing, isn't it?' And then the Harley.

195

What did I do wrong?"

"Nothing," Bethany said. "It wasn't your fault."

"How can you say that? This all happened because —"

Bethany swung Charlie around. She said, "Don't do this, Charles. What was the last thing he said to you?" She already knew, of course. It was one of the first things Charlie had told her, once the hysteria had subsided and the subsequent shock had settled in. She was asking only so that Charlie herself had to hear the words again and had to digest them.

" 'Remember, I'll always love you,' " she recited.

"He said that for a reason," Bethany declared.

"Then why —"

"There're some questions you never get answered in life. *Why?* is generally one of them." Bethany hugged her one-armed, a squeeze to tell her that she wasn't alone no matter how she felt, no matter how it seemed and was going to seem in the big, expensive, suburban house that they'd bought three years ago because "It's time for a family, Char, don't you think? And no one believes cities are good for kids." Declared with an infectious smile, declared with that spurt of Eric energy that had always kept him active, curious, involved, and alive.

Charlie said, looking at the assembled guests, "I can't believe his family didn't come. I phoned his ex-wife. I told her what happened. I asked her to tell the rest of his family — well, to tell his parents . . . who else is there, really? — but none of them even sent a message, Beth. Not his father, not his mother, not his own daughter."

"Maybe the ex didn't — what's her name?"

"Paula."

"Maybe Paula didn't pass on the word. If the divorce was nasty . . . was it?"

"Fairly. There was another man involved. Eric fought Paula for custody of Janie."

"That could've done the trick."

"It was *years* ago."

"Put the screws to him in death. Some people can never let go."

"D'you think she might not have told his parents?"

"Sounds about right," Bethany said.

It was the thought that Paula, in a last stroke of posthumous revenge upon her erstwhile husband, might have refused to pass along the news to Eric's parents that made Charlie decide to contact the elder Lawtons herself. The problem was that Eric had long been estranged from his parents, a sad fact that he'd revealed to Charlie during their first holiday season together. Close to her own family despite the distance that separated them all, she'd brought up "making arrangements for the holidays. D'you want to spend them with your family or mine? Or should we divide them up? Or have everyone here?"

Here at that time was a two-bedroom condo in the Hollywood Hills from which Eric ventured forth each day to his job in the distant suburbs while Charlie dashed off to her casting calls with the hope that something other than being the mom-with-the-perfect-family on WoW! soap commercials might be in her future. A two-bedroom condo with an airliner-sized kitchen and a single bathroom was not the ideal spot for entertaining mutual families, so she had prepared herself for the inevitable division of time between the end of November and the beginning of January: Thanksgiving in one location, Christmas Eve in another, Christmas Day at a third, and New Year's Eve together at home alone in front of the artificial fire, with fruit and champagne. Only, that wasn't how the holidays played out because Eric told her the painful story of his estrangement from his parents: about the hunting accident that had caused the estrangement and what had followed that accident.

"I tripped and the gun went off," he confessed one night in the darkness. "If I'd known what to . . . I didn't know what to *do*. I had no first aid. He bled to death, Char. With me shaking him and yelling his name and crying and telling him, *begging* him, to hold on, to just hold on."

"I'm so sorry," she'd said and she'd pulled his head to her breast because his voice had broken and his body trembled and he clung to her and she wasn't used to a man showing emotion. "Your own brother. Eric, what a horrible thing."

"He was eighteen. They tried to forgive me. But he was . . . Brent was like the crown prince to them. I couldn't take his place. I drifted off eventually. Just a bit at first. Then more and more. They decided to let me. It was best for us all. We couldn't get over it. We couldn't get past it."

Charlie tried to imagine what it had been like for him: growing to adulthood and then toward middle age and always knowing he'd shot his own brother. They'd been birding, out at dawn at the edge of the desert where the doves wintered. They'd hunted birds from childhood, first with their father and then — when Brent was old enough to drive — on their own. And on their second such trip together, the worst had happened.

"They probably forgave you years ago," she'd said to her husband loyally. "Have you tried to contact them?"

"I don't want to see it in their eyes. The looking at me and trying to seem like there's nothing beneath that look but love."

"Well, there's not hate beneath it."

"No. Just sorrow, which I put there. Being dumb. Being slipshod. Not holding the gun right. Not watching my feet."

"You were only fifteen," Charlie protested.

"I was old enough."

For what? she'd wondered. But she worked out the answer eventually: old enough to disappear.

They had a right to know that he was dead, however. So even though Charlie had no idea where Marilyn and Clark Lawton lived, she determined she would find them and give them the information. She knew that Eric would want it that way.

The very fact that he had a virtual gallery of family pictures told her that he had never stopped feeling the aching loss of a place in his parents' hearts.

She went to these pictures the day after his funeral, light-headed and sore-muscled after the trauma of the past week. The grieving tightness in her throat was still there — had been there since the night Eric died — and so was the sickly, feverish sensation she'd had for days. She couldn't remember how it was to feel normal any longer. But things had to be done.

The pictures were in the living room, standing like deliberate, intrusive thoughts at intervals among the books on either side of the fireplace. She knew who every individual was because Eric had told her several times. But he'd identified most of them by first name only, which wasn't helpful in the present circumstances: Aunt Marianne at her high school graduation, Great-Aunt Shirley with Great-Uncle Pat, Grandma Louise (*on which side of the family, Eric?*), Uncle Ross, Brent at seven, Mom at ten, Dad at thirteen, Mom and Dad on their wedding day, Grandpa and his brothers, Nana Jessie-Lynn. But aside from his parents' last name, she knew no one else's. And a look in the phone book told her no Lawtons named Clark or Marilyn lived nearby.

Not that she had expected them to be near. She'd hoped for that, but at the same time she'd already realized that hunting trips taken by teenaged boys to the edge of the desert suggested a town not far away from a place even more arid than the LA suburb where she and Eric had bought their home.

She got out a map of California and considered beginning her search in the south, right at the state border. She could call information for every town that sided the slice of land that was Highway 805. But she got not much farther than Paradise Hills before she reconsidered this painstaking approach.

She went back to the pictures and took them down. She carried them into the kitchen and set them carefully on the granite counter. They were all old pictures, the most recent being Brent at seven, and some of them were tintypes assiduously preserved. Still, sometimes, she knew, families made note of the subjects of photographs and the locations where the pictures had been taken as well. And if that was the case with Eric's family pictures, there might be a clue as to the current whereabouts of his relatives.

So she eased off the back of each of the frames, and examined the reverse side of the photographs. Only two provided writing. A delicate hand had written *Brent Lawton, seven years old, Yosemite* on the back side of the picture of Eric's brother. A spidery pen had placed *Jessie-Lynn just before Merle's wedding* on the picture of one of the grandmothers in Eric's life. But that was it.

Charlie sighed and began to reassemble the frames and their contents: glass, photograph, cardboard filler, and velvet-covered backing. When she got to the Lawtons' wedding picture, however, she discovered that something besides the glass, the photo, the filler, and the backing had been put into the frame. Perhaps it was because the more recent the photo, the thinner the paper on which it had been printed. But the wedding picture had required something extra to fill up the space between it and the backing. This something was a folded paper, which unfolded turned out to be a blank receipt. Printed at the top of this was *Time on My Side* and an address on Front Street in Temecula, California.

Charlie got out her map again. A shot of excitement and certainty flashed through her when she found Temecula at the edge of the desert, sitting alongside another desert freeway, as if waiting for her to discover its secrets.

She didn't go at once. She planned to head out the very next day, but she awakened to find that the tightness in her throat had become a burning and the soreness in her muscles had metamorphosed into chills. It was more than simply exhaustion and grief, she realized. She'd come down with the flu.

She felt resignation but very little surprise. She'd been running on nerves alone for days: with virtually no food and even less sleep. It was no shock to find herself become a breeding ground for illness.

She forced herself to the drugstore and prowled the length of the cold-and-flu aisle, blearily reading the labels on medicines that promised a quick fix for — or at least temporary relief from — the nasty little bug that had invaded her body. She knew the routine: lots of liquids and bed rest, so she stocked up on Cup of Soup, Cup of Noodles, Lipton's, and Top Ramen. As long as the microwave worked, she would be all right, she told herself. Eric's family could wait the twenty-four or forty-eight hours it would take for her to regain her strength.

Thus, it was two days later when Charlie set out for Temecula. Even then, she did so in the company of Bethany Franklin. For although she felt somewhat buoyed by the forty-eight hours of bed rest interrupted only by forays to the refrigerator and the microwave, she didn't trust herself to drive such a distance without a companion.

Bethany didn't like the idea of her going at all. She said bluntly, "You look like hell," when she roared up in her pride and joy, a silver BMW sports car. "You should be in bed, not traipsing around the state looking for . . . who're we looking for?" She'd brought a bag of Cheetos with her — "absolute nectar of the gods," she announced, waving the sack like a woman flagging down a taxi — and she munched them as she followed Charlie from the front door into the kitchen. There, the family pictures stood where Charlie had left them. Charlie took up the photo of Eric's parents, along with the receipt from Time on My Side.

She said, "I want to tell his family what happened. I don't know where they are, and this is the only clue I have."

Bethany took the picture and the receipt

as Charlie explained where she'd found the latter. She said, "Why don't we just phone this place, Charles? There's a number."

"And if Eric's parents own it? What do we say?" Charlie asked. "We can't just tell them about . . ." She felt tears threaten, again. Again. *Remember, I'll always love you, Char.* "Not on the phone, Beth. It wouldn't be right."

"No. You're right. We can't do it on the phone. But you're in no shape to cruise up and down freeways. Let me go if you're so set on this."

"I'm fine. I'm okay. I'm feeling better. It was just the flu."

The compromise was that they would travel with the top up and Charlie was to bring with her a Thermos of Lipton's chicken noodle and a carton of orange juice as well, which she was to use to minister to herself during the long drive to the southeast. In this fashion, they made their way to Temecula, down Highway 15 which squeezed a concrete valley through the rock-strewn hills that divided the California desert from the sea. Here, greedy developers had raped the dusty land, planting it with the seed of their neighborhoods, each identical to the last, all colored a uniform shade of dun, all unshaded by even a single tree, all roofed in a pantiled fashion that had prompted the builder of one site to name the monstrosity, ludicrously, "Tuscany Hills."

They arrived in Temecula just after one in the afternoon, and it was no difficult feat for them to find Front Street. It comprised what the city council euphemistically called "The Historic District" and it announced itself from the freeway some mile and a half before the appropriate exit.

"The Historic District" turned out to be several city blocks separated from the rest of the town — its modern half — by a railroad track, the freeway, a smallish industrial park, and a public storage site. These city blocks stretched along a two-lane street, and they were lined with gift shops, restaurants, and antique stores, with the occasional coffee, candy, or ice-cream house thrown in for good measure. In short, "The Historic District" was another name for tourist attraction. It might have once been the center of the town, but now it was a magnet for people seeking a day's respite from the indistinguishable urban sprawl that oozed out from Los Angeles in all directions like a profitable oil slick. There were wooden sidewalks and structures of adobe, stucco, or brick. There were colorful banners, quirky signs, and a you-are-here billboard posted at the edge of the public parking lot. It was Disneyland's Main Street without having to pay the exorbitant entrance fee.

"And you ask me why I hate to venture out of LA," Bethany commented as she pulled into a vacant space and gazed around with a shudder. "This is SoCal at its best. Phony history for fun and profit. It reminds me of Calico Ghost Town. You ever been there, chickadee? The only ghost town on earth that someone's managed to turn into a shopping mall."

Charlie smiled and pointed at the you-are-here billboard. "Let's look at that sign."

They found Time on My Side listed as one of the shops in the first block of the historic district. Between them, they'd decided on the drive that it was probably an establishment selling clocks but when they got to it, they discovered that it was — like so many of its companion businesses — an antique shop. They went inside.

A low growl greeted them, followed by a man's voice admonishing, "Hey you, Mugs. None of that," which was directed to a Norwich terrier who was curled on a cushion on an old desk chair. This stood next to an ancient rolltop desk at which a man was sitting beneath a bright light, studying a porcelain bottle through a jeweler's lens. He looked over the countertop at Bethany and Charlie, saying, "Sorry. Some folks take her amiss. It's just her way of saying hello. You go back to sleep, Mugs." The dog apparently understood. She sank her head back to her paws and sighed deeply. Her eyelids began to droop.

Charlie scanned the man's face, seeking a likeness, hoping to see projected on its elderly features an Eric who would never be. He was the right age to be Eric's dad: He looked about seventy. And he was wiry like Eric, with Eric's frank gaze and an Eric energy that expressed itself in a foot that tapped restlessly against the rung of his chair.

"Make yourself to home," the old gentleman said. "Have a spec around. You looking for anything special?"

"Actually," Charlie said as she and Bethany approached the counter, "I'm looking for a family. My husband's family."

The man scratched his head. He set the porcelain bottle down on his desk and placed the jeweler's lens next to it. "Don't sell families," he said with a smile.

"This one's called Lawton," Bethany said.

"Marilyn and Clark Lawton," Charlie added. "We were . . . Well, *I* was hoping that you might . . . Are you Mr. Lawton, by any chance?"

"Henry Leel," he said.

"Oh." Charlie felt deflated. More, the knowledge that the man wasn't Eric's father struck her more forcefully than she thought it would. She said, "Well, it was always only a chance, driving out here. But I hoped . . . You don't happen to know any family called Lawton in town, do you?"

Henry Leel shook his head. "Can't say as I do. They antiques people?" He gestured at the shop around him, crowded to a claustrophobic degree with furniture and bric-a-brac.

"I don't . . ." Charlie felt a slight dizziness come over her, and she reached for the counter.

Bethany took her arm. She said, "Here. Take it easy," and to Henry Leel, "She's just getting over the flu. And her husband . . . He died about a week ago. His parents don't know about it and we're looking for them."

"They the Lawtons?" Henry Leel said, and when Bethany nodded, he cast a sympathetic gaze on Charlie. "She looks mighty young to be a widow, poor thing."

"She *is* mighty young to be a widow. And like I say, she's been sick."

"Bring her behind here then and sit her down. Mugs, get off that chair and give it to the lady. Go on. You heard me. Here. Let me get the pillow off, Miss . . . Mrs. . . . What'd you say the name was?"

"Lawton," Charlie said. "Forgive me. I haven't been feeling well. His death . . . It was sudden."

"I'm sure sorry about that. Here. I'm making you some tea with a tot of brandy in it. It'll set you up. You stay where you are."

He locked the front door of the shop and disappeared into the back. When he returned with the tea, he brought a local telephone directory with him, eager to be of help to the ladies. But a search through its pages turned up no Lawtons in the area.

Charlie quelled her disappointment. She drank her tea and felt revived enough to tell Henry Leel how she and Bethany had come to choose this shop in Temecula as the jumping-off point to find Eric's family. When she'd completed the story and brought forth the wedding picture of Eric's parents, Henry gazed at it long and hard, his brow furrowed as if he could force recognition out of his skull. But he shook his head after a minute of study. He said, "They look a touch familiar, I'll give you that. But I wouldn't want to say that I know them. 'Sides, I sell old pictures not much different from this, so after a while *everyone* in a picture looks like someone I've seen somewhere. Here. Let me show you."

He went to a dark far corner of the shop and brought out a small bin that stood on the shelf of a kitchen dresser. He carried this back to Charlie and Bethany saying, "I don't sell many. Mostly to tearooms, theater groups, frame shops wanting to use them for display. That sort of thing. Here. Have a look-see yourself." He plopped the bin on the desk. "See. This here one of yours . . . it fits right in with this last bunch in the bin. A little more recent, but I've got some that age. Looks like . . . let me see for a second. Yep. It looks like a fifties shot. Late fifties. Maybe early sixties."

Charlie had begun to feel uneasy with the first mention of the photographs. She didn't want to look at Bethany, afraid of what her own face might reveal. She fingered through the photographs cooperatively, unable to avoid noticing the fact that they represented all styles and all periods of time. There were tintypes, there were old black and white snapshots, there were studio studies, there were hand-tinted portraits. Some of them had hand-writing on the back, identifying either the subjects or the places. Charlie didn't want to think what this meant. *Jessie-Lynn just before Merle's wedding.*

Henry Leel said, "So how'd you come to think these Lawton folks'd be here? At this shop in Temecula."

"There was a receipt," Bethany responded. "Charlie, show him what you found in that frame."

Charlie handed over the slip of paper. As Henry Leel squinted down at it, she said, "It must have been a coincidence. The picture . . . this one of his parents . . . it was a bit loose in the frame, and he must have been just using it to fill in the gap. I saw it and . . . Since I was hoping to track down his family, I made a leap that wasn't warranted. That's all."

Henry Leel pulled thoughtfully at his chin. He cocked his head to one side and tapped his index finger — its nail blackened by some sort of fungus — against the receipt. He said, "These're numbered. See here? One-oh-five-eight in the top right-hand corner? Just hang on a minute. I

213

might be able to help you." He rustled within his rolltop desk, rousing Mugs from her slumber at its side. She lifted her head and blinked at him sleepily before pillowing herself once again in her paws. Her master brought forth a worn, black, floppy-covered book of an official nature and he plopped it onto his desktop, saying, "Let's see what we can come up with in here."

In here turned out to be copies of the sales receipts for merchandise for Time on My Side. Within a moment, the shop owner had leafed back through them to find what was on either side of 1058. 1059 had been made out to a Barbara Fryer with a home address in Huntington Beach. "Not much help there," Henry Leel said regretfully, but he added, "Say now. Here's what we want," when he saw the receipt that preceded it. "Here's who you're looking for. You said Lawton, didn't you? Well, I've got myself a Lawton right here."

He swung the accounts book in Charlie's direction, and she saw what she'd anticipated seeing — without knowing or understanding *why* she would be seeing it — the moment she began fingering through the old pictures. *Eric Lawton* was written on receipt number 1057. Instead of an address anywhere at all, there was only a phone number: Eric's work number at the pharmaceutical company where he'd been director of sales for the seven years that Charlie had known him.

Beneath Eric's name was a list of purchases. Charlie read *gold locket (14 ct), 19th century porcelain box, woman's diamond ring,* and *Japanese fan.* Beneath this last was the number ten and the word *pix.* Charlie didn't need to ask what that final notation meant.

Bethany pointed to it, saying, "Charles, is this —"

Charlie cut her off. Her limbs felt like lead, but she moved them anyway, turning the account book back to the shop owner and saying, "No. It's . . . I'm looking for Clark or Marilyn Lawton. This is someone else."

Henry Leel said, "Oh. Well, I s'pose it wouldn't be this fellah. He was too young to be who you're looking for anyway. I remember him, and he was . . . say . . . fortyish? Forty-five. I remember because look here, he spent near seven hundred dollars — the ring and the locket were the big-money items — and you don't see that kind of sale every day. I said to him, 'Some lady's going to get lucky,' and he winked. 'Every lady's lucky when she's my lady,' he said. I remember that. Cocky, I thought. But cocky in a good way. You know what I mean?"

Charlie smiled faintly. She got to her feet. She said, "Thanks. Thanks so much for your help."

"Sorry I couldn't've been more of a one," Henry Leel replied. "Say, you want to head off right now? You're looking green around the gills. Ask me, you need a straight shot of brandy."

"No, no. I'm fine. Thanks," Charlie said. She gripped Bethany's arm and drew her steadily from the shop.

Outside, an old-time hitching rail ran along the wooden sidewalk, and Charlie clutched onto this, looking out into the street. She thought about *10 pix* and what that meant: a family conveniently purchased in Temecula, California. But what did *that* mean? And what did it tell her about her husband?

She felt Bethany come close to her side and she blessed her friend for the gift of her silence. It continued while out in the bright street, cars cruised by and pedestrians dodged between them to dart into yet another shop.

When she was finally able to speak, Charlie said, "What happened was that I accused him of having an affair. Not that night. A week or so before."

Bethany said, voice glum, "He never gave you that locket, I guess. Or the ring."

"Or the porcelain box. No. He didn't."

"Maybe he sent them to Janie? Trying to be a good dad?"

"He never said." In spite of an attempt to control them, Charlie's tears welled anyway, spilling onto her cheeks in a silent trail of misery. "He'd been acting different for about three months. At first I thought it was work — sales being down or something. But there were the phone calls he hung up on when I walked into the room. There were the times he came home late. He always phoned me, but the excuses were . . . Beth, they were so transparent."

Bethany sighed. "Charles, I don't know. It looks bad. I can see that for myself. But it just doesn't *seem* like Eric."

"Did a Harley-Davidson seem like Eric? A tattoo of a snake crawling up his arm?" Charlie began crying in earnest then, and the rest of her fears, her suspicions, and her covert activities in the final week before Eric's death spilled out of her for her friend's ears. He'd denied an affair earlier when confronted, she told Bethany. He'd denied it with such incredulous outrage that Charlie had decided to believe in him. But three weeks later, he suggested casually that she slow down in her decorating of their house and especially that she hold off on their plans for a nursery since "we don't really know how much longer we're going to live in this place," which set fire to her suspicions again.

She'd hated the part of herself that had doubts about Eric, but she'd not been able to stop herself from dwelling on them. They led her to snooping in a despicable fashion she was embarrassed to admit to, stooping so low as to even go through his bathroom — for God's sake — for signs that there was another woman who might have been in the house with Eric when she herself was gone.

As she told the tale, Charlie wiped her eyes and even laughed shakily at her own behavior: She'd been like a character in an afternoon soap opera, a woman whose life goes from bad to worse but all the time at her own hands. She'd studied telephone bills for strange numbers; she'd gone through her husband's address book, looking for cryptic initials that stood in place of a mistress's name; she'd examined his dirty laundry for telltale signs of lipstick that was not her own; she'd rustled through his dresser drawers for mementos, receipts, letters, messages, ticket stubs, or anything else that might give him away; she'd picked the lock of his briefcase and read every document inside it as if the convoluted reports from Biosyn Inc. were love letters or diaries written in code.

She'd been forced to confess to all of this, however, when she sank to the depths of opening up a prescription cough syrup she'd found in his bathroom — not even knowing *why* she was opening it . . . what did she expect to find in there? A genie who would tell her the truth? — only to have it slip from her fingers and smash and spill upon the limestone floor. That had served to bring her to her senses: that rising sense of frustration at not being able to prove what she believed to be true, that muttered *aha!* when she saw the bottle, that clutching to her bosom of the medicine itself and unscrewing its top with unsteady hands and watching dumbly as it flew from her fingers and broke on the floor, spilling out the syrup in an amber pool. When this occurred, she had realized how futile her investigation was and how ugly it was making her. Which was why she finally confessed to her husband. It seemed the only way to get herself beyond what was troubling her.

"He listened. He was terribly upset. And after we talked, he just went into himself. I thought he was punishing me for what I'd done, and I knew I deserved it. What I did was wrong. But I thought he'd get past it, we'd both get past it and that would be the end of it. Only, a week later he was dead. And now . . ." Charlie glanced at the door of Time on My Side. "We know, don't we? We know what. We just don't know who. Let's go home, Beth."

Bethany Franklin was reluctant to believe the worst of Eric Lawton. She pointed out to Charlie that Charlie's own search had turned up nothing and that, for all she knew, Eric had been squirreling away Christmas presents for her. Or birthday presents. Or Valentine's presents. Some people buy things when they see them, Bethany pointed out, and just hang on to them till the appropriate day.

But that hardly explained the pictures, Charlie said. He'd "bought" his family at Time on My Side. And what did *that* mean?

That he had another family somewhere, she decided. Beyond his earlier marriage to Paula, beyond his daughter Janie, and beyond herself.

★ ★ ★

For the next two days, Charlie fought off a relapse of the flu and used her bed time to sort out who among Eric's limited number of friends might be able and willing to tell her the truth about her husband's private life. She decided that Terry Stewart would be the man: Eric's attorney, his regular tennis partner, and his buddy from their days in kindergarten. If there was a hidden side to Eric Lawton, Terry Stewart had to know it.

Before she could phone him and make an arrangement to see him, however, she received her first hint of what Eric's second life might be. One of his colleagues came to call, a woman Charlie had never met, had never even heard of. She was named Sharon Pasternak ("No relation," she said with a smile when she introduced herself at the front door), and she apologized for stopping by without phoning. She wondered if she could have a look through Eric's work papers, she said. The two of them had been assembling a report for the board of directors, and Eric had taken most of the paperwork home to put it together in a logical fashion.

"I know it's awfully soon after . . . well, you know. And I'd wait if I could, hon-

221

estly," Sharon Pasternak said as Charlie admitted her into the house. "But the board meets next month and since I'll be putting this together by myself now . . . I'm *really* sorry to have to come around . . . But I need to get going on it." She looked earnest, regretful about having even to say Eric's name, not wishing to cause his widow further grief. She made all the right noises. On the other hand, she also said she was a molecular biologist, which prompted Charlie to ask herself why one of Biosyn's scientists and its director of sales would be writing a report together.

Cautiously, all her senses on alert, Charlie showed Sharon Pasternak to Eric's study where, on his desk, his briefcase lay. Sharon flashed her a smile, said, "May I . . . Is it all right if I sit here?" and put one hand on Eric's swivel chair. "It might take a while." She gestured around the room. "He's got so many files."

"Sure," Charlie said as pleasantly as she could. "Take your time. I have to go through all of this eventually, but you can take whatever relates to . . ." She made the pause deliberate. "To your work."

Sharon flushed and dropped her gaze. She said, "Thanks so much," and she lifted her head when she went on with, "I'm so sorry about . . . everything, Mrs. Lawton. He was a good man. He was *such* a good man." Her eyes bored meaningfully into Charlie's, fastening upon her for far too long.

So this was it, Charlie thought in reaction. This was how it played out when you came face-to-face with the object of your husband's secret passion. Except Sharon Pasternak wasn't Eric's type. Plump, a head of no-nonsense dark hair, a smattering of makeup, ankles too thick. She wasn't his type. Yet, it had to be asked: What *was* Eric Lawton's type? Who was his type? Did his wife even know?

Charlie went to her bedroom and closed the curtains. She lay in the darkness and listened to the sounds of Eric's colleague sifting through whatever she wanted to sift through in the study. Charlie herself had already been through much of the contents of the room during her frenzy of searching for evidence of her husband's infidelity. If Sharon indeed was the mystery woman, Charlie wanted to tell her, her secret was safe, or at least it had been safe till she'd showed up at Eric Lawton's front door. Dumb move, Ms. Pasternak.

"As in Boris?" Bethany asked Charlie later. "That's not exactly a name hanging on every tree. Did you see her ID? She could've given you an alias."

"Why? If she was Eric's lover, what difference does it make whether I know her name or not?"

"She might not be Eric's lover, Charles. She might be someone else altogether."

Charlie considered this point and all its implications. "I need to talk to Terry Stewart," she decided. "Terry must know who Eric was seeing."

"*If* he was seeing anyone at all. But why do *you* need to know?"

"Because I . . ." Charlie drew a deep breath. "I need absolution. The truth will give me absolution."

"For what?"

"For not knowing what to believe."

"There's no sin in that."

"For me, there is."

Eric's oldest friend, so often declared "my best friend on earth . . . he didn't desert me . . . he never would," Terry Stewart, Charlie knew, had to be confronted without having had the time to prepare a cover for whatever it was he might be hiding about Eric. As he was an attorney — Eric's own lawyer, in fact — she knew how likely it was that he would be set upon taking his clients' secrets to the grave. So she didn't want her visit to him to be official. Which meant she would need to waylay him in a location some distance from his glass-towered office.

The gym turned out to be that location. She saw his car parked in front of it when she was on her way to the tennis courts to check for him, and she recognized its vanity plate: IOS NEI. So she pulled into the lot, saw him sweating on the Stairmaster through the plate-glass windows of the establishment, and decided to wait for him to emerge. There was a Starbucks next door, and she went there.

She was in a window seat sipping a chai latte when Terry swung open the door of the gym. He headed for his car, straightening his tie as he walked. He looked freshly showered: all damp hair and glowing skin. She knocked on the window. He swung around, saw her, stopped, and smiled. He came in her direction and, in short order, joined her.

"How are you, Charlie?" His face was grave and kind.

Charlie shrugged. "I'm okay. I've been better, but I'll survive."

"I'm sorry I haven't phoned. I'm a coward, I guess. If I talk about it, she'll cry,

225

I told myself. And I can't avoid talking about it because if I do, it'd be like ignoring an alligator in your bathtub. But I don't want to make her cry. She's cried enough already. She might even be feeling better and there I'd be, making her live through everything again." He pulled out a chair and sat. "I'm sorry."

"He was having an affair, wasn't he?"

Terry jerked back against his seat, apparently startled by this frontal attack. *"Eric?"*

"I'd thought he was at first. Then I'd changed my mind. Well, he convinced me, really. But now . . . He *was* having an affair, wasn't he?"

"No. God, no. What makes you think —"

"All the changes, Terry. The Harley and the tattoo for starters."

"This county's *filled* with guys in their forties who spend their weekends riding around on Harleys. They've got wives, kids, cats, dogs, car payments, and mortgages and they wake up one morning and say, This is all there is? And they want more. Midlife crisis. They want the edge back. Harleys give it to them. That's it."

"There were phone calls. Late nights he supposedly spent at work. And a woman came by the house to look through his things. She said she was Sharon Pasternak, a molecular biologist at Biosyn. She said they were working on a report — she and Eric, Terry, why would Eric have been working on a report with a biologist, for God's sake? — and he had some data she said she needed in order to put the report together by herself now he's gone. But when she left, she took nothing with her. What's that supposed to tell me?"

"I don't know."

"I think it's obvious enough. She was looking for traces."

"Of what?"

"You know. He was seeing someone. Maybe it was her."

"That's impossible."

"Why? Why is it impossible?"

"Because . . . God, Charlie. He was crazy about you. I mean *crazy* about you. Had been since the day you two met."

"Then she was looking for something else. What?"

"Charlie, jeez. Take it easy, okay? You look like shit, pardon my French. Have you been sleeping? Are you eating? Have you thought about getting away for a few days?"

"He lied to me about his family. He had pictures. He used them to pretend . . . You saw them, Terry. You've been at our house. You saw those pictures and you know his family. You grew up with him. So you must have known . . ." Charlie clutched the table as a cramp gripped her stomach. Her bowels felt loose. Her palms were wet. She was falling apart and she *hated* the fact, and the hate made her raise her voice and cry, "I want the information. I have the right to it. Tell me what you know."

Terry looked puzzled more than anything else. "What pictures?" he asked. "What're you talking about?"

Charlie told him. He listened, but he shook his head, saying, "Sure, I knew Eric's family. But that was just his mom, his dad, and his brother. Brent. And even if I studied those pictures — which I didn't . . . I mean, who studies family pictures in other people's houses? You just glance at them when you walk by, don't you? — I wouldn't have recognized anyone. Eric's mom died when we were around eight and even before that she was in bed for five years with a stroke. I saw her what? maybe once, so in a picture. . . . No way. I wouldn't even know her. And I haven't set eyes on Brent or Eric's dad for years. At least ten, maybe more. So if there was a picture of either of them or all of them or someone else, I wouldn't have known the difference."

Charlie listened through a roar in her ears. "Brent?" she said in a whisper. "He *died*. The accident. And then Eric's mother and his father —"

"What accident?" Terry asked.

"The shotgun. Hunting birds. The desert. Eric tripped and Brent was . . ." She couldn't finish because Terry's face was telling her more than she wanted to know. She felt her own face crumple. "Oh God. Oh *God*."

Terry said, "Jeez. Jeez, Charlie." Awkwardly, he patted her hand. "Jeez. I don't know what to say."

"Tell me what you know. Tell me why he lied. Tell me who she is. Tell me who he was."

"I swear to God —"

She smacked her hand on the table. "He was your best friend!"

Terry glanced over his shoulder to the counter, where the Starbucks clerk was beginning to show more interest in them than in the lattes she was making. He turned back to Charlie. "There was a blowup in his family. This was years ago. That's all I know. He didn't talk about it and I didn't ask."

"So why didn't he tell me that? Why'd he pretend —"

"I don't know. Maybe it sounded . . . more glamorous or something."

"To have *shot* your own brother? I don't believe that. The only reason a man would tell a woman that tale would be to keep her from wondering why he never mentioned a family, why he never saw them or heard from them. And why would he do that in the first place, Terry? You know as well as I: if he had another life that they knew about. Right?"

"That's not the case."

"How do you know?"

"Look. Do you know how much planning it would take to have a double life like the kind you're imagining? Jeez. Do you know how much plain old cash it would take? He didn't have that kind of money, Charlie. All he had was pipe dreams like the rest of us."

"What sort of pipe dreams?"

"He talked through his hat. You *know* how he was."

"Talked about what?"

"I need a cup of coffee." Terry got up and went to the counter, where he placed an order, dug out his wallet, and waited.

Biding his time, Charlie thought. Establishing his story. For the first time since

Eric's death, she wondered if there was anyone whom she could trust and at this thought, she sank back in her seat and felt ill to her soul.

"He talked about Barbados. Grenada. The Bahamas." Terry set a cappuccino on the table and tore the top off a packet of sugar. "He talked about putting his money there, having a new life, sleeping in a hammock on the beach, drinking piña coladas."

"Dear God, what was going on?" Charlie cried.

"Don't you see? *Nothing.* He was forty-two. *That's* what was going on. He was talking, that's all. That's what guys do. They talk about investments. About offshore banking. About fast cars and women with big boobs and yachts and racing in the America's Cup. About hiking in the Himalayas and renting a palazzo in Venice. He was talking, Charlie. That's what guys do when they're forty-two."

"Do you do that?"

Terry colored brightly. "It's a guy thing."

"Do you do it?"

"Not all guys are the same." And as he read the despair on her face, he hastened on with, "Charlie, it was nothing. It was going to blow over."

"He felt trapped and he'd done something about it."

"No way."

"Except something happened to prevent him from going through with what he intended to do and then he was really trapped and then —"

"No! That's not it."

"What is it, then? What *was* it?"

He grasped his cappuccino but he didn't drink it. "I don't know," he said.

"I don't believe you."

"I'm telling you the truth." He gazed at her long, hard, and earnestly as if his look carried the power to convince and reassure her. "You need to come to the office," he said. "We've got to go over his will. And there's probate to be handled . . . Charlie, I want to help you through this. I'm devastated, too. He was my closest friend. Can't we be there for each other?"

"Like Eric was there for both of us? What does that even mean, Terry?"

He was gone and that was difficult enough for Charlie to cope with. The manner of his going — the suddenness and the inexplicable horror of it — made the coping even more difficult. But now to have to face the fact that the man she'd loved and lost had not even been who she'd thought he was . . . It was too much to bear and far too much to assimilate. She drove home feeling as if she'd been struck by the plague, a virulent interloper that was forcing her body to suffer what her mind could not begin to face.

Somatizing. Somehow she remembered the term from Psych all those years ago. She couldn't bring herself to embrace the full truth, but her body *knew* what that full truth was and it reacted accordingly. She wasn't suffering from the flu at all. She was somatizing. And now her body was trying to purge her of Eric's lies, because as she drove home, she was overcome by a nausea so fierce that she didn't think she would make it into her house without vomiting.

She didn't. Once pulled into her driveway, she shoved open the door of the car and stumbled out. On the pristine front lawn, she fell to her knees and spasm after spasm wracked her stomach, forcing its meager contents upward and outward in a humiliating and malodorous plume. She gagged on the taste and the smell of it, and she vomited more, until all that was left was the wretched heaving itself which she couldn't bring under control. Finally, she fell onto her side, panting, sweat heavy on her neck and her eyelids. She stared at the house and she felt the vomit slide across the sloping lawn and graze her cheek. *Remember, I'll always love you.*

She pulled herself up and staggered to the porch, thankful that like so many up-scale suburban neighborhoods in Southern California, her own was deserted at this time of day. The two-income families who were her neighbors wouldn't return to their homes before night, so she hadn't been seen. There was blessing in that.

She didn't notice anything wrong until she got to her front door. There, she had her key extended when she saw the deep gouges around what remained of the lock.

Weakly, she pushed the door open but she had the presence of mind not to enter. From the porch, she could see all she needed to see.

"Jesus H," the policeman muttered. "Fucking mess." He'd introduced himself to Charlie as Officer Marco Doyle, and he'd arrived within ten minutes of her phone call with his lights flashing and his siren blaring as if that's what she paid her taxes for. His partner was a dog called Simba, a European import that looked like a cross between a German shepherd and the hound of the Baskervilles. "She's on duty," Doyle had commented as he stepped inside the house. "Don't pet her."

Charlie hadn't considered doing so.

Simba remained on the front porch on the alert as Doyle went inside. It was from the living room that he'd made the comment which Charlie, clutching at her cell phone like a life preserver, heard from just inside the entry.

Doyle said, "Simba, come," and the dog bounded into the house. He directed her to sniff out intruders and while she did so — with Doyle on her heels going from room to room — Charlie examined the destruction.

It was obvious that the intent had been search and not robbery because her possessions were thrown around in a way that suggested someone moving quickly, knowing what he was looking for, and tossing things over his shoulder to get them out of his way when he did not find what he wanted. Each room appeared identical in its pattern of chaos: Everything was moved away from the walls; the contents of drawers and closets were dumped into the center. Pictures had been removed and books had been opened and flung to one side.

"No one here," Doyle said. "Whoever it was, he moved fast. There're too many scents for her to pick up anything useful, though. You have a party lately?"

A party. "People were here. After a funeral. My husband . . ." Charlie lowered herself to a chair, her knees going and the rest of her following.

"Oh. Hey. I'm sorry," Doyle said. "Hell. Rotten luck. Anything missing, can you tell?"

"I don't know. I don't think so. It seems like . . . I don't know." Charlie felt so used up that all she could think about was crawling into her bed and sleeping for a year. Sleeping away the nightmare, she thought.

Doyle said that he'd be radioing for the crime scene people. They'd come and fingerprint and take what evidence they could find. Charlie would want to phone her insurance company in the meantime, though. And was there anyone who could help her clean up the mess when the crime scene people were finished?

Yes, Charlie told him cooperatively. She had a friend who would help.

"Need me to call her?"

No, no, Charlie said. She'd place the call. No point in doing so till the crime scene people looked for evidence, though.

Doyle said this was sensible and he told her he'd wait outside with the dog for the crime scene team to show up. Which they did in an hour, pulling up in a white sedan with *Crime Scene Investigation* printed in subtle gray on the doors.

While they went through the motions of looking for evidence in the debris that was Charlie's house, Charlie herself sat in the backyard, staring numbly at the pictur-esque fountain that she and her husband had two years ago debated removing "once the babies come." It all seemed so much a part of another life now, a life that not only bore no resemblance to her present one but also had been a fabrication.

"Wow, this guy's too good to be *true*," her sister Emily had murmured the first time she'd met Eric.

And that had apparently been the case.

When the crime scene people were done with their work, they left Charlie with the name and phone number of someone who specialized in "fixing up after this kind of thing," they said. "You can get her to help you clean up. She's reasonable."

Charlie didn't know if they meant her personality or her expense.

In either case, it didn't matter. She

wanted no other professionals traipsing through the wreckage of her world.

So she forced herself to deal with the wreckage alone, and she began where she knew, without wanting to admit it to herself, that the intruder had begun: in Eric's study.

This was owing to Sharon Pasternak, Charlie thought as she stood in the doorway, slumped against its jamb. She would have to be every which way a complete fool not to put together this break-in with Sharon Pasternak's visit "to find some papers." Failing to find whatever she'd been looking for, she'd called in someone with a little more imagination in the searching arena. And here before Charlie was the result.

She stepped over a pile of file folders and went to Eric's desk. She began with the easiest task: putting the drawers back in and reassembling their contents. And it was in the midst of doing this that she found an indication of where — if not what — the "papers" were that Sharon Pasternak and the intruder who followed her had wanted. For dumped alongside Eric's desk, as if they'd been contained in one of its lower drawers, was a set of documents that were out of place: the deed to the house, the pink slips to the cars, insurance papers, birth certificates, and passports. All of this belonged in their safe-deposit box at the bank, not here at home. Which made Charlie wonder what, if anything, had replaced these documents in that protected vault.

She didn't go until the following day. In the afternoon, following a morning in which she lay in bed fighting against an inertia that threatened to keep her there permanently, she fumbled her way to the bathroom, shuffled through the debris, and ran the water in the tub. She soaked until the water was cool, when she refilled the tub and languidly washed. She tried to remember another time when everything — even the slightest movement — had been such an effort. She couldn't.

It was two o'clock when she finally walked into the bank with her key to the safe-deposit box in her hand. She tapped the bell for assistance and a clerk came to help her, a girl who couldn't have been much older than college age, with jet-black hair, jet-black eyeliner, and a name tag identifying her as Linda.

Charlie filled out the appropriate card. Linda read her name and the number of her deposit box and then looked back up from the card to Charlie's face. She said, "Oh! You're . . . I mean, you've never —" She stopped herself as if remembering her place. "It's this way, Mrs. Lawton," she settled on saying.

The deposit box was one of the large ones on the bottom row. Charlie inserted her key in its right lock as Linda inserted her key in its left. A twist and the box slid out of its compartment. Linda heaved it up and onto the counter. She said, "Is there anything else I can do for you, Mrs. Lawton?" And she watched Charlie so intently when she asked the question that Charlie wondered if the girl was part of Eric's secret life.

"Why do you ask?" Charlie said.

"What?"

"Why do you ask if there's anything else you can do for me?"

Linda backed away, as if suddenly aware that she was in the presence of a crazy woman. "We always ask that. We're supposed to ask. Would you like some coffee? Or tea?"

Charlie felt her anxiety dissipate. She said, "No. Sorry. I haven't been well. I didn't mean . . ."

"I'll leave you then," Linda said and

seemed glad to be doing so.

Alone in the vault, Charlie took a deep breath. It was an airless space, overheated and silent. She felt watched inside, and she looked around for cameras, but there was nothing. She had all the privacy she needed.

It was time to know what Sharon Pasternak had wanted in Eric's study. It was time to know why an intruder had broken into her house and torn it apart.

She eased the top of the deposit box open, and she drew in a sharp breath when she saw its contents: Neatly stacked in rows and bound in their centers by rubber bands, thick packets of one-hundred-dollar bills shot the odor of age, use, and malefaction into the air.

Charlie whispered, "Oh my God," and slammed the lid of the deposit box home. She leaned over the counter, breathing like a runner and trying to account for what she'd just seen. The packets looked to be fifty bills thick. There were . . . what? . . . fifty, seventy, one hundred packets in the deposit box? Which meant . . . ?What? It was more money than she'd ever seen outside of a motion picture. God in heaven, *who* was her husband? What had he done?

A movement at the edge of her vision

prompted Charlie to turn her head. In the crack that existed between the side of the vault and its door, the girl Linda was watching. She moved away quickly — back-to-business personified — when she saw Charlie's gaze fall upon her.

Charlie hustled out of the vault and called the girl's name. Linda turned, her expression striving for professional indifference. She failed at this, a deer-caught-in-the-headlights look in her eyes. She said quietly, "Yes, Mrs. Lawton? Is there something else?"

Charlie indicated with a motion of her head that she wanted Linda to accompany her back into the vault. The girl looked around as if for rescue but apparently found none. A couple sat at a far desk opening an account with the accounts manager. The tellers were occupied at their windows. The branch manager's office door was closed. Otherwise, the bank was experiencing the typical midday languor that preceded the final rush of the afternoon.

"I've got to . . ." Linda twisted a ring on her hand. It was a diamond. Engagement or something else? Charlie wondered.

"I don't imagine you're supposed to spy on customers in the vault," Charlie said.

"I'd hate to have to report you to the manager. Do you want to come back here with me, or should I knock on his door?"

Linda swallowed. She shoved a lock of hair behind her ear. She followed Charlie.

The deposit box sat on the counter where Charlie had left it. Linda's glance went to it compulsively. She gripped her hands in front of her and waited for whatever Charlie would say.

"You knew my husband. You recognized his name. You as much as said he was in here often."

"I didn't mean you to think —"

"Tell me what you know about this." Charlie opened the deposit box. "Because you knew it was here. You were watching me. You were waiting to see what my reaction was going to be."

Linda said in a rush, "I shouldn't have watched. I'm *sorry*. I don't want to lose my job. It's been hard. I've got a little girl, see."

Eric's child? Charlie braced herself.

"She's only eighteen months old," Linda continued. "Her dad won't give us anything and *my* dad won't let us move in with him. I've been here a year and I'm doing pretty good and if I get fired . . ."

"How long had you and my husband . . . How did you know each other?"

"Know . . . ?" Linda looked appalled as she made the connection. "He's *nice,* is all. He . . . Well, he likes to flirt, but that's it. I didn't even know he was married till I saw your name on the card one time. And . . . really, it was *nothing.* He's just sort of cute and he comes and goes and I got curious about him, is all."

"So you watched him in the vault."

"Only once. I swear it. Once. The rest of the time . . . Well, when he first came in to make his deposits — for the checking account, you know? — he'd just wait for me. He'd let other people go past him till I was available. He saw the picture of Brittany once — that's my little girl? — that I keep at my window — right over there? — and he asked me about her and that's how we got to know each other. He said he had a little girl as well only she was older and they hadn't seen each other in years and he missed her and that's what we talked about. He was divorced. I knew that because he said 'my ex-wife' and I thought at first . . . Well, he made me feel special and I thought wouldn't it be neat if I met someone right here at the bank? So I watched him and I was friendly. And he didn't seem to mind."

"He's dead."

"Dead. Oh my *gosh*. I'm sorry. I didn't know." She gestured to the metal box. "I was curious about this, is all. Really. That's it."

"How long has this been here?" Charlie asked. "The money, I mean."

"I don't really . . . Two weeks? Three?" Linda said. "It was in between times when he usually came in with his paycheck."

"What happened? Why did you watch him?"

"Because he was . . . He was all lit up that day. He was high."

"On *drugs?*"

"Not like that. Just happy high. Flying. He had this briefcase with him and he rang the bell just like you did and I went over and he signed the card. He said, 'I'm glad it's you, Linda. I wouldn't trust *this* day to anyone else.' "

" 'This day?' "

"See, I didn't know what he meant, which is why I watched him. And what he did was put the briefcase on the counter. He opened the deposit box and took out a slew of papers and he put them in the briefcase and put what was in the briefcase in the box. And *that* was the money. And that's what I saw. I thought he was . . . Well, it looked like he'd sold drugs or something because why else would he be carrying around so much cash. And I couldn't believe it because he seemed so straight. And that's all I saw. I didn't talk to him when he left, and I didn't ever see him again."

Eric selling drugs. Charlie snatched at the thought. Drugs. Yes. That was the answer. But not the type Linda was thinking about. The girl pictured Eric dealing in those bricklike bags of cocaine one saw on TV or in movies. She fancied him pushing marijuana to high school kids outside the local liquor store. She thought he was supplying yuppies with heroin, Ecstasy, or some other designer drug. But she didn't imagine him stealing from Biosyn — an efficacious immunosuppressant, a cutting-edge form of chemotherapy with no side effects, an AIDS vaccine ready to be marketed, a Viagra for women . . . What was it, Eric? — and selling it on the international black market to the highest bidder, who would make a fortune manufacturing it.

Terry Stewart's words came back to Charlie as she stood looking down at the closed deposit box in the airless confines of the bank's secure vault: *Pipe dreams, Charlie. That's all they were.* Except they hadn't been. Not for Eric. He'd been forty-

246

two years old with the majority of his life behind him. He'd seen his chance and he'd taken it. One negotiation, one sale, and a vast accumulation of cash. So many things were beginning to make sense now. Things he'd said. Things he'd done. Who he had become.

Charlie locked the deposit box and returned it to its space in the vault. She felt sick at heart, but at least she was uncovering the truth about her husband. The only question remaining for her was: What had Eric stolen from Biosyn? And the only possible answer seemed to be: nothing at all.

He'd taken money — perhaps a down payment? — for something which he had promised to deliver. He'd failed to procure what he had sold, and as a result, he'd died. With him gone, her house had been searched in an attempt to find the drug, and that search presaged danger for her as long as the promised substance wasn't placed into the palm of whoever had paid for it. Charlie knew that she had to get her hands on that drug and hand it over if she wanted her own security to be inviolate. That being impossible, her only recourse was to track down the person who had paid in the first place and return the money.

★ ★ ★

Sharon Pasternak seemed the likeliest source of information. She'd been the first person to search Eric's study, after all. Having made the unexpected discovery of money, Charlie knew she'd be a fool to believe that Sharon had come looking for *anything* unrelated to that money in the safe-deposit box.

She left the bank and headed for the freeway.

Biosyn was located on a stretch of highway called the Ortega, which snaked over the coastal mountains, linking the dreary town of Lake Elsinore with the more upscale San Juan Capistrano. It was a dusty road that attracted bikers by the thousands on Sundays. During the week, it was a mostly treeless, boulder-strewn thoroughfare traveled by men and women who worked in service jobs in the restaurants and high-price hotels on the coast.

The company itself was some twelve miles into the hills, an unwelcoming low building the color of dirt that was separated from the rest of the environment by a high chain-link fence with coils of barbed wire springing from its top. Charlie had never been to Biosyn, and she would have missed the turnoff altogether had she not had to brake for a FedEx truck that was making a left turn from Biosyn's concealed entrance into the highway.

It was an odd place altogether to find a pharmaceutical company, Charlie thought as she turned into the narrow drive. It was an odd place to find any company. Most of the industry was miles away, erupting from unsightly industrial parks and strung like bad teeth along the county's multitude of freeways.

There was a guard shack some fifty yards up the drive and iron gates closing off entry to anyone unexpected. Charlie braked there and gave Sharon Pasternak's name as well as her own. She had an anxious minute while the guard phoned into the sprawling building on the hill ahead of her. For all she knew, Sharon Pasternak was a phony name, which certainly seemed likely if the woman was in on Eric's deal.

But that wasn't the case. The guard returned to Charlie's car with a pass, saying, "She'll meet you in the lobby. Park in visitors. Go straight in, hear? Don't wander around."

Why on earth would she want to wander around? Charlie wondered as she took the visitor's pass. The place was a wasteland of dust, boulders, cactus, and chaparral. Not her idea of a spot for a saunter.

She pulled in front of the main entrance to the building and went inside. It was frigidly cool, and a shudder went through her. She was momentarily lost, blinded by the contrast between the bright light outside and the darkly painted walls.

Someone said, "Yes? May I help you?" from a dim corner.

Before Charlie's eyes could adjust, another voice came from the other side of the room. "She's here to see me, Marion. This is Eric Lawton's wife."

"Dr. Lawton's . . . ? Oh, I'm awfully sorry. About . . . How d'you do? I *am* sorry. He was . . . Such a lovely man."

"Thanks, Marion. Mrs. Lawton . . . ?"

Charlie finally began to make out the shapes of things: the white-haired woman behind a mahogany reception desk and reflected in the mirror behind her, Sharon Pasternak who'd just come through a heavy-looking, metal-plated door. She was wearing a lab coat over black leggings, Nike running shoes, and athletic socks.

Sharon Pasternak came to Charlie's side and put a hand on her arm. "Have you actually found that paperwork we were missing?" she asked determinedly, fixing her eyes on Charlie. "You'll be saving my life if you say yes." She squeezed Charlie's arm, and it felt like a warning. So Charlie nodded and forced a smile.

"Great," Sharon said. "What a relief. Come on back."

"She doesn't have clearance, Dr. Pasternak," Marion protested.

"It's okay, Mar. Don't worry. I'll take her over to the coffee room."

"Dr. Cabot won't —"

"It's cool," Sharon said. "We'll be less than five minutes. Time us."

"I'll be watching the clock," Marion warned.

Sharon guided Charlie across the lobby, not to the heavy door through which she herself had emerged but rather to a less secure door that led to a cafeteria-style room that was, at this time of day, deserted. She made no preamble when they got inside. She said tersely, "You've figured it out. Someone must have phoned your house. Did they leave a name? A number I can call?"

"Someone *searched* my house," Charlie said. "Someone tore it apart. After you were there."

"*What?*" Sharon glanced around hastily. "This is serious trouble. We can't talk here, then. The walls have ears. If you'll give me the name, I'll contact them myself. It's what Eric would've wanted."

"I don't have any name." Charlie was feeling hot now, and she was growing confused. "I thought *you* had it. I assumed that because when you came to the house and then left with nothing and then the house was searched again . . . What were you looking for? Whose name? All I have is the . . ." She couldn't bring herself to say it, so horrible and low it seemed to her that her husband — a man she had adored and had thought she knew — had actually stolen from his employer. "I want to return the money," she said in a rush before she could think of an excuse not to speak.

Sharon said, "What money?"

"I've got to return it because they're not going to let up if I don't. Whoever they are. They've searched the house once, and they'll be back. No one puts out that kind of money without expecting . . . what do you want to call it? . . . the goods?"

"But that's not how it works," Sharon said. "They never pay. So if there's money somewhere —"

"Who *are* they?" Charlie heard her voice grow louder as her anxiety increased. "How do I contact them?"

Sharon said, "Ssshhhh. Please. Look, we can't talk here."

"But you came to my house. You searched. You were looking —"

"For their names. Don't you see? I didn't know who Eric was talking to. He just said that it was CBS. But CBS where? LA? New York? Was it *Sixty Minutes* or just the local news?"

Charlie stared at her. "*Sixty Minutes?*"

"Keep your voice down! Good grief! I'm on the line here, about six steps away from losing my job or going to jail or who the hell knows what else, and then what good will I be to anyone?" She looked to the doorway, as if expecting a camera crew to come barreling through. "Look, you've got to leave."

"Not till you tell me —"

"I'll meet you in an hour. In San Juan. Los Rios district. D'you know it? Behind the Amtrak station. There's a tea place there. I don't know the name, but you'll see it when you cross the tracks. Turn to the right. It's on the left. Okay? An hour. I *can't* talk here."

She shoved Charlie toward the door of the coffee room and quickly walked her back to reception. In the lobby she said heartily, "You've saved me about ten days of work. I can't thank you enough," and she strong-armed her right out into the sunlight, where she said, "An hour," in a low voice before disappearing back into the building where the door clicked shut behind her.

Charlie stared at the darkened glass, feeling her body like an unwieldy weight that she was supposed to propel to her car in some way. She tried to assimilate what Sharon had said — CBS, *60 Minutes*, the local news — and she set the information next to what had happened and what she already knew. But none of it made sense. She felt like a passenger on the wrong airplane without a passport to show at her destination.

She stumbled to her car. The shivers came upon her there, so badly that she couldn't for a moment get the key into the ignition. But she finally managed to steady one hand with the other and in this manner, she started the engine.

Back down the drive and onto the highway, she wove her way in the direction of the coast. As she drove, she thought about all the things she'd heard about this stretch of road in the years she'd been in Southern California: how it was the ideal place for dumping bodies, frequented by such notable serial killers as Randy Kraft;

how contract killings took place in its pull-outs and abandoned vehicles were set fire to in the gullies that bordered its sides; how drunks ran off the road and died at cliff bottoms, their bodies not to be recovered for months; how big rigs crossed the double yellow line and smashed head-on to obliterate anything in their paths. What did it mean that Biosyn, Inc. was located here, of all places? And what did it mean that Eric Lawton was talking to someone from CBS?

Charlie had no answers. Only more questions. And the only option available to her was to find the tea house in the Los Rios district of San Juan Capistrano and hope that Sharon Pasternak was as good as her word.

She was. Seventy-one minutes after Charlie left Biosyn, Eric's colleague walked into the tea house, a building from the early 1900s, once the home of a founding family of the town. It was a good place for an assignation, the least likely spot any individual would choose with surreptitious activity on her mind. Coyly decorated with lace, teapots, antiques, hat stands, and *chapeaux* for the sartorial entertainment of its customers, it offered, at exorbitant prices, an American version of English afternoon tea.

Sharon Pasternak looked over her shoulder as she came into the building, where Charlie was seated at a table for two just inside the door. There was another table occupied in the room, a round one at which five women in hats borrowed from the establishment were having a merry birthday tea, looking in their anachronistic *chapeaux* as if Alice and the March Hare were about to join them.

"We need a different table," Sharon told Charlie without preamble. "Come on." She led the way to a second room and from there to a third at the back of the house. This was furnished with five small tables, but they were all empty, and Sharon strode to the one that was farthest from the door. "You can't come to Biosyn again," she told Charlie in a low voice. "Especially if you come asking for me. It's risky and obvious. If you'd come to talk to the Human Resources people — about Eric's retirement package or insurance or something — you might have gotten away with it. You and I running into each other in the hall or something. But this? No way. Marion's going to remember and she's going to tell Cabot. She's worked for him for thirty-five years — since he was just out of grad school, if you can believe it — and she's more loyal to him than she is to her husband. She calls him David, all stars in her eyes. By now, he knows you've put in an appearance and asked for me."

"You said CBS," Charlie began. "You said *Sixty Minutes*."

"He came to me about Exantrum. His lab was working on something different, but he knew about Exantrum. Everyone in Division II knew. Everyone knows even if they pretend they don't."

"His lab? Whose lab?"

"Eric's."

"What're you talking about?"

"What d'you mean?"

"Why would Eric have had a lab? He was director of sales. He had meetings and business trips all over the country and . . . Why would he have a lab? He isn't . . . He wasn't . . ."

"Sales?" Sharon asked. "That's what he told you? You never knew?"

"What?"

"He's a molecular biologist."

"A molecular . . . No. He was director of sales. He *told* me." But what had he told her? And what, from his behavior and allusions, had she merely assumed?

"He's a biologist, Mrs. Lawton. I mean, he was. I ought to know since I worked with him. And he . . . listen, I have to ask this. I'm sorry, but I don't know how else to make sure. . . . Did he die the way they said he died? He wasn't . . . ? I wouldn't put it past Cabot to have him snuffed out. He's a secrecy freak. And even if he weren't, this stuff's so nasty that if Cabot knew Eric was taking it to CBS, believe me, he'd do something to stop him."

"To stop him from what?"

"Contributing to the exposé. Eric was blowing the whistle on Biosyn. He was scared shitless to do it — we both were scared shitless — but he'd made up his mind. I smuggled out a sample of Exantrum one night — and I can't even tell you how freaked out I was to get close to the stuff without a safety suit on — and I gave it to Eric. He was set to meet with the journalists, to hand it over so they could get it tested for themselves in Atlanta, and then . . . This was three weeks ago. I guess he might've met with them but he didn't say and then he was dead. There hasn't been even a *sign* at Biosyn that anything's the least bit wrong, so I started to think Eric never made contact and I wanted to get the name of the journalist myself to find out. That's what I was looking for at your house. The name of the journalist. Either that or the Exantrum. Because if he didn't make contact, I've got to get that stuff back into a controlled environment. Fast."

Charlie stared at the woman. She couldn't digest the information she was being given quickly enough to make a coherent reply.

"I can see he didn't tell you any of this. He must've wanted to protect you. I admire that. It was decent of him. Typical, too. He was a great guy. But I wish he'd confided in you because then at least we'd know what we were dealing with here. We could set our minds at rest. As it is . . . Either that stuff's out there waiting to wreak havoc on the state of California or it's safe at the Centers for Disease Control. But in either case, I need to know."

The Centers for Disease Control. "What is it?" Charlie asked, and the words sounded hollow to her ears and dry in her throat. "I thought Biosyn made pharmaceuticals. Cancer drugs. Medication for asthma and arthritis. Maybe sleeping pills and antidepressants."

"Sure. That's part of it. That's Division I. But Division II is where the real money is, where Eric and I worked, where Exantrum is."

"What is it?" Charlie repeated, dread rising up in her throat like bile.

Sharon looked around. She said, "We need to order something. If we don't and if someone sees us here, it's going to look suspicious. We've got to get a waitress's attention."

They managed to do so, each of them asking for scones and tea which both of them knew they would not touch. When their order came, Sharon poured from the pot and said, "Exantrum is Cabot's key to immortality. It's a virus. It was discovered in standing water in a cave . . . this was about two years ago. A hiker went inside a cave in the Blue Ridge Mountains. A hot day. He finds a pool of water. He splashes himself on the face with it. He's dead in twenty-one days. Hemorrhagic fever. The doctors in North Carolina don't know where the virus came from but it looks enough like Ebola to make people freak. Atlanta gets onto it and everyone starts tracing where this guy has been, who he's seen, what he's been up to. They're looking at his associates through a microscope, they're looking at his passport to see if he's been out of the country, they're looking at his family to see which of them might've passed something on from someone else. They can't figure it out. Cabot follows all this but does his own detective work because he thinks this is something different from Ebola and what he's wanted from the day he graduated from UCLA is to have a name that gets associated with *something* that changes the world, like Jonas Salk or Louis Pasteur or Alexander Fleming. He's probably thinking *cure* at first, but the government comes calling once Cabot has the stuff isolated and it gets twisted into *disease*. Uncle Sam'll pay big bucks for a weapon like Exantrum. You put it into water, you drink it, you splash it onto your face and it gets into your eyes, you let it touch a hangnail, you get it in your nose, you have a scratch on your body, you step in it, you breathe it . . . take your choice. It doesn't matter how you come into contact with it because the end's the same. You die. It's for biological warfare. For use against the Iraqis if they get out of line. Or the Chinese if they start shaking their sabers. Or the North Koreans. Cabot stands to make a fortune from it, and Eric was going to let the world know." Sharon looked at her teacup and turned it in its saucer. She finished with, "He was a really good man. A decent good man. I only wish I'd had his courage. But the truth of the matter is I don't. So I need to get the Exantrum back to the lab if Eric hadn't made contact with the journalist yet."

"He . . . he wouldn't have kept it at our house, though," Charlie said, because she wanted desperately to believe it. "Not if it's as dangerous as you say it is. He wouldn't have kept it at home, would he?"

"Hell no. That's why when I showed up, I was looking for the journalist's name, not the virus. He would've put the virus somewhere safe till he had a meeting time and a place to hand it over. And if he *did* put it somewhere safe, I need to know where it is. Or I need to confirm that it's in Atlanta which I can only do by talking to the journalist that Eric was talking to."

Charlie heard the words but she was thinking of other things: what Terry had said about midlife crisis and what Linda had told her about Eric's last visit to the bank. She was thinking of all that money in the vault, the search of her house, and the expression on her husband's face when she had penitently related her suspicions about the love affair which he'd never had. Especially this last, Charlie considered. And the horrible possibilities it presented.

"How did you smuggle Exantrum out of Biosyn?" she asked Sharon Pasternak, steeling herself to hear the answer.

"I put the safe suit on and transferred it into a cough syrup bottle," Sharon told her. "It was risky as hell, but believe me if I'd been caught leaving with anything besides that bottle, it would've been the end of me."

"Yes," Charlie said. "I do see that." And more, in fact. What she saw with absolute clarity at last was the end of Charlie Lawton.

She went to the mission. She said to Sharon, "I'll go to the bank and check our safe-deposit box. Eric may have put the bottle in there."

Sharon was grateful. She said, "That would be a godsend. But if it *is* there, for God's sake don't open it whatever you do. Try not to touch it, even. Just call me. Here. Let me give you my home number. And leave a message, okay? Say you're from Sav-on, just in case Cabot's bugged my phone. Say, 'Your medication's arrived,' and I'll know what you mean and I'll come to your house. Okay? Got it?"

"Yes," Charlie said faintly. "Sav-on. I've got it."

"Good."

And so they parted, Sharon zooming off in the direction of Dana Point and Charlie walking not to her car in the city parking structure but rather around the block and down the street to Mission San Juan Capistrano.

She made her way along the uneven path within the mission walls, between the mis-shapen cacti and the thirsty poppies. She wandered mostly, not caring about her destination because her destination didn't matter any longer. She ended up in the narrow chapel built three centuries earlier by the hands of the California Indians and under the direction of that single-minded taskmaster, Junípero Serra.

The light inside was muted . . . or per-haps, she thought, it was her vision which might be going to fail her along with the rest of her body now. Perhaps that was an-other effect of exposure to Exantrum — loss of vision — or perhaps she had been suffering from that loss from the moment she'd begun to believe that her husband was having an affair.

How clear it all was now. How neatly Terry Stewart's description of male midlife crisis fit in with what Eric Lawton had done. How obvious were the reasons why Eric manufactured not only his present but his past. How easy it was to understand why he'd become estranged from his first wife, from his daughter, and from the rest of a family who no doubt knew exactly what he did for a living. Better to pretend one had no family, better to act the part of injured party, better to *anything* than to live openly as a scientist who made his salary developing weapons of death. And not weapons for war to be used by the military on opposing troops but weapons to decimate innocent civilians or, in the hands of someone else — a terrorist, for instance — to bring an entire population to its knees.

Charlie knew two things at the end of her conversation with Sharon Pasternak: She knew that Eric — who had talked about not living in this area much longer, who had talked about fast cars and off-shore banking and racing in the America's Cup — had not made contact with any journalist and had never intended to do so. He had done what she'd first thought he'd done: He had sold a substance from Biosyn. It just hadn't been the cure for AIDS or cancer or anything else that she'd assumed when she'd seen the money. Whether that made him a bad man, a mis-guided man, a greedy man, or the devil himself was of no consequence to Charlie. Because Eric Lawton was also a dead man and she finally knew the reason for that as well.

She worked her way into one of the hard-backed pews. She sat. There was a kneeler that she could have used to pray from, but she was beyond casting petitions heavenward. There was no help — divine or otherwise — for what ailed her. This was something Eric had known the moment she confessed to him the depth to which her suspicions about him had taken her. And she'd *had* to confess — had felt the *need* to confess — once he'd come home triumphant from "the biggest sale in my whole career, Char, wait'll you hear about the bonus, how does a cruise sound to you for a celebration? Or even a complete lifestyle change? We can have that now. We can have it all. Hell, I'm sorry I've been so out of it lately."

She'd known then that her fears had been groundless, that there was no other woman in his life. And, knowing this and seeking absolution for her sin of doubting him, she'd told him the truth.

"Char, God, we went through this once already, didn't we? I'm *not* having an affair!" He'd said it all with an earnestness that, combined with the joy with which he'd told her about his impending good fortune, had made it impossible to disbelieve him. "You're the only one . . . You've *always* been the only one. How could you think anything else? I know I've been preoccupied. And in and out at weird hours. And taking phone calls and disappearing. But that all was because of this deal and you can't ever think . . . Hell, *never*, Char. You're the reason I've been doing all this. So that we can have a better life. For us. For our kids. Something more than suburbia. You deserve it. I deserve it. And now that this deal I've been concentrating on at work has gone through . . . I haven't wanted to talk about it because I didn't want to jinx it. I never thought it'd get you all upset. Come here, Char. Hell. God. I'm sorry, babe."

And she'd known from the sound of his voice that he meant it. And from the sound of his voice and the look in his eyes, she'd drawn the comfort that told her her fears were groundless. So she'd given herself up to his love that evening and later, at dawn, she'd confessed the rest of her sins. She owed him that confession, she thought. Only by telling him how low she had sunk would she be able to forgive herself.

"I finally stopped it all when I spilled medicine all over the floor in your bathroom." She laughed at herself and at all of her fears, groundless now. "It was like I regained consciousness all of a sudden, standing in a pool of Robitussin."

He smiled and kissed the tips of her fingers. "Robitussin? Char. What were you *up* to?"

"Insanity," she said. "I was so sure. I thought, 'There's got to be evidence somewhere. Of *some*thing.' So I was searching through everything. Even your medicine cabinet. I broke that bottle of cough syrup on your bathroom floor. I'm sorry."

He continued to smile but in Charlie's mind's eye — now, in the chapel in San Juan Capistrano — she could see how fixed that smile had become. She could see how he'd attempted to clarify what she was telling him.

"There wasn't cough syrup in my bathroom, Char. You must've been in —"

"You've probably forgotten it. The label was old. It's actually just as well it got thrown out. Don't they say medicine over six months old isn't right to take?"

Had his lips looked stiff? Had that smile stayed fixed? He said, "Yeah, I think they do say that."

"Sorry I broke it, though."

Had he averted his eyes, then? "How'd you clean it up?"

"On my hands and knees, doing penance."

Had he laughed? Weakly or otherwise? "Well, I hope you wore rubber gloves, at least."

"Nope. I didn't want anything to get in the way of me and my sin. Why? Was it not really cough syrup? Have you been disguising poison in a medicine bottle just in case you decide to off your wife?" And she'd tickled him to force him to answer. And they'd laughed and begun to make love again.

He hadn't been able to.

"Getting old," he said. "Everything goes to hell after forty. Sorry."

And it had got worse from there. He'd been gone more; he'd become preoccupied once again — more than ever this time — he'd closeted himself away and spent hours on the phone; he'd invested days, it seemed, on the Internet "doing research," he'd told her when she asked him. Finally, when the phone had rung one evening, she'd overheard him say, "Look, I can't *make* it tonight, all right? My wife's not well," and she'd suffered a rebirth of all her suspicions.

It was two days later that he'd come home from work and found her under a blanket on the sofa, dozing off a combination of headache and muscle pain that she'd assumed she'd brought on herself with a lengthy hike on the slopes of Saddleback Mountain. She'd been asleep and hadn't awakened upon his entry. Only when he dropped to his knees beside the couch did she stir with a start.

"What is it?" he'd asked her. Was it fear in his voice and not concern as she'd thought at the time? "Char, what's wrong?"

"Achy all over," she replied. "Too much exercise today. Got a headache, too."

"I'm going to make you some soup," he told her.

He'd gone into the kitchen and banged about. Ten minutes later, he brought a tray into the living room where she lay.

"Sweet," she murmured. "But I can get up. I can eat with you."

"I'm not eating," he said. "Not right now. You stay put." And he'd lovingly and gently fed tomato soup to her a slow and patient spoonful at a time. He'd even wiped her mouth with a paper napkin. And when she'd laughed a little and said,

"Really, Eric, I'm all right," he hadn't made a reply.

Because he'd known, Charlie thought. The process had begun. First the sudden onset marked by headache and muscle pain. A slight fever to accompany them. Chills and an inability to eat hard upon the heels of the fever.

And after that? What she'd marked as mourning first and denial second, both of them made manifest in her body: sore throat, dizziness, nausea, and vomiting. But she hadn't been reacting to her husband's death. She'd been reacting to what he'd done in his life. Or what he'd tried to do and what he would have done had she not broken the bottle in which the virus was sealed before he had the chance to give it to its purchaser.

How torn he must have been, she realized. There he was: caught in the middle of something gone terribly wrong, the best-laid plans come to nothing. With nothing to give in exchange for the down payment he'd received for the Exantrum, with a wife fatally exposed to the virus he himself had stolen. And knowing that that wife was going to die, as surely as he must have known thousands — millions — of others would have died had fate, in the person of

Charlie's jealousy, not stepped in to prevent that from occurring.

He'd fed her the soup and studied her face as if such a study would allow him to take the image of her into the grave and beyond. When she was finished eating, when she could swallow no more, he put the spoon in the bowl and the bowl on the tray. He'd leaned forward and kissed Charlie on the forehead. He'd adjusted the covers up to her chin.

"Remember, I'll always love you," he'd said.

"Why're you telling me that? Like that?"

"Just remember."

He'd taken the tray from the room. She heard the sound of it being set on the counter in the kitchen. A moment later he returned and sat opposite her, in an easy chair, with a pillow behind his head.

"Do you remember?" he asked.

"What?"

"What I said. Remember. I'll always love you, Char."

Before she could respond, he took the revolver from within his jacket. He put the barrel in his mouth, and he blew off the back of his head.

So this, Charlie thought, was what it felt

like to know you were going to die. This sense of drifting. No panic as she'd once thought she might panic if handed a death sentence like pancreatic cancer. But instead a numbness and a going through the motions: getting up from the pew in the mission chapel, approaching the altar, pausing at a statue of a yellow-and-green-robed saint to light a candle, then standing deep in the sanctuary and knowing there was nothing to ask God for or about any longer.

What had Eric thought? she wondered. There he was at forty-two. Had he thought, This is it, this is all there is to my life unless I take this one chance to change it all, to have more, to be more, to ride the wave of opportunity that I see rising in front of me and to discover upon what shore that wave will deposit me? If I only take a risk, that's all, one little risk. And really, not much of a risk at all if I play it right and figure the angles: Involve Sharon Pasternak in scoring the virus so if anyone's caught smuggling it out of Biosyn, it'll be Sharon and not me. Play the part of whistle-blower so Sharon will think I've got a selfless goal in mind. Make contact with an interested party but make sure I set the whole deal up so that there's a down payment first, some lag time second to make my plans to escape should my contact try to eliminate me, and then a second meeting to hand over the Exantrum followed by a hasty exit and a flight to . . . where? Tahiti, Belize, south of France, Greece. It didn't matter. What mattered was that "the rest of my life" would have new meaning to Eric, more meaning than a Harley-Davidson motorcycle and a tattoo on his arm had been able to give him.

"Eric, Eric," Charlie whispered. Where, when, and why had he gone so wrong?

She didn't know. She didn't know him. She wasn't sure if she even knew herself.

She left the chapel and made her way back to her car in the city parking structure next to the train station. She climbed inside, feeling weary now, feeling as if the virus inside her were a presence she could actually sense in her veins. And it *was* there. She knew that without checking into a hospital or traveling out to Biosyn to offer herself to Dr. Cabot as proof that his weapon of war was as efficacious as he had hoped.

Eric had known she was going to die. He'd known how the virus would work. He'd known there was no cure for what was going to attack her, so he'd taken himself away from having to face what evil he'd brought down upon them both.

What's to do? she asked herself. But she knew the answer. Write it all out clearly so that no one would take any risks with her body afterwards. And then do as Eric had done but for an entirely different set of reasons. It wasn't the noble solution although it might be seen as such. It was the only solution. She still had the gun. It would create a mess and a mess was dangerous to other people, but the note she would write — and would post on the doorway so no one could miss it before they entered the room — would explain the situation.

Odd, she thought. She wasn't angry. She wasn't afraid. She wasn't anything. Perhaps that was good.

On the freeway, she drove with more care than usual. Every car that hurtled by her was an obstacle that she had to avoid at any cost. It was growing dark and she was having trouble seeing through the glare of oncoming headlights, but she made it home without incident and she parked in the driveway and felt a heaviness come over her, knowing what deed faced her when she got inside.

More than anything she just wanted to sleep. But there wasn't time for that. If she wasted eight hours, that would be a third of a day which the virus would have to work in her body. Who knew what condition she would be in tomorrow if she gave in to exhaustion today.

She got out of the car. She stumbled up the walk. The porch light wasn't on, so she didn't see the form emerge from the shadows till she was upon it. And then she saw a faint glimmer of the streetlight shining on something metallic that he held. A gun, a knife? She couldn't tell.

He said, "Mrs. Lawton, you have something that belongs to me, I think," and his accent was as dusky as his complexion and his tone was as black as his hooded eyes.

She had no fear of him. What was there to fear? He could do no more to her than Exantrum was already doing.

She said, "Yes, I have it. But not in the form you were hoping for. Come inside, Mr. . . . ?"

"Names do not matter. I want what I'm owed."

"Yes. I know you do. So come inside, Mr. Names Do Not Matter. I'm only too happy to give it to you."

She'd have to write the letter first, she

thought. But something told her Mr. Names Do Not Matter was desperate enough to be willing to give her the time that writing the letter required.

Introduction to

I, Richard

I first developed an affinity for Richard III, England's most controversial king, when I was a college student taking my first Shakespeare course. In it, we read *Richard III* — interestingly titled *The Tragedy of King Richard III* — and through this process, I came into contact with a fascinating group of historical figures who have never been far from my imagination since those autumn mornings in 1968 when we as a class discussed them.

I watched my first production of the play at the Los Gatos Shakespeare Festival a short time thereafter, but it wasn't until I read Josephine Tey's famous novel *The Daughter of Time* that I began to see King Richard in a light other than that in which Shakespeare's famous play bathed him. After that, I became more intrigued with this much maligned king and more reading followed: *Richard III, The Road to Bosworth*

Field; *The Year of Three Kings 1483*; *The Mystery of the Princes*; *Richard III, England's Black Legend*; *The Deceivers*; and *Royal Blood* became a permanent part of my library. And when I created the continuing characters for my crime novels, I decided to make one of them a Ricardian Apologist, the better to have opportunities to take potshots at the man I eventually came to believe was the real black heart at the heart of what happened in 1485: Henry Tudor, Earl of Richmond, later Henry VII.

All along, I wanted to write my own story of what might have happened to the Princes in the Tower, a story that would exonerate Richard and put blame where it rightfully belonged. But the problem was that everyone I read had a different take on who the real culprit was. Some thought it likely that Henry Tudor had had the boys put to death after ascending the throne himself. Others thought the Duke of Buckingham was responsible, seeking to grease his own way to accession. Still others saw the involvement of the Stanleys, of the Bishop of Ely, of Margaret Beaufort. Some claimed the disappearance and death of the boys a conspiracy. Others declared it the work of a single hand. And some remained convinced that the deed was perpetrated by the man upon whom blame had been cast for five hundred years: that bunch-backed toad himself, Richard, Duke of Gloucester, later Richard III.

I knew that I wanted neither to write a historical novel nor to change my career and become a medieval historian. But I did want to write a story about people who were, like me, interested in that period of time, and I wanted to call it "I, Richard," taking my title from the manner in which documents began that were written by the reigning monarchs of the time.

The challenge for me was to write a story in the present time that dealt with another story five hundred years old. I didn't want to approach it as Tey had done, using a character in a hospital bed who is distracted from his condition through the means of being given a mystery to solve. At the same time, I did want to create a story in which something existed — something fictional, of course — that proved irrefutably that Richard was guiltless of the death of his nephews.

My first task was to decide what that something was.

My second task was to decide what kind

of modern-day story could embrace that something.

I approached the plot the way I approach every plot: I decided to go to the location in which I'd decided to set my tale. So in a frigid February, I trekked up to Market Bosworth in the company of a girlfriend from Sweden. Together we walked the perimeter of the battle site, Bosworth Field, where Richard III died as a result of treachery, betrayal, and greed.

Bosworth Field is much the same as it was over five hundred years ago when the armies met in August 1485. It hasn't been plowed over for housing estates, and Wal-Mart hasn't managed to put an unsightly megastore anywhere near it. Thus, it remains a forsaken, windswept place marked only by flagpoles that show visitors where the various armies were encamped and by plaques that explain along an established route exactly what happened at each spot.

It was when I reached a plaque that directed my gaze toward the distant village of Sutton Cheney where King Richard prayed in St. James Church on the night before the battle that I saw my story take shape. And what happened to me as I stood before that plaque was something that had never happened before nor has it happened since. It was this:

I read the words that told me to look for the windmill some mile or so in the distance and to recognize this structure as marking the village of Sutton Cheney where King Richard had prayed the night before battle. And as I lifted my eyes and found that windmill, the entire short story that you will read here dropped into my mind. All of a piece. As simple as that.

All I had to do was recite the facts of the story into my hand-held tape recorder as the wind buffeted me and the temperature challenged me to stay out of doors long enough to do so.

I came home to California and created the characters who would people the small world of "I, Richard." Once I did that, the story virtually wrote itself.

The guilt or innocence of the parties in history is lost to all of us, pending the discovery of a document whose veracity cannot be disputed. Indeed, I wasn't interested in trying to prove anyone did anything. What I was interested in writing about was one man's obsession with a long-dead King and the extremes he was willing to go to in order to advance himself under the banner of that defeated white boar.

I, Richard

Malcolm Cousins groaned in spite of himself. considering his circumstances, this was the last sound he wanted to make. A sigh of pleasure or a moan of satisfaction would have been more appropriate. But the truth was simple and he had to face it: No longer was he the performance artist he once had been in the sexual arena. Time was when he could bonk with the best of them. But that time had gone the way of his hair and at forty-nine years old, he considered himself lucky to be able to get the appliance up and running twice a week.

He rolled off Betsy Perryman and thudded onto his back. His lower vertebrae were throbbing like drummers in a marching band, and the always-dubious pleasure he'd just taken from Betsy's corpulent, perfume-drenched charms was quickly transformed to a faint memory. Jesus God, he thought with a gasp. Forget justification altogether. Was the end even *worth* the bloody means?

Luckily, Betsy took the groan and the gasp the way Betsy took most everything. She heaved herself onto her side, propped her head upon her palm, and observed him with an expression that was meant to be coy. The last thing Betsy wanted him to know was how desperate she was for him to be her lifeboat out of her current marriage — number four this one was — and Malcolm was only too happy to accommodate her in the fantasy. Sometimes it got a bit complicated, remembering what he was supposed to know and what he was supposed to be ignorant of, but he always found that if Betsy's suspicions about his sincerity became aroused, there was a simple and expedient, albeit back-troubling, way to assuage her doubts about him.

She reached for the tangled sheet, pulled it up, and extended a plump hand. She caressed his hairless pate and smiled at him lazily. "Never did it with a baldy before. Have I told you that, Malc?"

Every single time the two of them — as she so poetically stated — did it, he recalled. He thought of Cora, the springer spaniel bitch he'd adored in childhood, and the memory of the dog brought suitable fondness to his face. He eased Betsy's fingers down his cheek and kissed each one of them.

"Can't get enough, naughty boy," she said. "I've never had a man like you, Malc Cousins."

She scooted over to his side of the bed, closer and closer until her huge bosoms were less than an inch from his face. At this proximity, her cleavage resembled Cheddar Gorge and was just about as appealing a sexual object. God, another go-round? he thought. He'd be dead before he was fifty if they went on like this. And not a step nearer to his objective.

He nuzzled within the suffocating depths of her mammaries, making the kinds of yearning noises that she wanted to hear. He did a bit of sucking and then made much of catching sight of his wristwatch on the bedside table.

"Christ!" He grabbed the watch for a feigned better look. "Jesus, Betsy, it's eleven o'clock. I told those Aussie Ricardians I'd meet them at Bosworth Field at noon. I've got to get rolling."

Which was what he did, right out of bed before she could protest. As he shrugged into his dressing gown, she struggled to transform his announcement into something comprehensible. Her face screwed up and she said, "Those Ozzirecordians? What the hell's that?" She sat up, her blonde hair matted and snarled and most of her makeup smeared from her face.

"Not Ozzirecordians," Malcolm said.

"Aussie. Australian. Australian Ricardians. I told you about them last week, Betsy."

"Oh, that." She pouted. "I thought we could have a picnic lunch today."

"In this weather?" He headed for the bathroom. It wouldn't do to arrive for the tour reeking of sex and Shalimar. "Where did you fancy having a picnic in January? Can't you hear that wind? It must be ten below outside."

"A bed picnic," she said. "With honey and cream. You *said* that was your fantasy. Or don't you remember?"

He paused in the bedroom doorway. He didn't much like the tone of her question. It made a demand that reminded him of everything he hated about women. Of *course* he didn't remember what he'd claimed to be his fantasy about honey and cream. He'd said lots of things over the past two years of their liaison. But he'd forgotten most of them once it had become apparent that she was seeing him as he wished to be seen. Still, the only course was to play along. "Honey and cream," he sighed. "You brought honey and cream? Oh Christ, Bets. . . ." A quick dash back to the bed. A tonguely examination of her dental work. A frantic clutching between her legs. "God, you're going to drive me

288

mad, woman. I'll be walking round Bosworth with my prong like a poker all day."

"Serves you right," she said pertly and reached for his groin. He caught her hand in his.

"You love it," he said.

"No more'n you."

He sucked her fingers again. "Later," he said. "I'll trot those wretched Aussies round the battlefield and if you're still here then . . . You know what happens next."

"It'll be too late then. Bernie thinks I've only gone to the butcher."

Malcolm favoured her with a pained look, the better to show that the thought of her hapless and ignorant husband — his old best friend Bernie — scored his soul. "Then there'll be another time. There'll be hundreds of times. With honey and cream. With caviar. With oysters. Did I ever tell you what I'll do with the oysters?"

"What?" she asked.

He smiled. "Just you wait."

He retreated to the bathroom, where he turned on the shower. As usual, an inadequate spray of lukewarm water fizzled out of the pipe. Malcolm shed his dressing gown, shivered, and cursed his circumstances. Twenty-five years in the classroom, teaching history to spotty-faced hooligans who had no interest in anything beyond the immediate gratification of their sweaty-palmed needs, and what did he have to show for it? Two up and two down in an ancient terraced house down the street from Gloucester Grammar. An ageing Vauxhall with no spare tyre. A mistress with an agenda for marriage and a taste for kinky sex. And a passion for a long-dead King that — he was determined — would be the wellspring from which would flow his future. The means were so close, just tantalising centimetres from his eager grasp. And once his reputation was secured, the book contracts, the speaking engagements, and the offers of gainful employment would follow.

"Shit!" he bellowed as the shower water went from warm to scalding without a warning. "Damn!" He fumbled for the taps.

"Serves you right," Betsy said from the doorway. "You're a naughty boy and naughty boys need punishing."

He blinked water from his eyes and squinted at her. She'd put on his best flannel shirt — the very one he'd intended to wear on the tour of Bosworth Field, blast the woman — and she lounged against the doorjamb in her best attempt at a seductive pose. He ignored her and went about his showering. He could tell she was determined to have her way, and her way was another bonk before he left. Forget it, Bets, he said to her silently. Don't push your luck.

"I don't understand you, Malc Cousins," she said. "You're the only man in civilisation who'd rather tramp round a soggy pasture with a bunch of tourists than cozy up in bed with the woman he says he loves."

"Not says, does," Malcolm said automatically. There was a dreary sameness to their postcoital conversations that was beginning to get him decidedly down.

"That so? I wouldn't've known. I'd've said you fancy whatsisname the King a far sight more'n you fancy me."

Well, Richard was definitely more interesting a character, Malcolm thought. But he said, "Don't be daft. It's money for our nest egg anyway."

"We don't need a nest egg," she said. "I've told you that about a hundred times. We've got the —"

"Besides," he cut in hastily. There couldn't be too little said between them on the subject of Betsy's expectations. "It's good experience. Once the book is finished, there'll be interviews, personal appearances, lectures. I need the practice. I need" — this with a winning smile in her direction — "more than an audience of one, my darling. Just think what it'll be like, Bets. Cambridge, Oxford, Harvard, the Sorbonne. Will you like Massachusetts? What about France?"

"Bernie's heart's giving him trouble again, Malc," Betsy said, running her finger up the doorjamb.

"Is it, now?" Malcolm said happily. "Poor old Bernie. Poor bloke, Bets."

The problem of Bernie had to be handled, of course. But Malcolm was confident that Betsy Perryman was up for the challenge. In the afterglow of sex and inexpensive champagne, she'd told him once that each one of her four marriages had been a step forward and upward from the marriage that had preceded it, and it didn't take a hell of a lot of brains to know that moving out of a marriage to a dedicated inebriate — no matter how affable — into a relationship with a schoolteacher on his way to unveiling a piece of mediaeval history that would set the country on its ear was a step in the right direction. So Betsy would definitely handle Bernie. It was only a matter of time.

Divorce was out of the question, of course. Malcolm had made certain that Betsy understood that, while he was desperate mad hungry and all the etceteras for a life with her, he would no more ask her to come to him in his current impoverished circumstances than would he expect the Princess Royal to take up life in a bedsit on the south bank of the Thames. Not only would he not ask that of her, he wouldn't allow it. Betsy — his beloved — deserved so much more than he would be able to give her, such as he was. But when his ship came in, darling Bets. . . . Or if, God forbid, anything should ever happen to Bernie. . . . This, he hoped, was enough to light a fire inside the spongy grey mass that went for her brain.

Malcolm felt no guilt at the thought of Bernie Perryman's demise. True, they'd known each other in childhood as sons of mothers who'd been girlhood friends. But they'd parted ways at the end of adolescence, when poor Bernie's failure to pass more than one A-level had doomed him to life on the family farm while Malcolm had gone on to university. And after that . . . well, differing levels of education *did* take a toll on one's ability to communicate with one's erstwhile — and less educated —

mates, didn't it? Besides, when Malcolm returned from university, he could see that his old friend had sold his soul to the Black Bush devil, and what would it profit him to renew a friendship with the district's most prominent drunk? Still, Malcolm liked to think he'd taken a modicum of pity on Bernie Perryman. Once a month for years, he'd gone to the farmhouse — under cover of darkness, of course — to play chess with his former friend and to listen to his inebriated musings about their childhood and the what-might-have-beens.

Which was how he first found out about The Legacy, as Bernie had called it. Which was what he'd spent the last two years bonking Bernie's wife in order to get his hands on. Betsy and Bernie had no children. Bernie was the last of his line. The Legacy was going to come to Betsy. And Betsy was going to give it to Malcolm.

She didn't know that yet. But she would soon enough.

Malcolm smiled, thinking of what Bernie's legacy would do to further his career. For nearly ten years, he'd been writing furiously on what he'd nicknamed *Dickon Delivered* — his untarnishing of the reputation of Richard III — and once The Legacy was in his hands, his future was going to be assured. As he rolled towards Bosworth Field and the Australian Ricardians awaiting him there, he recited the first line of the penultimate chapter of his magnum opus. "It is with the alleged disappearance of Edward the Lord Bastard, Earl of Pembroke and March, and Richard, Duke of York, that historians have traditionally begun to rely upon sources contaminated by their own self-interest."

God, it was beautiful writing, he thought. And better than that, it was the truth as well.

The tour coach was already there when Malcolm roared into the car park at Bosworth Field. Its occupants had foolishly disembarked. All apparently female and of depressingly advanced years, they were huddled into a shivering pack, looking sheeplike and abandoned in the gale-force winds that were blowing. When Malcolm heaved himself out of his car, one of their number disengaged herself from their midst and strode towards him. She was sturdily built and much younger than the rest, which gave Malcolm hope of being able to grease his way through the moment with some generous dollops of charm. But then he noted her short clipped hair, elephantine ankles, and massive calves . . . not to mention the clipboard that she was smacking into her hand as she walked. An unhappy lesbian tour guide out for blood, he thought. God, what a deadly combination.

Nonetheless, he beamed a glittering smile in her direction. "Sorry," he sang out. "Blasted car trouble."

"See here, mate," she said in the unmistakable discordant twang — all long *a*'s becoming long *i*'s — of a denizen of the Antipodes, "when Romance of Great Britain pays for a tour at noon, Romance of Great Britain expects the bleeding tour to begin at noon. So why're you late? Christ, it's like Siberia out here. We could die of exposure. Jaysus, let's just get on with it." She turned on her heel and waved her charges over towards the edge of the car park where the footpath carved a trail round the circumference of the battlefield.

Malcolm dashed to catch up. His tips hanging in the balance, he would have to make up for his tardiness with a dazzling show of expertise.

"Yes, yes," he said with insincere joviality as he reached her side. "It's incredible that you should mention Siberia, Miss . . . ?"

"Sludgecur," she said, and her expression dared him to react to the name.

"Ah. Yes. Miss Sludgecur. Of course. As I was saying, it's incredible that you should mention Siberia because this bit of England has the highest elevation west of the Urals. Which is why we have these rather Muscovian temperatures. You can imagine what it might have been like in the fifteenth century when —"

"We're not here for meteorology," she barked. "Get on with it before my ladies freeze their arses off."

Her ladies tittered and clung to one another in the wind. They had the dried-apple faces of octogenarians, and they watched Sludgecur with the devotion of children who'd seen their parent take on all comers and deck them unceremoniously.

"Yes, well," Malcolm said. "The weather's the principal reason that the battlefield's closed in the winter. We made an exception for your group because they're fellow Ricardians. And when fellow Ricardians come calling at Bosworth, we like to accommodate them. It's the best way to see that the truth gets carried forward, as I'm sure you'll agree."

"What the bloody hell are you yammering about?" Sludgecur asked. "Fellow who? Fellow what?"

Which should have told Malcolm that the tour wasn't going to proceed as smoothly as he had hoped. "Ricardians," he said and beamed at the elderly women surrounding Sludgecur. "Believers in the innocence of Richard III."

Sludgecur looked at him as if he'd sprouted wings. "What? This is the Romance of Great Britain you're looking at, mate. Jane Bloody Eyre, Mr. Flaming Rochester, Heathcliff and Cathy, Maxim de Winter. Gabriel Oak. This is Love on the Battlefield Day, and we mean to have our money's worth. All right?"

Their money was what it was all about. The fact that they were paying was why Malcolm was here in the first place. But, Jesus, he thought, did these Seekers of Romance even know where they were? Did they know — much less care — that the last King to be killed in armed combat met his fate less than a mile from where they were standing? *And* that he'd met that same fate because of sedition, treachery, and betrayal? Obviously not. They weren't here in support of Richard. They were here because it was part of a package. Love Brooding, Love Hopeless, and Love

Devoted had already been checked off the list. And now he was somehow supposed to cook up for them a version of Love Deadly that would make them part with a few quid apiece at the end of the afternoon. Well, all right. He could do that much.

Malcolm didn't think about Betsy until he'd paused at the first marker along the route, which showed King Richard's initial battle position. While his charges took snapshots of the White Boar standard that was whipping in the icy wind from the flagpole marking the King's encampment, Malcolm glanced beyond them to the tumbledown buildings of Windsong Farm, visible at the top of the next hill. He could see the house and he could see Betsy's car in the farmyard. He could imagine — and hope about — the rest.

Bernie wouldn't have noticed that it had taken his wife three and a half hours to purchase a package of minced beef in Market Bosworth. It was nearly half past noon, after all, and doubtless he'd be at the kitchen table where he usually was, attempting to work on yet another of his Formula One models. The pieces would be spread out in front of him and he might have managed to glue one onto the car before the shakes came upon him and he had to have a dose of Black Bush to still them. One dose of whiskey would have led to another until he was too soused to handle a tube of glue.

Chances were good that he'd already passed out onto the model car. It was Saturday and he was supposed to work at St. James Church, preparing it for Sunday's service. But poor old Bernie'd have no idea of the day until Betsy returned, slammed the minced beef onto the table next to his ear, and frightened him out of his sodden slumber.

When his head flew up, Betsy would see the imprint of the car's name on his flesh, and she'd be suitably disgusted. Malcolm fresh in her mind, she'd feel the injustice of her position.

"You been to the church yet?" she'd ask Bernie. It was his only job, as no Perryman had farmed the family's land in at least eight generations. "Father Naughton's not like the others, Bernie. He's not about to put up with you just because you're a Perryman, you know. You got the church *and* the graveyard to see to today. And it's time you were about it."

Bernie had never been a belligerent drunk, and he wouldn't be one now. He'd say, "I'm going, sweet Mama. But I got the most godawful thirst. Throat feels like a sandpit, Mama girl."

He'd smile the same affable smile that had won Betsy's heart in Blackpool where they'd met. And the smile would remind his wife of her duty, despite Malcolm's ministrations to her earlier. But that was fine, because the last thing that Malcolm Cousins wanted was Betsy Perryman forgetting her duty.

So she'd ask him if he'd taken his medicine, and since Bernie Perryman never did anything — save pour himself a Black Bush — without having been reminded a dozen times, the answer would be no. So Betsy would seek out the pills and shake the dosage into her palm. And Bernie would take it obediently and then stagger out of the house — sans jacket as usual — and head to St. James Church to do his duty.

Betsy would call after him to take his jacket, but Bernie would wave off the suggestion. His wife would shout, "Bernie! You'll catch your death —" and then stop herself at the sudden thought that entered her mind. Bernie's death, after all, was what she needed in order to be with her Beloved.

So her glance would drop to the bottle of

pills in her hand and she would read the label: *Digitoxin. Do not exceed one tablet per day without consulting physician.*

Perhaps at that point, she would also hear the doctor's explanation to her: "It's like digitalis. You've heard of that. An overdose would kill him, Mrs. Perryman, so you must be vigilant and see to it that he never takes more than one tablet."

More than one tablet would ring in her ears. Her morning bonk with Malcolm would live in her memory. She'd shake a pill from the bottle and examine it. She'd finally start to think of a way that the future could be massaged into place.

Happily, Malcolm turned from the farmhouse to his budding Ricardians. All was going according to plan.

"From this location," Malcolm told his audience of eager but elderly seekers of Love on the Battlefield, "we can see the village of Sutton Cheney to our northeast." All heads swivelled in that direction. They may have been freezing their antique pudenda, but at least they were a cooperative group. Save for Sludgecur who, if she had a pudendum, it was no doubt swathed in long underwear. Her expression challenged him to concoct a Romance out of the Battle of Bosworth. Very well, he thought, and picked up the gauntlet. He'd give them Romance. He'd also give them a piece of history that would change their lives. Perhaps this group of Aussie oldies hadn't been Ricardians when they'd arrived at Bosworth Field, but they'd damn well be neophyte Ricardians when they left. *And* they'd return Down Under and tell their grandchildren that it was Malcolm Cousins — *the* Malcolm Cousins, they would say — who had first made them aware of the gross injustice that had been perpetrated upon the memory of a decent King.

"It was there in the village of Sutton Cheney, in St. James Church, that King Richard prayed on the night before the battle," Malcolm told them. "Picture what the night must have been like."

From there, he went onto automatic pilot. He'd told the story hundreds of times over the years that he'd served as Special Guide for Groups at Bosworth Field. All he had to do was to milk it for its Romantic Qualities, which wasn't a problem.

The King's forces — 12,000 strong — were encamped on the summit of Ambion Hill where Malcolm Cousins and his band of shivering neo-Ricardians were standing.

The King knew that the morrow would decide his fate: whether he would continue to reign as Richard III or whether his crown would be taken by conquest and worn by an upstart who'd lived most of his life on the continent, safely tucked away and coddled by those whose ambitions had long been to destroy the York dynasty. The King would have been well aware that his fate rested in the hands of the Stanley brothers: Sir William and Thomas, Lord Stanley. They had arrived at Bosworth with a large army and were encamped to the north, not far from the King, but also — and ominously — not far from the King's pernicious adversary, Henry Tudor, Earl of Richmond, who also happened to be Lord Stanley's stepson. To secure the father's loyalty, King Richard had taken one of Lord Stanley's blood sons as a hostage, the young man's life being the forfeit if his father betrayed England's anointed King by joining Tudor's forces in the upcoming battle. The Stanleys, however, were a wily lot and had shown themselves dedicated to nothing but their own self-interest, so — holding George Stanley hostage or not — the King must have known how great was the risk of entrusting the security of his throne to the whimsies of men whose devotion to self was their most notable quality.

The night before the battle, Richard would have seen the Stanleys camped to the north, in the direction of Market Bosworth. He would have sent a messenger to remind them that, as George Stanley was still being held hostage and as he was being held hostage right there in the King's encampment, the wise course would be to throw their lot in with the King on the morrow.

He would have been restless, Richard. He would have been torn. Having lost first his son and heir and then his wife during his brief reign, having been faced with the treachery of once-close friends, can there be any doubt that he would have wondered — if only fleetingly — how much longer he was meant to go on? And, schooled in the religion of his time, can there be any doubt that he knew how great a sin was despair? And, having established this fact, can there be any question about what the King would have chosen to do on the night before the battle?

Malcolm glanced over his group. Yes, there was a satisfactorily misty eye or two among them. They saw the inherent Romance in a widowed King who'd lost not only his wife but his heir and was hours away from losing his life as well.

Malcolm directed a victorious glance at Sludgecur. Her expression said, Don't press your luck.

It wasn't luck at all, Malcolm wanted to tell her. It was the Great Romance of Hearing the Truth. The wind had picked up velocity and lost another three or four degrees of temperature, but his little band of Antique Aussies were caught in the thrall of that August night in 1485.

The night before the battle, Malcolm told them, knowing that if he lost, he would die, Richard would have sought to be shriven. History tells us that there were no priests or chaplains available among Richard's forces, so what better place to find a confessor than in St. James Church. The church would have been quiet as Richard entered. A votive candle or rushlight would have burned in the nave, but nothing more. The only sound inside the building would have come from Richard himself as he moved from the doorway to kneel before the altar: the rustle of his fustian doublet (satin-lined, Malcolm informed his scholars, knowing the importance of detail to the Romantic Minded), the creak of leather from his heavy-soled battle shoes and from his scabbard, the clank of his sword and dagger as he —

"Oh my goodness," a Romantic neo-Ricardian chirruped. "What sort of man would take swords and daggers into a church?"

Malcolm smiled winsomely. He thought, A man who had a bloody good use for them, just the very things needed for a bloke who wanted to prise loose a stone. But what he said was, "Unusual, of course. One doesn't think of someone carrying weapons into a church, does one? But this was the night before the battle. Richard's enemies were everywhere. He wouldn't have walked into the darkness unprotected."

Whether the King wore his crown that night into the church, no one can say, Malcolm continued. But if there was a priest in the church to hear his confession, that same priest left Richard to his prayers soon after giving him absolution. And there in the darkness, lit only by the small rushlight in the nave, Richard made peace with his Lord God and prepared to meet the fate that the next day's battle promised him.

Malcolm eyed his audience, gauging

their reactions and their attentiveness. They were entirely with him. They were, he hoped, thinking about how much they should tip him for giving a bravura performance in the deadly wind.

His prayers finished, Malcolm informed them, the King unsheathed his sword and dagger, set them on the rough wooden bench, and sat next to them. And there in the church, King Richard laid his plans to ruin Henry Tudor should the upstart be the victor in the morrow's battle. Because Richard knew that he held — and had always held – the whip hand over Henry Tudor. He held it in life as a proven and victorious battle commander. He would hold it in death as the single force who could destroy the usurper.

"Goodness me," someone murmured appreciatively. Yes, Malcolm's listeners were fully atuned to the Romance of the Moment. Thank God.

Richard, he told them, wasn't oblivious of the scheming that had been going on between Henry Tudor and Elizabeth Woodville — widow of his brother Edward IV and mother of the two young Princes whom he had earlier placed in the Tower of London.

"The Princes in the Tower," another

voice remarked. "That's the two little boys who —"

"The very ones," Malcolm said solemnly. "Richard's own nephews."

The King would have known that, holding true to her propensity for buttering her bread not only on both sides but along the crust as well, Elizabeth Woodville had promised the hand of her eldest daughter to Tudor should he obtain the crown of England. But should Tudor obtain the crown of England on the morrow, Richard also knew that every man, woman, and child with a drop of York blood stood in grave danger of being eliminated — permanently — as a claimant to the throne. And this included Elizabeth Woodville's children.

He himself ruled by right of succession and by law. Descended directly — and more important legitimately — from Edward III he had come to the throne after the death of his brother Edward IV, upon the revelation of the licentious Edward's secret pledge of marriage to another woman long before his marriage to Elizabeth Woodville. This pledged contract of marriage had been made before a bishop of the church. As such, it was as good as a marriage performed with pomp and circumstance before a thousand onlookers, and it effectively made Edward's later marriage to Elizabeth Woodville bigamous at the same time as it bastardised all of their children.

Henry Tudor would have known that the children had been declared illegitimate by an Act of Parliament. He would also have known that, should he be victorious in his confrontation with Richard III, his tenuous claim to the throne of England would not be shored up by marriage to the bastard daughter of a dead King. So he would have to do something about her illegitimacy.

King Richard would have concluded this once he heard the news that Tudor had pledged to marry the girl. He would also have known that to legitimatise Elizabeth of York was also to legitimatise all her sisters . . . and her brothers. One could not declare the eldest child of a dead King legitimate while simultaneously claiming her siblings were not.

Malcolm paused meaningfully in his narrative. He waited to see if the eager Romantics gathered round him would twig the implication. They smiled and nodded and looked at him fondly, but no one said anything. So Malcolm did their twigging for them.

"Her brothers," he said patiently, and slowly to make sure they absorbed each Romantic detail. "If Henry Tudor legitimatised Elizabeth of York prior to marrying her, he would have been legitimatising her brothers as well. And if he did that, the elder of the boys —"

"Gracious me," one of the group sang out. "*He* would've been the true King once Richard died."

Bless you, my child, Malcolm thought. "That," he cried, "is exactly spot on."

"See here, mate," Sludgecur interrupted, some sort of light dawning in the cobwebbed reaches of her brain. "I've heard this story, and Richard killed those little blighters himself while they were in the Tower."

Another fish biting the Tudor bait, Malcolm realised. Five hundred years later and that scheming Welsh upstart was still successfully reeling them in. He could hardly wait until the day when his book came out, when his history of Richard was heralded as the triumph of truth over Tudor casuistry.

He was Patience itself as he explained. The Princes in the Tower — Edward IV's two sons — had indeed been long reputed by tradition to have been murdered by

311

their uncle Richard III to shore up his position as King. But there were no witnesses to any murder and as Richard was King through an Act of Parliament, he had no motive to kill them. And since he had no direct heir to the throne — his own son having died, as you heard moments ago — what better way to ensure the Yorks' continued possession of the throne of England than to designate the two Princes legitimate . . . after his own death? Such designation could only be made by Papal decree at this point, but Richard had sent two emissaries to Rome and why send them such a distance unless it was to arrange for the legitimatising of the very boys whose rights had been wrested from them by their father's lascivious conduct?

"The boys were indeed rumored to be dead." Malcolm aimed for kindness in his tone. "But that rumor, interestingly enough, never saw the light of day until just before Henry Tudor's invasion of England. He wanted to be King, but he had no rights to kingship. So he had to discredit the reigning monarch. Could there possibly be a more efficacious way to do it than by spreading the word that the Princes — who were gone from the Tower — were actually dead? But this is the question I pose to you, ladies: What if they weren't?"

An appreciative murmur went through the group. Malcolm heard one of the ancients commenting, "Lovely eyes, he has," and he turned them towards the sound of her voice. She looked like his grandmother. She also looked rich. He increased the wattage of his charm.

"What if the two boys had been removed from the Tower by Richard's own hand, sent into safekeeping against a possible uprising? Should Henry Tudor prevail at Bosworth Field, those two boys would be in grave danger and King Richard knew it. Tudor was pledged to their sister. To marry her, he had to declare her legitimate. Declaring her legitimate made them legitimate. Making them legitimate made one of them — young Edward — the true and rightful King of England. The only way for Tudor to prevent this was to get rid of them. Permanently."

Malcolm waited a moment to let this sink in. He noted the collection of grey heads turning towards Sutton Cheney. Then towards the north valley where a flagpole flew the seditious Stanleys' standard. Then over towards the peak of Ambion Hill where the unforgiving wind whipped Richard's White Boar briskly. Then down the slope in the direction of the railway tracks where the Tudor mercenaries had once formed their meagre front line. Vastly outnumbered, outgunned, and outarmed, they would have been waiting for the Stanleys to make their move: for King Richard or against him. Without the Stanleys' throwing their lot in with Tudor's, the day would be lost.

The Grey Ones were clearly with him, Malcolm noted. But Sludgecur was not so easily drawn in. "How was Tudor supposed to kill them if they were gone from the Tower?" She'd taken to beating her hands against her arms, doubtless wishing she were pummeling his face.

"He didn't kill them," Malcolm said pleasantly, "although his Machiavellian fingerprints are all over the crime. No. Tudor wasn't directly involved. I'm afraid the situation's a little nastier than that. Shall we walk on and discuss it, ladies?"

"Lovely little bum as well," one of the group murmured. "Quite a crumpet, that bloke."

Ah, they were in his palm. Malcolm felt himself warm to his own seductive talents.

He knew that Betsy was watching from

314

the farmhouse, from the first-floor bedroom from which she could see the battlefield. How could she possibly keep herself from doing so after their morning together? She'd see Malcolm shepherding his little band from site to site, she'd note that they were hanging onto his every word, and she'd think about how she herself had hung upon him less than two hours earlier. And the contrast between her drunken sot of a husband and her virile lover would be painfully and mightily on her mind.

This would make her realise how wasted she was on Bernie Perryman. She was, she would think, forty years old and at the prime of her life. She deserved better than Bernie. She deserved, in fact, a man who understood God's plan when He'd created the first man and woman. He'd used the man's rib, hadn't He? In doing that, He'd illustrated for all time that women and men were bound together, women taking their form and substance from their men, living their lives in the service of their men, for which their reward was to be sheltered and protected by their men's superior strength. But Bernie Perryman only ever saw one half of the man-woman equation. She — Betsy — was to work in his service, care for him, feed him, see to his well-being. He — Bernie — was to do nothing. Oh, he'd make a feeble attempt to give her a length now and again if the mood was upon him and he could keep it up long enough. But whiskey had long since robbed him of whatever ability he'd once had to be pleasing to a woman. And as for understanding her subtler needs and his responsibility in meeting them . . . forget that area of life altogether.

Malcolm liked to think of Betsy in these terms: up in her barren bedroom in the farmhouse, nursing a righteous grievance against her husband. She would proceed from that grievance to the realisation that he, Malcolm Cousins, was the man she'd been intended for, and she would see how every other relationship in her life had been but a prologue to the connection she now had with him. She and Malcolm, she would conclude, were suited for each other in every way.

Watching him on the battlefield, she would recall their initial meeting and the fire that had existed between them from the first day when Betsy had begun to work at Gloucester Grammar as the head-master's secretary. She'd recall the spark she'd felt when Malcolm had said, "Bernie Perryman's wife?" and admired her openly.

"Old Bernie's been holding back on me, and I thought we shared every secret of our souls." She would remember how she'd asked, "You know Bernie?" still in the blush of her newlywed bliss and not yet aware of how Bernie's drinking was going to impair his ability to care for her. And she'd well remember Malcolm's response:

"Have done for years. We grew up together, went to school together, spent holidays roaming the countryside. We even shared our first woman" — and she'd remember his smile — "so we're practically blood brothers if it comes to that. But I can see there might be a decided impediment to our future relationship. Betsy." And his eyes had held hers just long enough for her to realise that her newlywed bliss wasn't nearly as hot as the look he was giving her.

From that upstairs bedroom, she'd see that the group Malcolm was squiring round the field comprised women, and she'd begin to worry. The distance from the farmhouse to the field would prevent her from seeing that Malcolm's antiquated audience had one collective foot in the collective grave, so her thoughts would turn ineluctably to the possibilities implied by his current circumstances. What was to prevent one of those women from becoming captivated by the enchantment he offered?

These thoughts would lead to her desperation, which was what Malcolm had been assiduously massaging for months, whispering at the most tender of moments, "Oh God, if I'd only known what it was going to be like to have you, finally. And now to want you completely . . ." And then the tears, wept into her hair, and the revelation of the agonies of guilt and despair he experienced each time he rolled deliciously within the arms of his old friend's wife. "I can't bear to hurt him, darling Bets. If you and he were to divorce . . . How could I ever live with myself if he ever knew how I've betrayed our friendship?"

She'd remember this, in the farmhouse bedroom with her hot forehead pressed to the cold windowpane. They'd been together for three hours that morning, but she'd realise that it was not enough. It would never be enough to sneak round as they were doing, to pretend indifference to each other when they met at Gloucester Grammar. Until they were a couple — legally, as much as they were already a couple spiritually, mentally, emotionally, and physically — she could never have peace.

But Bernie stood between her and happiness, she would think. Bernie Perryman, driven to alcohol by the demon of fear that the congenital abnormality that had taken his grandfather, his father, and both of his brothers before their forty-fifth birthdays would claim him as well. "Weak heart," Bernie had doubtless told her, since he'd used it as an excuse for everything he'd done — and not done — for the last thirty years. "It don't ever pump like it ought. Just a little flutter when it oughter be a thud. Got to be careful. Got to take m' pills."

But if Betsy didn't remind her husband to take his pills daily, he was likely to forget there were pills altogether, let alone a reason for taking them. It was almost as if he had a death wish, Bernie Perryman. It was almost as if he was only waiting for the appropriate moment to set her free.

And once she was free, Betsy would think, The Legacy would be hers. And The Legacy was the key to her future with Malcolm. Because with The Legacy in hand at last, she and Malcolm could marry and Malcolm could leave his ill-paying job at Gloucester Grammar. Content with his research, his writing, and his lecturing, he would be filled with gratitude for her having made his new lifestyle possible. Grateful, he would be eager to meet her needs.

Which was, she would think, certainly how it was meant to be.

In the Plantagenet Pub in Sutton Cheney, Malcolm counted the tip money from his morning's labour. He'd given his all, but the Aussie Oldies had proved to be a niggardly lot. He'd ended up with forty pounds for the tour and lecture — which was an awesomely cheap price considering the depth of information he imparted — and twenty-five pounds in tips. Thank God for the pound coin, he concluded morosely. Without it, the tightfisted old sluts would probably have parted with nothing more than fifty pence apiece.

He pocketed the money as the pub door opened and a gust of icy air whooshed into the room. The flames of the fire next to him bobbled. Ash from the fireplace blew onto the hearth. Malcolm looked up. Bernie Perryman — clad only in cowboy boots, blue jeans, and a T-shirt with the words *Team Ferrari* printed on it — staggered drunkenly into the pub. Malcolm tried to shrink out of view, but it was impossible. After the prolonged exposure to the wind on Bosworth Field, his need for warmth had taken him to the blazing beechwood fire. This put him directly in Bernie's sight line.

"Malkie!" Bernie cried out joyfully, and went on as he always did whenever they met. "Malkie ol' mate! How 'bout a chess game? I miss our matches, I surely do." He shivered and beat his hands against his arms. His lips were practically blue. "Shit on toast. It's blowing a cold one out there. Pour me a Blackie," he called out to the publican. "Make it a double and make it double-quick." He grinned and dropped onto the stool at Malcolm's table. "So. How's the book comin', Malkie? Gotcher name in lights? Found a publisher yet?" He giggled.

Malcolm put aside whatever guilt he may have felt at the fact that he was industriously stuffing this inebriate's wife whenever his middle-aged body was up to the challenge. Bernie Perryman deserved to be a cuckold, his punishment for the torment he'd been dishing out to Malcolm for the last ten years.

"Never got over that last game, did you?" Bernie grinned again. He was served his Black Bush which he tossed back in a single gulp. He blubbered air out between his lips. He said, "Did me right, that," and called for another. "Now what was the full-on tale again, Malkie? You get to the good part of the story yet? 'Course, it'll be a tough one to prove, won't it, mate?"

Malcolm counted to ten. Bernie was presented with his second double whiskey. It went the way of the first.

"But I'm givin' you a bad time for nothing," Bernie said, suddenly repentant in the way of all drunks. "You never did me a bad turn — 'cept that time with the A-levels, 'course — and I shouldn't do you one. I wish you the best. Truly, I do. It's just that things never work out the way they're s'posed to, do they?"

Which, Malcolm thought, was the whole bloody point. Things — as Bernie liked to call them — hadn't worked out for Richard either, that fatal morning on Bosworth Field. The Earl of Northumberland had let him down, the Stanleys had out-and-out betrayed him, and an untried upstart who had neither the skill nor the courage to face the King personally in decisive combat had won the day.

"So tell Bern your theory another time. I love the story, I do, I do. I just wished there was a way for you to prove it. It'd be the making of you, that book would. How long you been working on the manuscript?" Bernie swiped the interior of his whiskey glass with a dirty finger and licked off the residue. He wiped his mouth on the back of his hand. He hadn't shaved that morning. He hadn't bathed in days. For a moment, Malcolm almost felt sorry for Betsy, having to live in the same house with the odious man.

"I've come to Elizabeth of York," Malcolm said as pleasantly as he could manage considering the antipathy he was feeling for Bernie. "Edward IV's daughter. Future wife to the King of England."

Bernie smiled, showing teeth in serious need of cleaning. "Cor, I always forget that bird, Malkie. Why's that, d'you think?"

Because everyone always forgot Elizabeth, Malcolm said silently. The eldest daughter of Edward IV, she was generally consigned to a footnote in history as the oldest sister of the Princes in the Tower, the dutiful daughter of Elizabeth Woodville, a pawn in the political power game, the later wife of that Tudor usurper Henry VII. Her job was to carry the seed of the dynasty, to deliver the heirs, and to fade into obscurity.

But here was a woman who was one-half Woodville, with the thick blood of that scheming and ambitious clan coursing through her veins. That she wanted to be Queen of England like her mother before her had been established in the seventeenth century when Sir George Buck had written — in his *History of the Life and Reigne of Richard III* — of young Elizabeth's letter asking the Duke of Norfolk to be the mediator between herself and King Richard on the subject of their marriage, telling him that she was the King's in heart and in thought. That she was as ruthless as her two parents was made evident in the fact that her letter to Norfolk was written prior to the death of Richard's wife, Queen Anne.

Young Elizabeth had been bundled out of London and up to Yorkshire, ostensibly for safety's sake, prior to Henry Tudor's invasion. There she resided at Sheriff Hutton, a stronghold deep in the countryside where loyalty to King Richard was a constant of life. Elizabeth would be well protected — not to mention well guarded — in Yorkshire. As would be her siblings.

"You still hot for Lizzie?" Bernie asked with a chuckle. "Cor, how you used to go on about that girl."

Malcolm suppressed his rage but did not forbid himself from silently cursing the other man into eternal torment. Bernie had a deep aversion for anyone who tried to make something of his life. That sort of person served to remind him of what a waste he'd made of his own.

Bernie must have read something on Malcolm's face because as he called for his third double whiskey, he said, "No, no, get on with you. I 'as only kidding. What's you doing out here today anyway? Was that you in the battlefield when I drove by?"

Bernie knew it was he, Malcolm realised. But mentioning the fact served to remind them both of Malcolm's passion and the hold that Bernie Perryman had upon it. God, how he wanted to stand on the table and shout, "I'm bonking this idiot's wife twice a week, three or four times if I can manage it. They'd been married two months when I bonked her the first time, six days after we were introduced."

But losing control like that was exactly what Bernie Perryman wanted of his old friend Malcolm Cousins: payback time for having once refused to help Bernie cheat his way through his A-levels. The man had an elephantine memory and a grudge-bearing spirit. But so did Malcolm.

"I don't know, Malkie," Bernie said, shaking his head as he was presented with his whiskey. He reached unsteadily for it, his bloodless tongue wetting his lower lip. "Don't seem natural that Lizzie'd hand those lads over to be given the chop. Not her own brothers. Not even to be Queen of England. 'Sides, they weren't even anywheres near her, were they? All speculation, 'f you ask me. All speculation and not a speck of proof."

Never, Malcolm thought for the thousandth time, never tell a drunkard your secrets or your dreams.

"It was Elizabeth of York," he said again. "She was ultimately responsible."

Sheriff Hutton was not an insurmountable distance from Rievaulx, Jervaulx, and Fountain Abbeys. And tucking individuals away in abbeys, convents, monasteries, and priories was a great tradition at that time. Women were the usual recipients of a one-way ticket to the ascetic life. But two young boys — disguised as youthful entrants into a novitiate — would have been safe there from the arm of Henry Tudor should he take the throne of England by means of conquest.

"Tudor would have known the boys were alive," Malcolm said. "When he pledged himself to marry Elizabeth, he would have known the boys were alive."

Bernie nodded. "Poor little tykes," he said with factitious sorrow. "And poor old Richard who took the blame. How'd she get her mitts on them, Malkie? What d'you think? Think she cooked up a deal with Tudor?"

"She wanted to be a Queen more than she wanted to be merely the sister to a King. There was only one way to make that happen. And Henry had been looking elsewhere for a wife at the same time that he was bargaining with Elizabeth Wood-ville. The girl would have known that. And what it meant."

Bernie nodded solemnly, as if he cared a half fig for what had happened more than five hundred years ago on an August night not two hundred yards from the pub in which they sat. He shot back his third double whiskey and slapped his stomach like a man at the end of a hearty meal.

"Got the church all prettied up for to-morrow," he informed Malcolm. " 'Maz-ing when you think of it, Malkie. Perry-mans been tinkering round St. James Church for two hundred years. Like a family pedigree, that. Don't you think? Re-markable, I'd say."

Malcolm regarded him evenly. "Utterly remarkable, Bernie," he said.

"Ever think how different life might've been if your dad and granddad and his granddad before him were the ones who tinkered round St. James Church? P'rhaps I'd be you and you'd be me. What d'you think of that?"

What Malcolm thought of that couldn't be spoken to the man sitting opposite him at the table. Die, he thought. Die before I kill you myself.

"Do you want to be together, darling?" Betsy breathed the question wetly into his ear. Another Saturday. Another three hours of bonking Betsy. Malcolm wondered how much longer he'd have to continue with the charade.

He wanted to ask her to move over — the woman was capable of inducing claustrophobia with more efficacy than a plastic bag — but at this point in their relationship he knew that a demonstration of postcoital togetherness was as important to his ultimate objective as was a top-notch performance between the sheets. And since his age, his inclinations, and his energy were all combining to take his performances down a degree each time he sank between Betsy's well-padded thighs, he realised the wisdom of allowing her to cling, coo, and cuddle for as long as he could endure it without screaming once the primal act was completed between them.

"We *are* together," he said, stroking her hair. It was wire-like to the touch, the result of too much bleaching and even more hair spray. "Unless you mean that you want another go. And I'll need some recovery time for that." He turned his head and pressed his lips to her forehead. "You take it out of me and that's the truth of it, darling Bets. You're woman enough for a dozen men."

She giggled. "You love it."

"Not it. You. Love, want, and can't be without." He sometimes pondered where he came up with the nonsense he told her. It was as if a primitive part of his brain reserved for female seduction went onto autopilot whenever Betsy climbed into his bed.

She buried her fingers in his ample chest hair. He wondered not for the first time why it was that when a man went bald, the rest of his body started sprouting hair in quadruple time. "I mean really be together, darling. Do you want it? The two of us? Like this? Forever? Do you want it more than anything on earth?"

The thought alone was like being imprisoned in concrete. But he said, "Darling Bets," by way of answer and he trembled his voice appropriately. "Don't. Please. We can't go through this again." And he pulled her roughly to him because he knew that was the move she desired. He buried his face in the curve of her shoulder and neck. He breathed through his mouth to avoid inhaling the day's litre of Shalimar that she'd doused herself with. He made the whimpering noises of a man *in extremis*. God, what he wouldn't do for King Richard.

"I was on the Internet," she whispered, fingers caressing the back of his neck. "In the school library. All Thursday and Friday lunch, darling."

He stopped his whimpering, sifting through this declaration for deeper meaning. "Were you?" He temporised by nibbling at her earlobe, waiting for more information. It came obliquely.

"You *do* love me, don't you, Malcolm dearest?"

"What do you think?"

"And you do want me, don't you?"

"That's obvious, isn't it?"

"Forever and ever?"

Whatever it takes, he thought. And he

did his best to prove it to her, although his body wasn't up to a full performance.

Afterwards, while she was dressing, she said, "I was so surprised to see all the topics. You c'n look up anything on the Internet. Fancy that, Malcolm. Anything at all. Bernie's playing in chess night at the Plantagenet, dearest. Tonight, that is."

Malcolm furrowed his brow, automatically seeking the connection between these apparently unrelated topics. She went on.

"He misses your games, Bernie does. He always wishes you'd come by on chess night and give it another go with him, darling." She padded to the chest of drawers where she began repairing her makeup. " 'Course, he doesn't play well. Just uses chess as an extra excuse to go to the pub."

Malcolm watched her, eyes narrowed, waiting for a sign.

She gave it to him. "I worry about him, Malcolm dear. His poor heart's going to give out someday. I'm going with him tonight. Perhaps we'll see you there? Malcolm, dearest, do you love me? Do you want to be together more than anything on earth?"

He saw that she was watching him closely in the mirror even as she repaired the damage he'd done to her makeup. She was painting her lips into bee-sting bows. She was brushing her cheeks with blusher. But all the time she was observing him.

"More than life itself," he said.

And when she smiled, he knew he'd given her the correct answer.

That night at the Plantagenet Pub, Malcolm joined the Sutton Cheney Chessmen, of whose society he'd once been a regular member. Bernie Perryman was delighted to see him. He deserted his regular opponent — seventy-year-old Angus Ferguson who used the excuse of playing chess at the Plantagenet to get as sloshed as Bernie — and pressed Malcolm into a game at a table in the smoky corner of the pub. Betsy was right, naturally: Bernie drank far more than he played, and the Black Bush served to oil the mechanism of his conversation. So he also talked incessantly.

He talked to Betsy, who was playing the role of serving wench for her husband that evening. From half past seven until half past ten, she trotted back and forth from the bar, bringing Bernie one double Black Bush after another, saying, "You're drinking too much," and "This is the last one, Bernie," in a monitory fashion. But he always managed to talk her into "just one more wet one, Mama girl," and he patted her bum, winked at Malcolm and whispered loudly what he intended to do to her once he got her home. Malcolm was at the point of thinking he'd utterly misunderstood Betsy's implied message to him in bed that morning when she finally made her move.

It came at half past ten, one hour before George the Publican called for last orders. The pub was packed, and Malcolm might have missed her manoeuvre altogether had he not anticipated that something was going to happen that night. As Bernie nodded over the chessboard, contemplating his next move eternally, Betsy went to the bar for yet another "double Blackie." To do this, she had to shoulder her way through the Sutton Cheney Dartsmen, the Wardens of the Church, a women's support group from Dadlington, and a group of teenagers intent upon success with a fruit machine. She paused in conversation with a balding woman who seemed to be admiring Betsy's hair with that sort of artificial enthusiasm women reserve for other women whom they particularly hate, and it was while she and the other chatted that Malcolm saw her empty the vial into Bernie's tumbler.

He was awestruck at the ease with which she did it. She must have been practising the move for days, he realised. She was so adept that she did it with one hand as she chatted: slipping the vial out of her sweater sleeve, uncapping it, dumping it, returning it to her sweater. She finished her conversation, and she continued on her way. And no one save Malcolm was wise to the fact that she'd done something more than merely fetch another whiskey for her husband. Malcolm eyed her with new respect when she set the glass in front of Bernie. He was glad he had no intention of hooking himself up with the murderous bitch.

He knew what was in the glass: the results of Betsy's few hours surfing the Internet. She'd crushed at least ten tablets of Digitoxin into a lethal powder. An hour after Bernie ingested the mixture, he'd be a dead man.

Ingest it Bernie did. He drank it down the way he drank down every double Black Bush he encountered: He poured it directly down his throat and wiped his mouth on the back of his hand. Malcolm had lost count of the number of whiskeys Bernie had imbibed that evening, but it seemed to him that if the drug didn't kill him, the alcohol certainly would.

"Bernie," Betsy said mournfully, "let's go home."

"Can't just yet," Bernie said. "Got to finish my bit with Malkie boy here. We haven't had us a chess-up in years. Not since . . ." He smiled at Malcolm blearily. "Why, I 'member that night up the farm, doanchew, Malkie? Ten years back? Longer was it? When we played that last game, you and me?"

Malcolm didn't want to get onto that subject. He said, "Your move, Bernie. Or do you want to call it a draw?"

"No way, Joe-zay." Bernie swayed on his stool and studied the board.

"Bernie . . ." Betsy said coaxingly.

He patted her hand, which she'd laid on his shoulder. "You g'wan, Bets. I c'n find my way home. Malkie'll drive me, woan-chew, Malkie?" He dug his car keys out of his pocket and pressed them into his wife's palm. "But doanchew fall asleep, sweet Mama. We got business together when I get home."

Betsy made a show of reluctance and a secondary show of her concern that Malcolm might have had too much to drink himself and thereby be an unsafe driver for her precious Bernie to ride along with. Bernie said, " 'F he can't do a straight line in the car park, I'll walk. Promise, Mama. Cross m' heart."

Betsy leveled a meaningful look at Malcolm. She said, "See that you keep him safe, then."

Malcolm nodded. Betsy departed. And all that was left was the waiting.

For someone who was supposed to be suffering from congenital heart failure, Bernie Perryman seemed to have the constitution of a mule. An hour later, Malcolm had him in the car and was driving him home, and Bernie was still talking like a man with a new lease on life. He was just itching to get up those farmhouse stairs and rip off his wife's knickers, to hear him tell it. Nothing but the Day of Judgement was going to stop Bernie from showing his Sweet Mama the time of her life.

By the time Malcolm had taken the longest route possible to get to the farm without raising Bernie's suspicions, he'd begun to believe that his paramour hadn't slipped her husband an overdose of his medication at all. It was only when Bernie got out of the car at the edge of the drive that Malcolm had his hopes renewed. Bernie said, "Feel a bit peaked, Malkie.

Whew. Nice lie down. Tha's just the ticket," and staggered in the direction of the distant house. Malcolm watched him until he toppled into the hedgerow at the side of the drive. When he didn't move after the fall, Malcolm knew that the deed had finally been done.

He drove off happily. If Bernie hadn't been dead when he hit the ground, Malcolm knew that he'd be dead by the morning.

Wonderful, he thought. It may have been ages in the execution, but his well-laid plan was going to pay off.

Malcolm had worried a bit that Betsy might muff her role in the ensuing drama. But during the next few days, she proved herself to be an actress of formidable talents. Having awakened in the morning to discover herself alone in the bed, she'd done what any sensible wife-of-a-drunk would do: She went looking for her husband. She didn't find him anywhere in the house or in the other farm buildings, so she placed a few phone calls. She checked the pub; she checked the church; she checked with Malcolm. Had Malcolm not seen her poison her husband with his own eyes, he would have been convinced that on the other end of the line was a woman anxious for the welfare of her man. But then, she *was* anxious, wasn't she? She needed a corpse to prove Bernie was dead.

"I dropped him at the end of the drive," Malcolm told her, help and concern personified. "He was heading up to the house the last I saw him, Bets."

So she went out and found Bernie exactly where he'd fallen on the previous night. And her discovery of his body set the necessary events in motion.

An inquest was called, of course. But it proved to be a mere formality. Bernie's history of heart problems and his "difficulty with the drink," as the authorities put it, combined with the fiercely inclement weather they'd been having to provide the coroner's jury with a most reasonable conclusion. Bernie Perryman was declared dead of exposure, having passed out on the coldest night of the year, teetering up the lengthy drive to the farmhouse after a full night of drink at the Plantagenet Pub, where sixteen witnesses called to testify had seen him down at least eleven double whiskeys in less than three hours.

There was no reason to check for toxicity in his blood. Especially once his doctor said that it was a miracle the man had lived to forty-nine, considering the medical history of his family, not to mention his "problem with the drink."

So Bernie was buried at the side of his forebears, in the graveyard of St. James Church, where his father and all the fathers before him for at least the past two hundred years had toiled in the cause of a neat and tidy house of worship.

Malcolm soothed what few pangs of guilt he had over Bernie's passing by ignoring them. Bernie'd had a history of heart disease. Bernie had been a notorious drunk. If Bernie, in his cups, had passed out on the driveway a mere fifty yards from his house and died from exposure as a result . . . well, who could possibly hold himself responsible?

And while it was sad that Bernie Perryman had had to give his life for the cause of Malcolm's search for the truth, it was also the truth that he'd brought his premature death upon himself.

After the funeral, Malcolm knew that all he needed to employ was patience. He hadn't spent the last two years industriously ploughing Betsy's field, only to be thwarted by a display of unseemly haste at the moment of harvest. Besides, Betsy was

339

doing enough bit chomping for both of them, so he knew it was only a matter of days — perhaps hours — before she took herself off to the Perrymans' longtime solicitor for an accounting of the inheritance that was coming her way.

Malcolm had pictured the moment enough times during his liaison with Betsy. Sometimes picturing the moment when Betsy learned the truth was the only fantasy that got him through his interminable lovemaking sessions with the woman.

Howard Smythe-Thomas would open his Nuneaton office to her and break the news in a suitably funereal fashion, no doubt. And perhaps at first, Betsy would think his sombre demeanour was an air adopted for the occasion. He'd begin by calling her "My dear Mrs. Perryman," which should give her an idea that bad news was in the offing, but she wouldn't have an inkling of how bad the news was until he spelled out the bitter reality for her.

Bernie had no money. The farm had been mortgaged three times; there were no savings worth speaking of and no investments. The contents of the house and the outbuildings were hers, of course, but only by selling off every possession — and the farm itself — would Betsy be able to avoid bankruptcy. And even then, it would be touch and go. The only reason the bank hadn't foreclosed on the property before now was that the Perrymans had been doing business with that same financial institution for more than two hundred years. "Loyalty," Mr. Smythe-Thomas would no doubt intone. "Bernard may have had his difficulties, Mrs. Perryman, but the bank had respect for his lineage. When one's father and one's father's father and his father before him have done business with a banking establishment, there is a certain leeway given that might not be given to a personage less well known to that bank."

Which would be legal doublespeak for the fact that since there were no other Perrymans at Windsong Farm — and Mr. Smythe-Thomas would be good about gently explaining that a short-term wife of a long-term alcoholic Perryman didn't count — the bank would probably be calling in Bernie's debts. She would be wise to prepare herself for that eventuality.

But what about The Legacy? Betsy would ask. "Bernie always nattered on about a legacy." And she would be stunned to think of the depth of her husband's deception.

Mr. Smythe-Thomas, naturally, would know nothing about a legacy. And considering the Perryman history of ne'er-do-wells earning their keep by doing nothing more than working round the church in Sutton Cheney . . . He would kindly point out that it wasn't very likely that anyone had managed to amass a fortune doing handywork, was it?

It would take some hours — perhaps even days — for the news to sink into Betsy's skull. She'd think at first that there had to be some sort of mistake. Surely there were jewels hidden somewhere, cash tucked away, silver or gold or deeds to property heretofore unknown packed in the attic. And thinking this, she would begin her search. Which was exactly what Malcolm intended her to do: Search first and come weeping to Malcolm second. And Malcolm himself would take it from there.

In the meantime, he happily worked on his magnum opus. The pages to the left of his typewriter piled up satisfactorily as he redeemed the reputation of England's most maligned King.

Many of the righteous fell that morning of 22nd August 1485, and among them was the Duke of Norfolk, who commanded the vanguard at the front of Richard's army. When the Earl of Northumberland refused to engage his forces to come to the aid of Norfolk's leaderless men, the psychological tide of the battle shifted.

Those were the days of mass desertions, of switching loyalties, of outright betrayals on the field of battle. And both the King and his Tudor foe would have known that. Which went far to explain why both men simultaneously needed and doubted the Stanleys. Which also went far to explain why — in the midst of the battle — Henry Tudor made a run for the Stanleys, who had so far refused to enter the fray. Outnumbered as he was, Henry Tudor's cause would be lost without the Stanleys' intervention. And he wasn't above begging for it, which is why he made that desperate ride across the plain towards the Stanley forces.

King Richard intercepted him, thundering down Ambion Hill with his Knights and Esquires of the Body. The two small forces engaged each other a bare half mile from the Stanleys' men. Tudor's knights began falling quickly under the King's attack: William Brandon and the banner of Cadwallader plummeted to the ground; the enormous Sir John Cheyney fell beneath the King's own ax. It was only a matter of moments before Richard might fight his way to Henry Tudor himself, which was what the Stanleys realised when they made their decision to attack the King's small force.

In the ensuing battle, King Richard was unhorsed and could have fled the field. But declaring that he would "die King of England," he continued to fight even when grievously wounded. It took more than one man to bring him down. And he died like the Royal Prince that he was.

The King's army fled, pursued hotly by the Earl of Oxford whose intent it would have been to kill as many of them as possible. They shot off towards the village of Stoke Golding, in the opposite direction from Sutton Cheney.

This fact was the crux of the events that followed. When one's life is hanging in the balance, when one is a blood relative of the defeated King of England, one's thoughts turn inexorably towards self-preservation. John de la Pole, Earl of Lincoln and nephew to King Richard, was among the fleeing forces. To ride towards Sutton Cheney would have put him directly into the clutches of the Earl of Northumberland who had refused to come to the

344

King's aid and would have been only too happy to cement his position in Henry Tudor's affections — such as they were — by handing over the dead King's nephew. So he rode to the south instead of to the north. And in doing so, he condemned his uncle to five hundred years of Tudor propaganda.

Because history is written by the winners, Malcolm thought.

Only sometimes history gets to be rewritten.

And as he rewrote it, in the back of his mind was the picture of Betsy and her growing desperation. In the two weeks following Bernie's death, she hadn't returned to work. Gloucester Grammar's headmaster — the sniveling Samuel, as Malcolm liked to call him — reported that Betsy was prostrate over her husband's sudden death. She needed time to deal with and to heal from her grief, he told the staff sorrowfully.

Malcolm knew that what she had to deal with was finding something that she could pass off as The Legacy so as to bind him to her despite the fact that her expectations of inheritance had come to nothing. Tearing through the old farmhouse like a wild thing, she would probably go through Bernie's wardrobe one thread at a time in an attempt to unearth some item of value. She'd shake open books, seeking everything from treasure maps to deeds. She'd sift through the contents of the half dozen trunks in the attic. She'd knock about the outbuildings with her lips turning blue from the cold. And if she was assiduous, she would find the key.

That key would take her to the safe-deposit box at that very same bank in which the Perrymans had transacted business for two hundred years. Widow of Bernard Perryman with his will in one hand and his death certificate in the other, she would be given access. And there, she'd come to the end of her hopes.

Malcolm wondered what she would think when she saw the single grubby piece of paper that was the long heralded Legacy of the Perrymans. Filled with handwriting so cramped as to be virtually illegible, it looked like nothing to the untrained eye. And that's what Betsy would think she had in her possession when she finally threw herself upon Malcolm's mercy.

Bernie Perryman had known otherwise, however, on that long-ago night when he'd shown Malcolm the letter.

"Have a lookit this here, Malkie," Bernie had said. "Tell ol' Bern whatchoo think of this."

He was in his cups, as usual, but he wasn't yet blotto. And Malcolm, having just obliterated him at chess, was feeling expansive and willing to put up with his childhood friend's inebriated ramblings.

At first he thought that Bernie was taking a page from out of a large old Bible, but he quickly saw that the Bible was really an antique leather album of some sort and the page was a document, a letter in fact. Although it had no salutation, it was signed at the bottom and next to the signature were the remains of a wax imprint from a signet ring.

Bernie was watching him in that sly way drunks have: gauging his reaction. So Malcolm knew that Bernie knew what it was that he had in his possession. Which made him curious, but wary as well.

The wary part of him glanced at the document, saying, "I don't know, Bernie. I can't make much of it." While the curious part of him added, "Where'd it come from?"

Bernie played coy. "That ol' floor always gave them trouble, di'n't it, Malkie? Too low it was, stones too rough, never a decent job of building. But what else c'n you expect when a structure's donkey's ears old?"

Malcolm mined through this non sequitur for meaning. The old buildings in the area were Gloucester Grammar School, the Plantagenet Pub, Market Bosworth Hall, the timbered cottages in Rectory Lane, St. James Church in —

His gaze sharpened, first on Bernie and then on his document. St. James Church in Sutton Cheney, he thought. And he gave the document a closer look.

Which was when he deciphered the first line of it — *I, Richard, by the Grace of God Kyng of England and France and Lord of Ireland* — which was when his glance dropped to the hastily scrawled signature, which he also deciphered. *Richard R.*

Holy Jesus God, he thought. What had Bernie got his drunken little hands on?

He knew the importance of staying cool. One indication of his interest and he'd be Bernie's breakfast. So he said, "Can't tell much in this light, Bernie. Mind if I have a closer look at home?"

But Bernie wasn't about to buy that proposal. He said, "Can't let it out of m' sight, Malkie. Family legacy, that. Been our goods for donkey's ears, that has, and every one of us swore to keep it safe."

"How did you . . . ?" But Malcolm knew better than to ask how Bernie had come to have a letter written by Richard III among his family belongings. Bernie would tell him only what Bernie deemed necessary for Malcolm to know. So he said, "Let's have a look in the kitchen, then. That all right with you?"

That was just fine with Bernie Perryman. He, after all, wanted his old mate to see what the document was. So they went into the kitchen and sat at the table and Malcolm pored over the thick piece of paper.

The writing was terrible, not the neat hand of the professional scribe who would have attended the King and written his correspondence for him, but the hand of a man in agitated spirits. Malcolm had spent nearly twenty years consuming every scrap of information on Richard Plantagenet, Duke of Gloucester, later Richard III, called the Usurper, called England's Black Legend, called the Bunch-Backed Toad and virtually every other obloquy imaginable. So he knew how possible it actually was that here in this farmhouse, not two hundred yards from Bosworth Field and little over a mile from St. James Church, he was looking at the genuine article. Richard had lived his last night in this vicinity. Richard had fought here. Richard had died here. How unimaginable a circumstance was it that Richard had also written a letter somewhere nearby, in a building where it lay hidden until . . .

Malcolm sifted through everything he knew about the area's history. He came up with the fact he needed. "The floor of St. James Church," he said. "It was raised two hundred years ago, wasn't it?" And one of the countless ne'er-do-well Perrymans had been there, had probably helped with the work, and had found this letter.

Bernie was watching him, a sly smile tweaking the corners of his mouth. "Whatchoo think it says, Malkie?" he asked. "Think it might be worth a bob or two?"

Malcolm wanted to strangle him, but instead he studied the priceless document. It wasn't long, just a few lines that, he saw, could have altered the course of history and that would — when finally made public through the historical discourse he instantaneously decided to write — finally redeem the King who for five hundred years had been maligned by an accusation of butchery for which there had never been a shred of proof.

I, Richard, by the Grace of God Kyng of England and France and Lord of Ireland, on thys daye of 21 August 1485 do with thys document hereby enstruct the good fadres of Jervaulx to gyve unto the protection of the beerrer Edward hytherto called Lord Bastarde and hys brother Richard, called Duke of Yrk. Possession of thys document wyll suffyce to identyfie the beerrer as John de la Pole, Earl of Lyncoln, beloved nephew of the Kyng. Wrytten in hast at Suton Chene. Richard R.

Two sentences only, but enough to redeem a man's reputation. When the King had died on the field of battle that 22nd of August 1485, his two young nephews had been alive.

Malcolm looked at Bernie steadily. "You know what this is, don't you, Bernie?" he asked his old friend.

"Numbskull like me?" Bernie asked. "Him what couldn't even pass his A-levels? How'd I know what that bit of trash is? But what d'you think? Worth something if I flog it?"

"You can't sell this, Bernie." Malcolm spoke before he thought and much too hastily. Doing so, he inadvertently revealed himself.

Bernie scooped the paper up and manhandled it to his chest. Malcolm winced. God only knew the damage the fool was capable of doing when he was drunk.

"Go easy with that," Malcolm said. "It's fragile, Bernie."

"Like friendship, isn't it?" Bernie tottered from the kitchen.

It would have been shortly after that that Bernie had moved the document to another location, for Malcolm had never seen it again. But the knowledge of its existence had festered inside him for years. And only with the advent of Betsy had he finally seen a way to make that precious piece of paper his.

And it would be, soon. Just as soon as Betsy got up her nerve to phone him with the terrible news that what she'd thought was a legacy was only — to her utterly unschooled eyes — a bit of old paper suitable for lining the bottom of a parakeet cage.

While awaiting her call, Malcolm put the finishing touches on his *The Truth About Richard and Bosworth Field*, ten years in the writing and wanting only a single, final, and previously unseen historical document to serve as witness to the veracity of his theory about what happened to the two young Princes. The hours that he spent at his typewriter flew by like leaves blown off the trees in Ambion Forest, where once a marsh had protected Richard's south flank from attack by Henry Tudor's mercenary army.

The letter gave credence to Malcolm's surmise that Richard would have told someone of the boys' whereabouts. Should the battle favour Henry Tudor, the Princes would be in deadly danger, so the night before the battle Richard would finally have had to tell someone his most closely guarded secret: where the two boys were. In that way, if the day went to Tudor, the boys could be fetched from the monastery and spirited out of the country and out of the reach of harm.

John de la Pole, Earl of Lincoln, and beloved nephew to Richard III, would have been the likeliest candidate. He would have been instructed to ride to Yorkshire if the King fell, to safeguard the lives of the boys who would be made legitimate — and hence the biggest threat to the usurper — the moment Henry Tudor married their sister.

John de la Pole would have known the gravity of the boys' danger. But despite the fact that his uncle would have told him where the Princes were hidden, he would never have been given access to them, much less had them handed over to him, without express direction to the monks from the King himself.

The letter would have given him that access. But he'd had to flee to the south instead of to the north. So he couldn't pull it from the stones in St. James Church where his uncle had hidden it the night before the battle.

And yet the boys disappeared, never to be heard of again. So who took them?

There could be only one answer to that question: Elizabeth of York, sister to the Princes but also affianced wife of the newly-crowned-right-there-on-the-battlefield King.

Hearing the news that her uncle had been defeated, Elizabeth would have seen her options clearly: Queen of England should Henry Tudor retain his throne or sister to a mere youthful King should her brother Edward claim his own legitimacy the moment Henry legitimatised her or suppressed the Act by which she'd been made illegitimate in the first place. Thus, she could be the matriarch of a royal dynasty or a political pawn to be given in marriage to anyone with whom her brother wished to form an alliance.

Sheriff Hutton, her temporary residence, was no great distance from any of the abbeys. Ever her uncle's favourite niece and knowing his bent for things religious, she would have guessed — if Richard hadn't told her directly — where he'd hidden her brothers. And the boys would have gone with her willingly. She was their sister, after all.

"I am Elizabeth of York," she would have told the abbot in that imperious voice she'd heard used so often by her cunning mother. "I shall see my brothers alive and well. And instantly."

How easily it would have been accomplished. The two young Princes seeing their older sister for the first time in who knew how long, running to her, embracing her, eagerly turning to the abbot when she informed them that she'd come for them at last . . . And who was the abbot to deny a Royal Princess — clearly recognised by the boys themselves — her own brothers? Especially in the current situation, with King Richard dead and sitting on the throne a man who'd illustrated his bloodthirst by making one of his first acts as King a declaration of treason against all who had fought on the side of Richard at Bosworth

Field? Tudor wouldn't look kindly on the abbey that was found to be sheltering the two boys. God only knew what his revenge would be should he locate them.

Thus it made sense for the abbot to deliver Edward the Lord Bastard and his brother Richard the Duke of York into the hands of their sister. And Elizabeth, with her brothers in her possession, handed them over to someone. One of the Stanleys? The duplicitous Earl of Northumberland who went on to serve Henry Tudor in the North? Sir James Tyrell, onetime follower of Richard, who was the recipient of two general pardons from Tudor not a year after he took the throne?

Whoever it was, once the Princes were in his hands, their fates were sealed. And no one wishing to preserve his life afterwards would have thought about levelling an accusation against the wife of a reigning monarch who had already shown his inclination for attainting subjects and confiscating their land.

It was, Malcolm thought, such a brilliant plan on Elizabeth's part. She was her mother's own daughter, after all. She knew the value of placing self-interest above everything else. Besides, she would have told herself that keeping the boys alive would only prolong a struggle for the throne that had been going on for thirty years. She could put an end to the bloodshed by shedding just a little more blood. What woman in her position would have done otherwise?

The fact that it took Betsy more than three months to develop the courage to break the sorrowful news to Malcolm did cause him a twinge of concern now and then. In the timeline he'd long ago written in his mind, she'd have come to him in hysterics not twenty-four hours after discovering that her Legacy was a scribbled-up scrap of dirty paper. She'd have thrown herself into his arms and wept and waited for rescue. To emphasise the dire straits she was in, she'd have brought the paper with her to show him how ill Bernie Perryman had used his loving wife. And he — Malcolm — would have taken the paper from her shaking fingers, would have given it a glance, would have tossed it to the floor and joined in her weeping, mourning the death of their dearly held dreams. For she was ruined financially and he, on a mere paltry salary from Gloucester Grammar, could not offer her the life she deserved. Then, after a vigorous and memorable round of mattress poker, she would leave, the scorned bit of paper still lying on the floor. And the letter would be his. And when his tome was published and the lectures, television interviews, chat shows, and book tours began cluttering up his calendar, he would have no time for a bumpkin housewife who'd been too dim to know what she'd had in her fingers.

That was the plan. Malcolm felt the occasional pinch of worry when it didn't come off quickly. But he told himself that Betsy's reluctance to reveal the truth to him was all part of God's Great Plan. This gave him time to complete his manuscript. And he used the time well.

Since he and Betsy had decided that discretion was in order following Bernie's death, they saw each other only in the corridors of Gloucester Grammar when she returned to work. During this time, Malcolm phoned her nightly for telesex once he realised that he could keep her oiled and proofread the earlier chapters of his opus simultaneously.

Then finally, three months and four days after Bernie's unfortunate demise, Betsy whispered a request to him in the corridor just outside the headmaster's office. Could he come to the farm for dinner that night?

She didn't look as solemn-faced as Malcolm would have liked, considering her impoverished circumstances and the death of her dreams, but he didn't worry much about this. Betsy had already proved herself a stunning actress. She wouldn't want to break down at the school.

Prior to leaving that afternoon, swollen with the realisation that his fantasy was about to be realised, Malcolm handed in his notice to the headmaster. Samuel Montgomery accepted it with a rather disturbing alacrity which Malcolm didn't much like, and although the headmaster covered his surprise and delight with a spurious show of regret at losing "a veritable institution here at GG," Malcolm could see him savouring the triumph of being rid of someone he'd decided was an educational dinosaur. So it gave him more satisfaction than he would have thought possible, knowing how great his own triumph was going to be when he made his mark upon the face of English history.

Malcolm couldn't have been happier as he drove to Windsong Farm that evening. The long winter of his discontent had segued into a beautiful spring, and he was minutes away from being able to right a five-hundred-year-old wrong at the same time as he carved a place for himself in the pantheon of the Historical Greats. God is good, he thought as he made the turn into the farm's long driveway. It was unfortunate that Bernie Perryman had had to die, but as his death was in the interests of historical redemption, it would have to be said that the end richly justified the means.

As he got out of the car, Betsy opened the farmhouse door. Malcolm blinked at her, puzzled at her manner of dress. It took him a moment to digest the fact that she was wearing a full-length fur coat. Silver mink by the look of it, or possibly ermine. It wasn't the wisest getup to don in these days of animal rights activists, but Betsy had never been a woman to think very far beyond her own desires.

Before Malcolm had a moment to wonder how Betsy had managed to finance the purchase of a fur coat, she had thrown it open and was standing in the doorway, naked to her toes.

"Darling!" she cried. "We're rich, rich, rich. And you'll never guess what I sold to make us so!"